Scurvy Goonda
CHRIS McCOY

A Yearling Book

Text copyright © 2009 by Chris McCoy
Cover art copyright © 2011 by Shutterstock
Photograph details copyright © 2009 by Mark Holthusen

All rights reserved. Published in the United States by Yearling, an imprint of Random House Children's Books, a division of Random House, Inc., New York. Originally published in hardcover in the United States by Alfred A. Knopf, an imprint of Random House Children's Books, a division of Random House, Inc., New York, in 2009.

Yearling and the jumping horse design are registered trademarks of Random House, Inc.

Visit us on the Web! www.randomhouse.com/kids

Educators and librarians, for a variety of teaching tools,
visit us at www.randomhouse.com/teachers

The Library of Congress has cataloged the hardcover edition of this work as follows:
McCoy, Chris.
Scurvy Goonda / Chris McCoy. — 1st ed.
p. cm.
Summary: Ted Merritt is eager to replace his imaginary friend, a bacon-loving pirate, with real friends, but soon he is led from Cape Cod, Massachusetts, into a world of discarded "abstract companions" who are intent on wreaking vengeance on the human race.
ISBN 978-0-375-85598-6 (trade) — ISBN 978-0-375-95598-3 (lib. bdg.) —
ISBN 978-0-375-89354-4 (ebook)
[1. Imaginary playmates—Fiction. 2. Pirates—Fiction. 3. Interpersonal relations—Fiction.
4. Adventure and adventurers—Fiction. 5. Family life—Massachusetts—Fiction.
6. Massachusetts—Fiction.] I. Title.
PZ7.M478414457Scu 2009
[Fic]—dc22
2008039290

ISBN 978-0-375-84739-4 (pbk.)

Printed in the United States of America

10 9 8 7 6 5 4 3 2 1

First Yearling Edition

Random House Children's Books supports the First Amendment and celebrates the right to read.

For Mom

Part One

On a black night, beneath a canopy of dense trees determined to prevent the moon from illuminating his route, Ted Merritt furiously pedaled his bike to his summer job at the local Stop to Shop supermarket. It was 11:05 p.m., he was late, and he had just launched himself down a steep, zigzagging road.

The wind whipped Ted's face and the glow from his bike lamp bounced off the eyes of animals hiding in the trees. He held his breath on the plunge down, hoping no cars would come barreling around the bend and send him flying into the woods, where he was certain he would become a slender meal for any number of ravenous sharp-toothed beasts. Reaching the bottom of the hill, he exhaled, took a sharp right onto a set of abandoned railroad tracks, and began pedaling through broken gravel and rusty metal stakes that poked up from the rails, eager to pop his tires. Two miles later, Ted cut up a dirt path that crossed the backyard of an old man who spent his nights etching designs onto seashells using an acid-dipped nail.

"Hello, Mr. Gamrecki!" called out Ted, receiving a *hrrmmph* in response. Scraping through some shrubbery, he boomed out onto Main Street, dodging flashy cars driven by barhopping tourists who liked to speed around and pretend they owned his town. Finally, Ted coasted to the front door of Stop to Shop.

Inside, the bacon was waiting.

As he entered the supermarket, Ted glimpsed his reflection in the glass of the automatic doors, and he experienced a familiar pang of dismay at how his appearance and the way he felt inside seemed to match up so perfectly. His brown bangs were sweat-mashed against his forehead. His white collared shirt was buttoned incorrectly. His earlobes were slightly uneven—one was attached to the base of his ear as it should be, but the other one dangled freely, which was the result of being nipped by a shar-pei puppy when he was a baby, and then being stitched up by an elderly, and unfortunately shaky, doctor. Too often, he felt like a platypus—a creature assembled from a mishmash of mismatched limbs and parts, compelled to hide in a burrow.

And as always, looking into the fingerprint-covered glass of the automatic doors, Ted saw *him*. Hovering behind his shoulder were the familiar black tricorne hat, sitting atop a greasy mop of hair, and the bearded, liver-spotted face highlighted by a large mouth filled with cracked and missing teeth. He saw the rotund body draped in a loose-fitting shirt that had been falling apart for the past three centuries. A pair of plump legs sported striped tailored trousers that had been the height of fashion in their day, and beneath these pants were two leather boots polished to a high shine.

This jumble of flesh and clothing and dirt and hair was Scurvy Goonda, a pirate who had been hanging out with Ted every moment of every day for seven of Ted's fourteen years. He was as much a part of Ted's life as Ted's own skin.

"Hello, Scurvy," sighed Ted.

"Ahoy, hello, and *yes*, Teddy m'boy!" said Scurvy. "It is time to *eat* some *animals*. Me goal tonight is tah not even chew. O, a *yo ho ho, and a yo ho ho*! Ya've never heard somebody go two yo ho hos in a row, have ya! To the bacon!"

3

II

In Ted's workstation of processed meats, Scurvy Goonda was stabbing packages of bacon with his dagger and sliding the raw slabs off the blade into his mouth. Scurvy loved the cured, smoked strips of pork with an insane enthusiasm.

For as long as Ted could remember, in the tradition of piratical pillagers, Scurvy had demolished Ted's sand castles and broken his toys and caused all manner of destruction for which Ted was inevitably blamed. Every night at the Stop to Shop, Ted was forced to conceal the pirate's meat-aisle carnage from Jed, the night manager, so that he didn't get fired.

"Please. Tell me again: why bacon?" asked Ted. "Why *raw* bacon?"

"Ah, a story, ya want! Y'see, I once survived on a lifeboat fer three weeks with a lovely pig named Alfie," said Scurvy, small globs of pink meat decorating his beard. "Alfie was a dear old friend, but there came a point where it was *him* or *me*. So I ate me dear piggy, I did. Roasted the lovely strips of him right on the blade of me sword. Alfie kept me company, and then kept me alive. Since that day, tah me bacon has tasted like friendship."

Ted nodded. Over the years he had learned it was best not to question Scurvy too vigorously about odd moments from his past.

"But it isn't good for you to eat it raw like that," said Ted, something he'd told Scurvy many times before. "Part of the point of cooking it is to *burn off* the fat."

"Don't ya worry about me, Teddy-boy," said Scurvy. "Whenever me heart stops, I just give it a wee pep talk—*Ahoy! Ticky-ticky thump pumper! Yer better than that! Buck up and do yer jobbie!*—and all of a sudden it's beatin' again like I'm a teenager in love."

Whether consuming cured meats, juggling chainsaws, cliff diving, or any other manner of questionable and dangerous activity, Scurvy approached everything he did as something to be *devoured*. When Ted went skiing for the first time, Scurvy slapped on his own skis and insisted they take the lift to the top of the highest peak, whereupon he told Ted that they needed to forge their own trail through the wooded backcountry.

"To the ledge!" he'd roared.

Ted had promised him it was certain death, but Scurvy launched himself over a sheer cliff and went tumbling down the mountain, head over leather boots, all the way to the bottom. Then he got up and brushed himself off, all fine and dandy.

"Yer turn!" he'd bellowed at Ted, but after one look at the cliff, Ted took the ski lift back down the mountain and spent the rest of the day on the beginner slope.

Then there was the time Ted had visited the Grand Canyon, and Scurvy had shown up wearing a parachute and had jumped over the edge of the chasm, yelling about how he would drink the entire Colorado River because he was that thirsty. Ted dropped a quarter into a tourist telescope at the top of the canyon and watched Scurvy howl through the empty air, plummet into the water, and be swept away by the current, whereupon he navigated deadly rapids by dog-paddling and using his face to absorb the impact of the boulders.

5

"Weren't no worse than boxin' fifteen rounds with an outback kangaroo!" Scurvy had explained later, while Ted was trying to jam the pirate's nose back into its correct position.

A great white shark had once swum to the shore near Ted's house. Scurvy hopped in the bay, grabbed on to the shark's fin, and disappeared for the next three days as he and the shark zoomed from Martha's Vineyard to Nantucket to the Maine shore and back to Cape Cod again. When he returned, Scurvy demanded that Ted start cooking him seal bacon, saying he'd developed a taste for aquatic mammals. Ted told him that Stop to Shop didn't carry it.

"Then ya gotta look at it as a *fantastic* business opportunity, me Teddy!" said Scurvy. "Melts on tha tongue, seal bacon! Ya'd never have tah work at a supermarket again! Seals are tha food of tha *future*, matey!"

Ted often wished that he was as brave as Scurvy—even though he knew that much of what Scurvy did was more stupid than brave.

Ted wasn't brave. At school, juniors and seniors picked on certain freshmen almost every day—headlocks and jibes and charley horses and . . . flushings. He didn't know why these kids singled him out, and he was jealous of Scurvy's gift for going unnoticed. Scurvy always explained that appearing invisible was a necessary skill for pirates, who had to be able to sneak up on enemies and slit their lousy throats.

"If you're going to eat free bacon," said Ted, "could you at least help me organize what's left? The night manager just moved me into this department, and I want to do a good job."

Scurvy stared down at the aisle. "What do ya want me tah do?"

"Stack the packages by brand, but make sure to stack the

newer packages on the bottom. We want the bacon closest to the expiration date on top."

Scurvy squinted at the crates. Then he sliced open a package of hot dogs with his dagger.

"Hey, thanks, Scurvy! That's really great!" Ted picked up the hot dogs and threw them in the trash. "How come no matter how much older I get, you always act the same as you did when I was *seven?*"

Scurvy looked down at his boots, avoiding eye contact with Ted, which was how he always acted when he felt bad about his actions.

"I'm sorry, Ted. I am. Sometimes I don't know why I do tha things I do. I admit I am a wee bit impulsive."

"Just think of it this way: if you get me fired, there won't be meat for you to plunder anymore. So let's clean up your mess, and then you can help me stack this stuff before the night manager comes by."

Jed had hired Ted even though state law required employees to be at least sixteen. Nobody wanted to work the night shift and Jed was desperate for help. But tonight, as he watched Ted pointing to the meat aisle, instructing the empty air on the finer points of stacking bologna, he wondered if he had lowered the job requirements a tad too much.

Then again, is it so wrong to employ the underage clinically insane? thought Jed. *Don't whack jobs like Ted deserve the chance to earn money and contribute to society?*

"What is *wrong* with you?" yelled Ted, at nothing. "Now all the packages are *dripping!*"

Okay, decided Jed. Ted was obviously far too nuts to be around the meat. It was time to call his mother.

7

III

"We've gone over this before. I am really, really not crazy."

Ted's family—his ancient grandmother, Rose; his mother, Debbie; and his seven-year-old sister, Adeline—was having breakfast and analyzing his mental condition. Despite his assurances, his mother and grandmother truly feared he was loony. Adeline simply thought that her brother was amazing.

The family home was an old whaling captain's quarters that had been battered by wind and saltwater spray for 150 years—shingles fell, leaks were constant, and the gardens awaited a tending to. Though the structure was three stories tall, the family never used the third floor because it lacked adequate insulation—drafts whirled through the dusty hallways even when there wasn't a hint of wind outside. The second floor held Debbie's bedroom and the guest rooms—but no guests. On the first floor, Ted's and Adeline's bedrooms were side by side, and Grandma Rose had converted the living room into a suite to give herself the shortest possible walk from her bed to the kitchen table, where she spent her long and sour-tempered days yelling about anything that crossed her mind:

"BUCKINGHAM PALACE HAS GOT TOO MANY ROOMS!"

"PEOPLE NEED TO SLOW DOWN THEIR SNEEZES!"

"CAPE COD NEEDS TO GET RID OF ALL THIS

SAND! BEACHES SHOULD BE MADE OF BRICKS! THEY'D LAST LONGER!"

Despite her advanced age, Grandma Rose supported the family—her husband had owned a fleet of fishing ships fifty years before, when the North Atlantic was still thick with bluefish and striped bass. He had invested his money wisely, but ever since his death, the ships had been sold off one by one, and now Debbie and her children lived off what would have been their inheritance. Debbie didn't work because she was afraid to leave her unpredictable mother alone.

The porch was perhaps the house's most striking feature, a long platform made from a mélange of exotic wood planks that had probably cost a fortune a century and a half ago. According to family lore, the wife of the whaling captain who'd built the house had liked to sit on the porch and wait for her husband's boat to return. Once in a while, Ted liked to sit out there too. The view was lovely, and sometimes he could see the backs of humpback whales as they glided by.

But now, back in the kitchen, Debbie was pleading with her son.

"The night manager told us he saw you ranting in the meat aisle," Debbie said. She had a small glob of chocolate stuck to her cheek, though they hadn't eaten anything containing chocolate for breakfast.

"I was *not* ranting," said Ted.

"This has come up before," said Debbie. "You remember the time you stole that boat in Falmouth Harbor, and you told the cops that it wasn't your idea?"

"Because it *wasn't.*"

"You ran a Jolly Roger up its mast," said his mother.

9

"No, I *didn't*."

"It was SCURVY," said Adeline. Ted smiled at her, and she smiled back.

"Sweetheart," said Debbie. "This Scurvy, he doesn't exist. Scurvy is just your brother's imaginary friend."

"Abstract companion," Ted mumbled.

"What'd you say?" said Debbie.

"Nothing, Ma," sighed Ted. "Never mind. I didn't say anything."

"He said ABSTRACT COMPANION," explained Adeline. "Imaginary friends don't CALL themselves imaginary friends, because they know they are not imaginary. They call themselves abstract companions because they're more than our friends and they're around all the time. Tell Mom what you told me, Ted!"

"Er," said Ted, "sometimes, they're not really friends with the kids they're assigned to. The word 'companion' works better. Or at least that's what I've been told."

"But Scurvy loves Ted," said Adeline. "That's why he has stuck around for so long!"

"Okay, Adeline," said Ted.

"They call themselves ab-coms for short!" said Adeline. "Don't they, Ted?"

"Um," said Ted.

Debbie stared at Ted. "What sort of nonsense are you telling your sister?"

"Just . . . it's just what I've learned."

"Well, you have completely lost your mind, and now you're turning Adeline into a batty little madwoman."

"Whatever you think," said Ted.

"Scurvy DOES exist," insisted Adeline. "He plays with my Eric."

Eric the Planda was Adeline's abstract companion, whom she described as an enormous panda that walked on his hind legs and had a bonsai tree growing out of the top of his head. Because of the plant, Adeline called Eric a "planda."

"All we want you to do is have a little chat with a professional," said Debbie.

"I don't want to."

"BECAUSE YOU'RE CRAZY," said Grandma Rose. "AND IF YOU ASK ME, YOU COULD USE A WHOLE NEW HEAD."

"Mom, tell Grandma that I'm not going to get a new head."

"Your grandma knows that. She's just trying to be helpful."

"MAKE HIM LOOK LIKE MARLON BRANDO IF HE GETS A NEW HEAD!"

"Ted, I went to a therapist when your father left. It helped me a lot to have somebody to talk to. I just think—"

"I have to go to bed," said Ted, getting up from the breakfast table, which for him was actually the dinner table, given that he'd just worked a full night shift.

"It isn't natural for a kid to sleep through his summer," said Debbie.

"LOTS OF THINGS AIN'T NATURAL ABOUT THAT BOY," said Grandma Rose.

"He's great! You leave him alone!" yelled Adeline, and ran after Ted.

Outside, standing on the porch, Scurvy Goonda looked at a dolphin frolicking and splashing, and wondered what it would taste like with a side of hash browns.

11

IV

No matter how tight Ted shut the curtains, light snuck in and bounced off his bedroom mirror, painting golden strips across his body. He was stretched out on his back, staring at the ceiling, which was covered with little glow-in-the-dark stars that his dad had given him when he was small.

As he always did, Scurvy lay in the bed next to Ted, breathing heavily, his face bright red. Scurvy didn't like the summer heat. Ted used to make him take off his boots before climbing under the covers, but Scurvy's feet were so shocking to look at—bent toes and explosive bunions, toenails the length of Ted's fingers—that Ted soon begged Scurvy to keep his boots on. This meant that whatever sludge Scurvy had been tramping through all day got smeared all over the bed.

Ted had thought about asking Scurvy to find another place to sleep, but he knew a secret—Scurvy was afraid of the dark. "If ya knew tha things that I've seen in tha dark, ya'd be afraid too," the pirate had once said. Ted figured that because Scurvy was so brave when it came to everything else, whatever he had seen must have been *really* alarming.

This morning, Ted and Scurvy were looking each other straight in the eye, faces six inches apart. Ted saw the grease in Scurvy's mustache and took in the smell of his breath. Scurvy frequently helped himself to the family liquor cabinet. Luckily,

Debbie and Grandma Rose always blamed each other for the missing booze, which allowed Scurvy to drink his fill. Tonight it smelled like he'd sampled the coconut-flavored rum. Scurvy loved all fruit-flavored cocktails.

"Roll over, Scurvy," said Ted. "It's too hard to sleep when you're staring at me."

"I like sleepin' on me left side," said Scurvy.

"Well, I like sleeping on my right side, and it's my bed, so I say you roll over."

"If ya want, we could sleep tha ol' head to toe. That way we could both sleep on tha side that we want, but we won't have tah look at each other."

Ted thought about this.

"But that would mean that I would have to smell what comes up out of your boots," said Ted. "Do you know what that smells like?"

13

"Smells like adventure, I reckon," said Scurvy.

Abruptly, Ted's door squeaked open, and Adeline peeked her little head inside the room.

"You awake, Ted?" she said.

"Come on in, Addie."

Adeline walked in, dragging her blanket behind her. She only carried the blanket, a relic of her baby days, when she was upset.

"What's wrong?" said Ted.

Adeline turned her head to her left, and Ted knew that she was looking at Eric. The planda always walked on her left.

"Is it something to do with Eric?" Ted said.

Adeline nodded.

"Tell me about it," said Ted.

"He's worried," said Adeline.

"How can you tell he's worried?"

"His fur."

Ted turned to Scurvy. "Could you take a look for me?"

"But I'm comfy in tha bed."

"C'mon, Scurv. This is important."

Adeline watched Scurvy heave himself off the mattress—she'd always been able to see Scurvy, for some reason. She talked a lot about all the ab-coms she could see, and there were times Ted wondered if she maybe could see everybody's abstract companions.

Ted sat up on the bed and watched Scurvy conducting his examination.

"Is he okay?" Adeline asked.

"Hold on, hold on," said Scurvy.

14

Being a planda, Eric always had black rings around his eyes, but today he looked downright exhausted. Even his bonsai was drooping.

"Strange, this," said Scurvy, poking a bare pink spot on the planda's belly. Eric recoiled. "It seems his baldish areas are a wee sensitive."

Eric tucked his head. He didn't like being the center of attention.

"What do you think we should do about it, Scurvy?" asked Addie.

"Not tah worry, m'lady! Yer planda is just a touch stressed! Probably worried about how he'll look in his bathing suit this summer!"

Adeline laughed.

"Ya know I won't let anything happen tah him," said

Scurvy. "If this is more than just a case of nerves, I will sail every ocean on Earth tah find him a cure fer his malady!"

"Thanks, Scurvy," said Adeline. Eric nodded gratefully.

As Adeline walked out of the room, holding Eric's hand, Scurvy saw more bald spots on his back and behind his legs. Dead bonsai leaves fell to the ground behind him.

"This isn't good at all, Teddy-boy. Somethin's brewin'," said Scurvy. But then he saw that Ted was already fast asleep.

Scurvy knew that Eric's fur was falling out because he was nervous, which made Scurvy nervous too. He reached under the mattress and pulled out a small envelope adorned with a silver seal blaring a portentous inscription:

From the office of
THE PRESIDENT OF MIDDLEMOST

15

The envelope had been delivered more than a week ago, brought in the middle of the night by an unseen courier and left inside Scurvy's boot.

Scurvy pulled a letter out of the envelope. The corners of the paper were bent and the sheet was dark with his fingerprints. Here's what it said:

ATTENTION
ALL ABSTRACT COMPANIONS!

THIS IS YOUR CALL TO ARMS!

ALL AB-COMS are to report back to
Middlemost within SIXTY DAYS or be
considered DESERTERS by the presidential

army! The humans are planning to
EXTERMINATE us! Return to Middlemost
before a grisly fate befalls you!

All check-ins will take place at Ab-Com City.
Do not tell anybody that you are leaving! We
have spies everywhere and we will know if
you are betraying your own kind!

The time is now! The future is ours!
Defend yourself and defend your real friends!
Onward!

Your Gorgeous Leader,
PRESIDENT PERSEPHONE SKELETON

"Not me leader, ya ain't," mumbled Scurvy, folding the letter and placing it back in the envelope. "Not me family. Not me friend. I won't ever leave me Ted."

Scurvy hadn't been to Middlemost in a very, very long time, and he wasn't going to be "called to arms" just because Persephone—*Persephone,* of all ab-coms—demanded it. His home was right here on lovely Cape Cod. With Ted.

V

Down a path from Ted's house, through the woods, and then up a hill was the crest of a sand dune—a big mound of fine, clean dirt. From the top of the dune, Ted could look down over two huge cranberry bogs and the big pond next to them. Bogs always had ponds next to them. To collect the cranberries, the farmers flooded the bogs using pond water, which caused the berries to float to the surface, making them easier to scoop. During the winter, the bogs were flooded to protect the plants from the cold, and when the water froze, Ted would skate on the surface, trying to slice the stray berries stuck in the ice. But now it was summer, and Ted was on top of the dune staring down at Carolina Waltz, who was sitting at its base.

When Ted and Carolina Waltz were in the same third-grade class, she had been the only girl to place a homemade card in his Valentine's Day mailbox. Ever since then, Ted had longed to be Carolina Waltz's boyfriend.

Here's a valentine, Ted, Carolina had written on that tremendous third-grade day. *I don't care that you talk to pirates. I like you.*

I like you too, Carolina, Ted had written back, which to this day was the best moment he'd ever had with a girl.

That is, it was the best moment he'd ever had in *real life* with a girl. But for years, in his mind, he and Carolina had been together. He saw them together in places around the world: There she was in a white dress, laughing as he steered their gondola through the canals of Venice en route to an art auction at which they hoped to pick up a new painting for their enormous Italian villa.

Che cosa comprare? Ted asked Carolina, because in this fantasy he spoke a little Italian, and he liked the way it made Carolina giggle.

Oh, Ted, you are my Da Vinci, said Carolina, twirling her parasol in her gloved hands. *We should buy whatever you want.*

Penso che un Cézanne sia sembrato piacevole, said Ted, because he knew that Cézanne was Carolina's favorite. She batted her eyelashes at him.

You're perfect, said Carolina.

Siete perfetti, said Ted, because he thought that Carolina was perfect too.

In his imagination.

In reality, since third grade Carolina had become *mean*. Today she was with two of her girlfriends, talking about guys from school, one of whom was walking toward them.

"Hello, ladies," said Duke.

"Duke!" shouted Carolina's friend Shelly LeShoot, who was awful.

Duke's usual method of beating up Ted started with Duke standing up in the middle of the high school lunchroom and demanding, "HEY, TED, SAY SOMETHING CRAZY!" which would cause hundreds of kids to turn toward wherever Ted was sitting, alone. Most kids believed Ted was nuts, and it frustrated them that he never actually *behaved* in a crazy manner.

And so Duke would continue: "YOU SHOULD SHOW EVERYBODY YOUR WEIRD BIRTHMARK."

Ted did have a strange birthmark that covered his right forearm. It stretched from his wrist to his elbow and was solid brown aside from three pale circles arranged in a triangle in its center. His mother used to tell him his father had one just like it. Ted had always been self-conscious about it. He never wore short-sleeved shirts, and when he had to change into his gym clothes, he always did so in one of the bathroom stalls.

"MAYBE HE'S SO CRAZY HE FORGOT HOW TO TALK!"

To which Ted would just silently reply, *Yes, Duke. I'm out of my mind. I now communicate via a system of grunts and whistles that you can only understand if you decipher the code I've written with my own earwax.*

Invariably, Duke would see Ted rolling his eyes, come storming over to the table, and tell Ted to meet him outside after lunch. So Ted would go outside after lunch, and Duke would beat him up in front of the student body. Duke was a master of the headlock.

"I love your new sneakers, Duke," said Carolina.

"Stole them from that Foot Locker at the mall," said Duke.

"That's so awesome," said Shelly.

Ted looked over at a rock lying nearby. It was almost perfectly round, about the size of a grapefruit, and it was covered in little shiny specks. It looked heavy, but not heavy enough that Ted couldn't hurl it from the top of the sand dune, if he were ever compelled to do such a thing.

He imagined himself hurling the rock at the group below,

19

and then, just as it was about to crash down upon them: *rrrrrkkk!* It would come to a screeching halt above Duke and his groupies, crack open, and dump hair-removal liquid all over them, so that when they came into school the next day, they would be grotesquely bald. Ted bet that under his luxurious blond hair, Duke had a lumpy caveman skull.

"Aye, Ted. From here, ya could knock Duke's head completely *off*," said Scurvy, nodding at the rock.

"I'd miss," said Ted. "And then he'd come up here and destroy me."

"Nah. We have tha high ground, matey. At tha very least, ya'd be able to roll some of these larger boulders down and take off running. Might kill some of the girls, but no great loss there. Not very bright, those pocky dollies."

"Oh, Duke, you're so funny!" yelled one of Carolina's friends.

"Mercy killin' is all it would be," said Scurvy. "Do it for the entire human race."

"Scurvy, you know it's not like it used to be in your time. You can't just go around murdering everyone you don't like."

"Watch yer mouth," said Scurvy. "This is *my* time as much as anyone else's."

"Let's go," said Ted, getting up from the sand.

"Help a pirate up, mate," said Scurvy.

Ted grabbed Scurvy's hand and pulled him to his feet. It was the first time he'd ever had to do that. Scurvy had always been terrifically strong.

"Are you okay to walk?" said Ted. "You look tired."

"I am that, a wee bit," said Scurvy. "Just haven't been sleepin'."

Ted took a final look at Carolina—geez, she was so beautiful. He couldn't believe that somebody who looked like that could be so mean. *Ahh . . . Carolina.*

For a second, Ted thought that she might be looking up the sand dune at him. But she was probably just tossing her hair, or making sure that her face was getting tanned. Girls like her always got all the sunshine.

21

VI

Ted's father, Declan, had left Cape Cod when Ted was seven, saying he was going camping with friends. When he didn't turn up a week later, Ted pictured his dad diving for sunken treasure, or releasing zoo wolves into the wild, or doing some other logical thing that would explain why he hadn't come home. But when inquiries to his dad's friends revealed that there was no camping trip, and credit card records showed that his father was in New York City, the truth hit young Ted: his father wasn't coming home. Shortly after that, even the credit card records stopped arriving.

Ted kept a photograph of his father in his bedroom. He had been a handsome man with a muscular physique, a receding hairline, and big hands. Ted remembered those hands gripping his ankles as he rode on his father's shoulders, way up high. The photo, from a fishing trip, showed his father helping him bait a hook. He remembered his father telling him stories about pirates and sea captains every night before he went to bed. He remembered that his father had loved him, though he was no longer quite sure if this was true. Maybe he just hoped he did?

Soon after Ted's dad left, Scurvy Goonda showed up.

These days, Ted found himself thinking of his dad a lot. Any time he saw one of his classmates getting picked up at school by a father, or he passed a sports field where fathers were cheering on their kids in soccer games or field hockey matches, he wondered what his life would have been like if his dad was still around to help him with everything.

It was hard being the only male in his family. His mother and Grandma Rose expected him to know how to change fuses and cut plants with the Weedwacker and get rid of mice. Even Adeline thought he should be a natural when it came to trapping spiders—indeed, *all* spider-disposal tasks fell on Ted's skinny shoulders.

Ted stared out the window. A windsurfer was skimming along the surface of the water. Ted remembered that his father used to love windsurfing. Even now, sitting at the kitchen table, Ted could almost picture his father holding up a big blue sail, buzzing along on top of the waves—

"WHY DO MEATBALLS HAVE TO BE ROUND ANYWAY?" said Grandma Rose. "I WANT MY MEAT IN A TRIANGLE!"

Debbie piled spaghetti onto Grandma Rose's plate, sprinkling the pasta with a few of her tears. Spaghetti had been Declan's favorite meal. Debbie still made the dish every Friday night, and it always made her cry.

"Why do you make spaghetti if it makes you sad?" asked Adeline.

"It was your father's favorite," Debbie explained, sniffling. "I want to have it ready when he comes home."

"How do you know he'll come home on a Friday?"

"PIPE DOWN, ADELINE," said Grandma Rose. "YOU SOUND LIKE A ZEPPELIN EXPLOSION."

"We scheduled an appointment for you to see a marvelous psychiatrist, Ted," said Debbie. Grandma Rose nodded and

23

spaghetti spilled from her mouth. She wasn't good at chewing anymore.

"No way," he declared.

"Sweetheart, you need friends who aren't imaginary pirates," said his mother.

"He's real to me."

"THEN WHY CAN'T ANYBODY BUT YOU SEE HIM?" asked Grandma Rose. "YOU WEARING GOGGLES MADE OF STUPID?"

"Maybe they can't see him because he's . . . shy?" he offered.

"PIRATES AREN'T SHY!" said Grandma Rose.

This was true. Scurvy was crazed and loud and consumed by bacon lust, and generally pretty much anything but shy.

"Maybe he hides from you 'cuz . . . 'cuz he just doesn't like you!" said Adeline, nodding to Scurvy, who was standing at the corner of the table observing the action. Scurvy tipped his tricorne and winked.

"Rightie-o, young Adeline," said Scurvy.

"Don't talk to invisible pirates, dear," said Debbie. "And finish your milk."

"Can I go now?" said Ted.

"Next Monday. Two o'clock. Dr. Winterhalter," said his mom.

"I have to go to work now, Mother."

Ted walked outside, got on his bike, and started pedaling madly. *There's nothing WRONG*, he thought. *Except for the fact that I'll spend the next eight hours at a lousy job where the bacon is going to be strewn around the meat aisle because our customers are MANIACS who ENJOY digging through piles of bacon, searching for the one PRIME PIECE that has only a SPECK OF FAT on it, messing up the PERFECT piles that I MADE last night.*

24

"Arrgh!" Ted roared at the road. But the road didn't say anything back.

Scurvy was riding on the bike's handlebars, and Ted had to keep pushing his head down to see where he was going. But each time he took his hand off Scurvy's head, the pirate would pop up and put his hands in the air, feeling free, and Ted had to lean far to the side to make sure that he didn't veer off the road or go careening into traffic.

"*Stay down*, Scurvy," said Ted.

"Bicycles are *brilliant*," said Scurvy, his long, dirty hair flapping behind him, whopping Ted in the face.

"But I can't see the road."

"I'll be yer eyes, Ted-o-mine!"

"Scurvy, please. I need my *own eyes*."

"Nonsense! Ya haven't spent a lifetime staring at tha horizon. Ya don't know what true vision is. Wait . . . a pothole coming up, starboard!"

25

Ted pulled on the handgrips, but he forgot which side was starboard, and then suddenly he was flying through the air, the gray asphalt beneath him and his brain firing off warning messages: *Pain coming! Try to fly!* The last thing Ted saw before he hit was Scurvy plummeting to the ground next to him.

"YER RIGHT," shouted Scurvy. "FROM NOW ON YA SHOULD BE YER OWN EYES!"

Before Ted could respond, he smacked into the hard earth.

VII

Each time Ted touched one of the freezing-cold packages of hot dogs or stacks of sliced bologna, his hands started to sting. Every part of his body was in pain—his elbows and knees were scraped, there were skid marks on his palms, he had a bump on his head, and he thought there might be a small pebble lodged way up his nostril.

"I asked politely, I tried to push you out of the way, I told you I *couldn't see*," said Ted.

"I tend tah lose my head when I feel tha wind through me hair," said Scurvy, uncharacteristically disappointed with himself. He was dirty from the crash, curled in a corner of the meat aisle, sitting on some smoked-turkey cold cuts. There were long smears of dirt across the Lunchables boxes he had assaulted.

"Yer upset with me," said Scurvy.

"*Yes, I'm upset.* If somebody sees me bleeding all over the meat aisle, I'm going to get in trouble."

"Then go to tha bathroom and get some Band-Aids. Or rub some mud into tha wounds."

"Mud won't help."

The truth was Ted didn't want to leave the meat aisle to get the first-aid kit because he was afraid of running into Jed. But he needed to tend to his oozier scrapes, so he grabbed a couple of empty cardboard cartons to make it look like he was doing *something* productive, and walked through a door marked EMPLOYEES ONLY.

The back of the store was packed with huge boxes filled with all the other products that would eventually make their way out to the unforgiving lights of the supermarket floor.

In the midst of all these boxes was the Crusher.

The Crusher was a giant vise that smashed whatever went into it into tiny cubes. Ted couldn't fathom how something so massive had ever been transported into the supermarket in the first place. He imagined instead that the Crusher had stood in the same place for thousands of years, built by druids or ancient pagans who had worshiped the machine as a god. The Stop to Shop had to have been built *around* the Crusher.

Ted tossed his empty cardboard boxes into the Crusher, put on a pair of protective goggles, and, with an enormous heave, pulled a long metal lever to turn on the machine. The Crusher roared to life and Ted jumped away like he always did, because the machine scared the heck out of him. Gears spun and levers creaked and Ted could almost hear the cardboard boxes screaming as they were smashed and compressed and obliterated out of their peaceful boxy existence.

Such was the power of the Crusher.

Ted popped a couple of aspirin and used the first-aid kit in the bathroom to smear his wounds with some sticky iodine. Meanwhile, Scurvy Goonda stared at himself in the mirror, using his dagger to pick bits of bacon out of his teeth.

"You messed me up pretty good, Scurv," said Ted.

"A lad needs scars."

Then came a pounding at the bathroom door and the sound of Jed shouting on the other side:

"Get back to work, Merritt! Whatever you're doing in there, you can do on your break!"

"Sorry, sorry."

Ted opened the door. Jed stood right in front of him. The night manager's eyes flicked from the bruises on Ted's arms to the raspberry on his forehead.

"Man, somebody beat the *crud* out of you," said Jed. "Kinda wish I had seen that."

"I just fell off my bike," said Ted.

"Guess that makes more sense. If you got into an actual fight, you'd probably be dead."

"I get into fights all the time."

"Oh, I'm sure you and your pirate pal are quite the dynamic duo."

"Give me three minutes and I'll turn him into chum," whispered Scurvy, poking the night manager's voice box with the tip of his dagger. "We'll fish for marlin with the scraps."

"Get back to work, Merritt," said Jed.

Ted knew that other kids were spending their vacations driving around in Jeeps with cute girls, or teaching tennis to the children of summer people for thirty dollars an hour, or sitting in lifeguard chairs and blowing their whistles at the bronzed and the bikinied. He wondered if his job would be more fun if he had the chance to blow a whistle every now and then. It would definitely be more fun if there were more bikinis around the Stop to Shop.

All of a sudden, Scurvy smacked him across the face.

"Snap out of it!" said Scurvy. "You only need tah do this job fer three months!"

"Don't hit me!" said Ted.

He grabbed a liverwurst pack and used it to cuff Scurvy on the ear.

"How do you like it when I smack *you?*" said Ted.

Ted stomped on Scurvy's tricorne hat, grinding it into the freshly waxed supermarket floor.

"And see that? *That's* for knocking me off my bike!"

"*ME HAT!*" Scurvy roared. He struck back by putting his head down and ramming it into Ted's chest, bull-rushing him into the next aisle, where they scraped and clawed each other into a tank of lobsters that crashed to the floor with a terrific explosion that sent water gushing and crustaceans scurrying toward the dairy section. Ted grabbed Scurvy's beard and wrapped it around his neck, but with a quick flip Ted was on his back and Scurvy was sitting on his chest.

"For tha past *three hundred and twenty-five years*," said Scurvy, breathing hard, "that *hat* has been through wars and battles and monsoons without losing its fine, handcrafted *shape!* Which ya've now *ruined!*"

"It serves you ri—" said Ted, but he never finished his sentence. Over Scurvy's shoulder he could see Carolina Waltz and the rest of the popular girls. They were all laughing at him.

"What are you DOING?" said Carolina.

"Oh. Hi, Carolina," said Ted.

"God, *that's* what its voice sounds like?" said Carolina's friend Bridget Skoke, which Ted thought was an awful name. "I didn't know it could *talk!*"

"I'm not an *it*," said Ted.

"Maybe that's his *pirate* voice," said Carolina.

"It's my normal voice," said Ted, who didn't think there was anything weird about the way he spoke.

29

"He talked *again*! He sounds so *weird*!" said another of Carolina's awful friends.

Sprawled on his back, Ted could see new girls continually popping into his sightline—he imagined girls piling up throughout the supermarket, clawing over cereal boxes and packets of toilet tissue, just to see him on the ground, looking stupid.

"You are so *weird*, Ed," said Carolina.

"My name is Ted."

"Little Teddy!"

"Carolina has a teddy!"

"That's not a teddy, that's *underwear*!"

Then a booming voice drowned out all the other voices. "Merritt!" shouted Jed.

With that, Ted knew he had been fired from his summer job. He also knew that Carolina Waltz would never, ever be his girlfriend. He didn't even notice when Scurvy—broken and bruised from the fight—put his arm over his shoulder.

"There are other fish in tha sea, Ted," said Scurvy, who often knew what Ted was thinking. "I've seen them many times. I'll get ya a mermaid."

VIII

Ted and Scurvy sat across from one another on the back porch of the house. Ted was sipping the can of Coca-Cola he was using to keep himself awake. He wanted to make sure he had the energy to yell at Scurvy. Scurvy was crushing a few strips of bacon between his molars. Ted had burned the bacon on purpose, a subtle punishment for Scurvy's actions at the supermarket.

Inside the house, Grandma Rose glanced out the window at Ted, who appeared to be yelling at a lawn chair.

"YOUR POOR BOY IS LOOPY," declared Grandma Rose. "AND I THINK HE'S BEEN CHEWING ON THE CARPET."

"The mice are doing the chewing, Mom," said Debbie.

"Ted is not loopy!" said Adeline, seated on the living room floor, reading a book with Eric.

"Quiet, Adeline," said Debbie.

Outside on the porch, all the caffeinated blood in Ted's body was rushing to his head.

"Which means that when school starts, Carolina is going to tell *everybody* about how she saw me on my back fighting some invisible—"

"I'm not invisible," said Scurvy, calmly eating another strip of bacon. "Ya know that. I could make meself visible tah everybody anytime I want. I choose not tah."

"Do you *know* how many times I'm going to get beat up because of last night? Because you had to *pick a fight* with me?"

"I know what ya look like when yer fallin' into one of yer funks. I tried tah smack ya out of it."

"That is *not* the way you deal with somebody who is feeling depressed."

"On tha contrary, boy-o-mine! On me ship, tha *Gallows Swan*, smackin' was tha second most popular way we cured our men from fallin' into depression. Tha first was rum, but ya seem tah be a bit too yellow fer liquor's sweet cure."

"I'm only fourteen, Scurvy. I'm not allowed to drink."

"By the time I was fourteen, I had wives on three continents—and that *includes* Antarctica. But that was only because I left one of them there when she started nagging me about my personal appearance. Cindy tha See-Saw, they called her."

"Scurvy, you embarrassed me in front of Carolina Waltz!"

"And yer better off!" said Scurvy, popping the final blackened bit of bacon into his mouth. "She's a wicked girl, that one, but yer too blinded by her looks to see that. I did ya a *favor*."

Looking at the bits of bacon plummeting from Scurvy's lips into his wild beard, Ted began to ponder something that he'd never truly pondered before: why the heck was he putting up with this guy?

Thoughts flashed through Ted's mind:

The reason I got hurt yesterday is because SCURVY refused to do what I told him to do! And the reason I was fired is because I got into a fight with SCURVY. I got into that fight because he was trying to slap me out of my depression. But the reason I'm depressed is because I don't have any friends and I've never had a girlfriend and everybody thinks I'm crazy because of SCURVY!

Carolina would never, ever hold his hand. All because of Scurvy.

But if Scurvy's existence was all in his mind, like his family insisted, if Scurvy *wasn't around* anymore—heck, if Ted didn't have an imagination *at all*—the other parts of his life would fall into place. Some of the most popular kids in his school were the dumbest and least imaginative.

His life could only be better if Scurvy—if his *whole imagination*—wasn't involved in it.

Ted didn't think he could get rid of his entire imagination, but he was beginning to think he might be able to do something about Scurvy.

"Are ya okay?" asked Scurvy, staring uneasily at Ted. "Yer face just got a wee bit strange."

"I'm fine. I'd say I'm great, actually," said Ted, giving Scurvy a big smile.

"Ya don't seem angry anymore."

"I'm not angry anymore."

Scurvy studied Ted's suddenly serene expression. Pirates were in the business of deception and Scurvy was, of course, a master of the trade. He couldn't figure out what exactly was going on inside Ted's head, but he knew he was lying.

"Feel like some more bacon?" said Ted.

"Ya complained when I asked ya tah cook me tha first batch."

"I'm feeling domestic," said Ted, smiling again in a way that Scurvy had never seen him smile before.

"Well, if yer offerin', perhaps just a slab . . . or ten?"

Ted walked into the house. Scurvy saw him lean over and tell his mother something that prompted Debbie to throw her arms around her son, and Ted to hug her back. But young Adeline scrunched up her face like she was about to cry and then ran off to her bedroom.

Scurvy was right. Something was up indeed.

IX

"And how long has zis pirate been with you?" asked Dr. Winter-halter. The thin, tweed-jacketed, foreign-accented doctor would occasionally jot something down on the yellow notepad sitting on his lap, but his decisions about when and when not to take notes seemed odd—for example, he made a note when Ted said that he needed to use the bathroom.

"About the last seven years," said Ted. He'd always thought that when you talked to a psychiatrist, you had to lie down, but there were no couches in this office. Instead, they were both sitting in hard-backed chairs, four feet apart from one another.

In the far corner of the room, Scurvy was leaning against the windowsill, shaking his head. Ted avoided eye contact with him—he had asked the pirate to stay away, but Scurvy had insisted on coming.

"Do you remember ze moment he first appeared?"

Ted did.

Though he had been only seven at the time, the memory of Scurvy Goonda's arrival was etched clearly into Ted's mind. He'd been walking around the cranberry bog with his mother, shortly after his father had left the family. His mother had started to put on weight, and she wanted the exercise. She was crying, but Ted didn't yet understand why she was so sad, so he was just holding her hand and watching the swans on the pond next to the bog.

And then, all of a sudden, there was Scurvy navigating a one-man frigate on the lake, hoisting up a Jolly Roger and roaring his way to the shore. He was completely scary, but also quite fantastic.

Reaching the bank of the pond, Scurvy leaped out of his boat, removed his hat, and bowed to the young Ted:

"Good Master Ted, Scurvy Gordon at yer service—Scurvy fer tha year and a half I went without fruit in tha East Indies, which cost me some of me teeth but none of me spirit, Gordon fer me dear late father."

"Goonda," said seven-year-old Ted, who had an ear infection and couldn't hear too well what Scurvy was saying.

"Gordon."

"Goonda."

"Gordon."

"GOOOON-DA!"

"Fine, Goonda. Whatever ya want."

"Hi."

"Hello there, Teddy m'boy."

"Who are you talking to, Ted?" asked Debbie.

"Goonda," said seven-year-old Ted. It was fun to say.

"Oh," said his mother. "Okay. Let's keep walking."

Ted still remembered Scurvy's big leather boots squashing the mud next to him and his mother, who had to stop every few minutes to stifle a cry or blow her nose or curse. Ted felt so safe next to those boots.

"You know, come to think of it, I don't exactly remember when he showed up," said Ted.

"Lies!" said Scurvy from the back of the room. "We've

talked about that fateful day many times. Ya've never been one fer falsehoods, Ted. Deception doesn't suit ya."

Dr. Winterhalter must have seen Ted's eyes flick over to the pirate, because he twisted in his chair to see if anything was there and then turned back to Ted.

"Is zis," started Dr. Winterhalter, searching his notepad, "er, *Scurvy Goonda* in ze room vith us right now?"

Ted nodded.

"And he is doing vat?"

"He's painting a skull and bones on the front of your desk using some of his own blood."

Indeed, it appeared that Scurvy had cut the tip of his finger using a letter opener and was now drawing symbols of his trade on the doctor's office furniture—swords, lusty wenches, Jolly Rogers, and so forth—though Ted wasn't quite able to discern some of the depictions. Scurvy had flair, but no true artistic talent.

"If yer giving him yer money, ya might as well give him me blood!"

"Quit it!" said Ted. "The way you're acting right now is the reason we're *here*."

"The reason we're here is that ya want tah get rid of me! I know what happens in these offices! They give people new brains! Pop out tha old and pop in tha new!"

"Can you blame me for being here? Look how you're acting!"

"*So it's true, it is! Mutiny!*"

"This can't be a mutiny because you're not in charge, Scurvy! I am the captain! Captain Ted! I'm the leader of my entire *fleet*! And I can't have you constantly following me around and getting in the way and making people think I'm out of my mind!"

"Then if yer so burdened by me and me company, be a man and ask me tah leave!"

"*LEAVE!*"

As soon as it popped out of his mouth, Ted couldn't believe what he'd just said—and neither could Scurvy. He just stared at Ted, arms slumped to his sides, blood dripping from his fingertip onto the carpeted floor.

"Ya . . . ya tellin' tha truth when ya say that?" said Scurvy, wounded.

Ted took a deep breath. "I am."

Scurvy took off his hat and held it over his chest.

"I'll start behaving, I will," said Scurvy.

"I've asked you to behave a thousand times."

"I don't want tah go."

"You aren't leaving me a choice here, Scurvy," said Ted. "I'm sorry."

Ted turned his attention to Dr. Winterhalter, who was staring at him over his glasses, slack-jawed.

"So I guess you think I'm nuts now too," said Ted.

"Do you always have zese arguments vith ze pirate?"

Ted took a deep breath. "I've been having a lot more of them recently."

Dr. Winterhalter tapped his pen against his notepad.

"Sorry about him staining the rug," said Ted.

"Vat do you mean?"

Ted pointed to a spot on the floor, and the psychiatrist leaned in close to see what he was talking about.

"Zere is no stain on zis carpet."

Ted got up from his chair to get a better look, and he saw that what the doctor was saying was true. On the spot where it had looked like Scurvy was bleeding, there was nothing except for clean, well-vacuumed carpeting.

"But it looked like blood was dripping from his finger," said Ted, quietly.

"Dripped on me boot, it did," said Scurvy.

"Is your family in ze vaiting room?" said the doctor.

"My mom should be out there," said Ted.

"Zen I'll be right back."

39

X

Debbie stood next to Dr. Winterhalter in a sterile white office, looking at his elegant hands.

"Hold on. It's around here somevere," said Dr. Winterhalter, opening and shutting drawers.

Debbie's nostrils were being overrun by some sort of *masculine* smell, and she was trying to figure out if the smell was aftershave, or deodorant, or perhaps a moisturizer the doctor applied each morning after getting out of the shower—he did seem to have good skin. And that *accent*. He was so dashing.

Snap out of it! thought Debbie.

She couldn't remember the last time she'd been this close to a man, and she was letting her senses get the best of her. She looked down at the shiny wedding ring on her finger. She always kept it polished. She loved her husband and still considered herself a married woman, even if he was gone.

"Here it is," said Dr. Winterhalter. "Zis should do ze trick."

The doctor held up something in front of Debbie that looked a bit like a Band-Aid, except that it was round and had a quarter inch of puffy thickness to it. It was printed with a picture of some kind of monster that had been circled and cut in half by a red slash, like a NO SMOKING sign.

"What is that?" asked Debbie.

"A rep from ze pharmaceutical company—a strange-looking

man—came by vith zem last week. Zey are brand-new. Zey are called Ab-Com Patches. Interesting, no?"

"What do they do?"

"Well, according to zis representative, zey don't do anything at all."

"I don't understand."

"Frequently, kids who have zese imaginary friends are very intelligent, and ze friend is simply a by-product of zeir overactive minds. Ze *last* thing ve vant to do is put zese kids on medication to slow zeir brains down—and zat's vere ze Ab-Com Patches come in. Ven ze kids vear zem, zey start to really *believe* zat zey are getting medicine to get rid of zeir imaginary friends—and because zey *vant* to get rid of zeir friends, ze friends simply go away. It's all a trick of ze mind, no drugs necessary. Look here."

41

Dr. Winterhalter picked up a pair of scissors and cut the Ab-Com Patch open. The patch lost its shape, and Debbie could see that there was nothing inside but a little bit of powder.

"See? Just a vee bit of placebo powder inside. Completely harmless."

"Extraordinary."

"Ted will be my first recommendation for ze Ab-Com Patch. But ze rep said zat ze patch vas nearly one hundred percent effective in ze test trials."

"What drug company makes it?"

"Ze rep said it vas a small subsidiary of one of those larger conglomerates—Middlemost Pharmaceuticals, I zink he called it."

Debbie looked at the Ab-Com Patch.

"Does it work on pirates?" she said.

"If it is one hundred percent effective," said the doctor, "zen you can be sure it vill vork on a pirate. And more good news: zey are as cheap as a box of bandages. You can pay at ze front desk."

"Thank you so much," said Debbie as the doctor handed her the Ab-Com Patches. A feeling of relief washed over her. Her Ted would be like other kids. He would be happy. These patches were going to fix everything.

42

XI

In addition to supplying the box of patches, the doctor instructed Ted to simply ignore Scurvy. He said the patches would take a few days to really start working, and during that time it would be better if Ted didn't talk to Scurvy, because it would make the break in their relationship easier. The doctor indicated that Scurvy, being predisposed to tantrums, might act up at the prospect of being ignored, but he encouraged Ted to stay strong and just let the medication run its course.

Ted attached an Ab-Com Patch to his shoulder. Debbie, thrilled by the recent changes in her son's attitude, patted the patch firmly onto his skin, trying hard to be helpful.

"Now move around a little," said Debbie. "Make sure it is really stuck on there."

The rest of Ted's family was sitting at the dinner table, the same as always, waiting to see what happened once the patch was fully attached to his arm. Would his head explode? Would his arm fall off?

"WHAT IF HE BECOMES A ZOMBIE?" said Grandma Rose. "I CAN'T RUN THAT FAST WHAT WITH MY HIP."

"He's not going to become a zombie, Mother," said Debbie.

"Take the patch off, Ted," said Adeline, pulling at the bottom of his T-shirt, her eyes wet. "You know this isn't right."

Ted hid the patch under his sleeve and bent down to talk to his sister.

"Everything is going to be fine, Addie," said Ted.

"That patch won't make you happy."

"Then *you'll* have to make me happy, squirt." Ted tousled Adeline's hair.

"You're being stupid," said Adeline.

"You just don't understand, Adeline," said Ted. "I'm doing what I need to do."

Ted tried not to make eye contact with Scurvy, who was leaning against the refrigerator, watching Ted adjust the patch.

"Ya don't know what yer doing, Ted," said Scurvy somberly, but Ted rolled his sleeve down around his wrist and walked to the refrigerator to get some orange juice. Scurvy shook his head, and so did Eric.

"It was good knowing you, Eric," said Scurvy.

Eric nodded. From the look in the planda's tired eyes, Scurvy could tell he felt bad about the whole situation.

"But heck, chances are I'll be seeing ya soon," said Scurvy. "I might need a mate up there in Middlemost."

Eric nodded again. He could also use a buddy if he had to leave. Scurvy walked out on the deck to look at the ocean.

Inside the house, Debbie embraced her son. "You did the right thing, Ted. School starts in a couple of weeks, and you want this year to be better."

"I know, Mom."

Ted heard the thud of something falling to the ground, and when he turned in the direction of the sound, he saw Scurvy lying crumpled on the deck, his legs having given out from under him. Scurvy crawled to one of the plastic patio chairs and tried to pull himself up into it. Ted struggled against the urge to run out and help his friend, but the psychiatrist had told him he was supposed to ignore Scurvy no matter what. So that was what he was going to do.

"You're so *mean*," said Adeline. "Can't you see you're hurting him?"

Adeline ran out onto the deck to help Scurvy up. Ted saw Scurvy fall again. The pirate's legs were suddenly too weak to support the weight of his body.

"His hands have green *bumps* on them!" yelled Adeline.

Ted wished the patch worked some other way. But at the same time, Ted noticed something peculiar. As Scurvy grew weaker, he felt himself getting more confident. This was the right thing to do. This was what had to happen. He had to take care of his life. His *real* life.

45

XII

Weeks passed, and though Ted tried to enjoy what was left of his summer, it was impossible because Scurvy was still always *around*. When Ted went to the harbor, he'd see Scurvy sitting out on the jetty rocks, looking shrunken, his face and arms now covered in green bumps. When Ted went to the library, Scurvy would be there slumped in a study cubicle, overhead light off, popping green boils while he flipped through his books. When Ted went for a walk around the cranberry bog, he'd see Scurvy sitting on a rock in the middle of the pond, which was his way of making sure Ted remembered that this was the spot where they'd first met. But no matter where Scurvy popped up, Ted never said a word to him, and after a while Scurvy stopped talking too.

At home, Ted's relationship with Debbie and Grandma Rose had never been better. Grandma Rose yelled that she'd written him back into her will, though he wasn't sure what she could possibly leave behind, given that all she owned in the world was her wheelchair, a stack of *Life* magazines, and the license plate from her old Chevy Nova.

"Scurvy is right *there*," said Adeline, glaring at Ted and pointing to the couch, where Scurvy lay sprawled over the cushions, reading a copy of *Cosmopolitan*. "He's reading a magazine for girls because he's too tired to do anything else!"

"Ask him about tha bacon," Ted heard Scurvy whisper to Adeline.

"Scurvy wants to know if you'll make him some bacon," said Adeline. "He hasn't been eating, and he's really hungry."

"Adeline, I . . ."

"NO! Make him the bacon, Ted! It's not a big deal, and he's your *friend*."

"Tell him he's rottin' from tha inside out like a fish on tha shore," said Scurvy.

"You're rotting like a fish!" said Adeline.

"Adeline—"

"Tell him his heart is as black as a crow."

"Your heart is a crow!" said Adeline.

"Stop it," said Ted, firmly.

"Tell him—"

"NO MORE," said Ted, whipping around to face Scurvy. "You will *not* turn my sister against me!"

47

"Oh, hello, Ted," said Scurvy. "Didn't see ya there."

"You know as well as I do that this is something that needs to happen."

"It's not right ta kill a pirate on tha land."

"I'm not killing you," said Ted. "You can't kill something that's only in your head."

"Ah, poor, poor Ted. Ya've always known that I'm much more than a figment of yer imagination. All of us—me and Eric here and tha rest of tha beings you call imaginary friends—we're all real, but there comes a day when most kids just decide that we aren't, and we leave because why would we stay around if we're no longer wanted? But ya never had that day, and ya know I'm real—otherwise, I wouldn't be here in front of ya."

"You're lying to me."

"Fer all my life, I was in tha business of lyin', Ted, but I've never lied to ya. If ya want ta believe I was ever untrue to ya, well then, put on another patch and give it a good squeeze tah make sure all those drugs get into yer system faster."

Ted walked into the kitchen, disappearing around the corner and clanking through the cabinets.

"Are you making him the bacon?" said Adeline, but when Ted reappeared, he was holding a glass of water and a fresh patch.

"Adeline, I want to be a basic, normal teenager. I want some control over who I am and who I become, and that's why I'm doing this."

"Ya were born fer something more than a normal life!" said Scurvy.

Ted's prescription called for him to use one patch per week, but now he slapped a new patch directly above the patch he already had on.

"Come on, Eric. You shouldn't see this," said Adeline, walking out of the room with her hand hanging in the air, leading Eric away by his invisible paw.

Ted and Scurvy looked at one another.

"If you'll just leave on your own, I promise I'll stop using the patches," said Ted.

"When I'm gone, you'll know," said Scurvy.

"I don't want to hurt you. Why are you staying?"

"Maybe there's something I need tah tell ya."

"Then say it."

Scurvy used the strength he had been saving for the rest of

the day to stand up so that he could look Ted directly in the eye.

"I still think . . . ya should consider . . . making bacon from seals," said Scurvy, with a wink. "It's delicious."

"You wasted my time for THAT?" said Ted, beyond irritated. As he walked away, he heard Scurvy laughing behind him:

"Maybe I'll tell ya tha other thing later!"

49

XIII

The night before the first day of school, Scurvy Goonda disappeared. Ted was laying out what he was going to wear on his bed, all the new things that he'd bought with what was left of his supermarket money, eager to start off the year on the right foot. He was a sophomore now, which meant that he was no longer at the absolute *bottom* of the social totem pole.

He was about to shut off the light and go to bed when he looked out the window—sure enough, there was Scurvy, limping slowly down the middle of the road to town. Ted felt bad. Whether his pirate was imaginary or not, he was still worried that Scurvy might get hit by a car walking in the middle of the road like that. He put on his shoes and went outside.

"Scurvy!" he yelled, standing on the house's front steps, causing the pirate to stop for a moment. But then Scurvy just shook his head and kept walking.

"At least use the side of the road!" yelled Ted, but Scurvy continued on his way the same as before. There was something about the way he was moving that made Ted nervous.

"Scurvy!"

No response.

"Where are you going?" yelled Ted. The question made Scurvy stop in his tracks and turn to look at him. When he spoke, Ted barely recognized the sandpaper voice that coarsely filled the night: "Middlemost," said Scurvy.

"The middle of what—"

"Don't ya worry about tha middle of what!" snapped Scurvy. He turned back toward the road.

"Am I going to see you again?" said Ted.

Scurvy looked at him.

"If I was right about ya," he said, "then ya will see me again."

And with that, Scurvy took the final few steps around the bend in the road and disappeared from sight. Gone gone gone.

51

XIV

Rumor had it that the architect who had designed Ted's high school had also designed the state prison in South Walpole, where Massachusetts's hardest criminals were locked away. The high school was filled with long hallways and small windows that refused to let in any natural light, and the lockers lining the corridors were thin and gray, invoking the same parallel lines as the bars of a cell.

Inside the sterile, cavernous cafeteria, Ted stood in place holding his tray, surrounded on all sides by tables full of kids who were talking about vacations and hookups and parties and other things that had happened to them on the Cape and elsewhere. He looked for a table where he could make new, unimaginative friends, and spotted one nearby that was filled with guys of average intelligence and social standing. Ted sometimes heard them in the hallway talking about televised no-holds-barred fighting championships. In terms of the social strata, they were *just there*, and that was all that Ted wanted to be—just there, just a part of a herd shuffling from class to class, normal and going through the days without getting beaten up or picked on or singled out as a freak.

Ted put down his lunch tray in front of an empty seat. The boys sitting at the table turned to look at him.

"I'm Ted," said Ted. "And I'm letting everybody know that my pirate is gone."

The boys looked at each other.

"I truly did not know he could talk," said a guy wearing a Bud Light T-shirt and warm-up pants.

"I'm talking," said Ted. "I'm turning over a new leaf."

"Well, that's super-duper, Ted," said another guy, who was wearing a beaded hemp necklace. "We can't wait to have some conversations with you, and help you turn that leaf."

"We're huge leaf-turners," said the Bud Light guy. "I can't walk past a leaf on the *street* without wanting to know what's on the other side."

"Nothing better than a mutual exchange of ideas with an interesting new friend," said the hemp-necklace guy, and Ted's heart jumped a little at the word *friend*. His instincts were right—these were his people.

53

"You say you got rid of your pirate? Take some medication for that?"

"Uh-huh," said Ted. "I used a patch."

"Well, that's a *fantastic* thing, Ted. Being pirate-less is going to help you a lot. Actually, Charlie here"—the Bud Light guy pointed to a kid who was laughing on the other side of the table—"Charlie just got rid of his imaginary antelope. Isn't that right, Charlie?"

"Sure is," said Charlie.

"And if I'm not mistaken, that antelope liked to dress like a paratrooper—isn't that right?"

"Thought he had served in Nam," said Charlie. "And actually, he claimed to have fought alongside Sully's friend—what was it again, Sully? Wasn't it a dolphin, or something?"

"That's exactly right," said Sully. "War dolphin. It fought in a couple of battles, which screwed it up in the head, which is why I had to get rid of it. Post-traumatic stress disorder."

"You see, Ted?" said Bud Light. "You're surrounded by a *whole table* of guys who had to get rid of their crazy imaginary friends, just the same as you. Heck, it took forever to get Jimmy there to give up his Pegasus."

"I still sleep with a feather from its wing. I miss its smell."

The table erupted with laughter, the howling loud enough to draw the attention of much of the lunchroom. By now, Ted had figured out that he was being mocked, and rivers of nervousness were running up his back and all over his body. He picked up his tray.

"If you didn't want me to sit here," he said, "you could have just said so."

Ted was about to walk to an empty table, but other kids were already filling it up. All the kids at tables with open seats were staring at him, *imploring* him with their eyes not to sit there. Ted turned in a circle, with nowhere to go, and then—

"A YO HO AND A BOTTLE OF RUM!" said bully Duke. "HEY, TED, SAY SOMETHING CRAZY!"

Oh, man.

"MAYBE HE'S SO CRAZY HE FORGOT HOW TO TALK!" said Duke, who apparently hadn't learned new taunts during the summer.

"You were a senior last year," said Ted. "I thought you graduated."

"What did you say?" said Duke, stepping forward.

"You were a senior. You should have graduated."

"Plenty of guys do a FIFTH YEAR, you moron. SPORTS!

Colleges want older players, and I'm gonna get NOTICED. If it wasn't for me, nobody would CARE about the cross-country team in this town."

Ted thought about this. "Wait, what?" he said. "You're running cross-country instead of playing football?"

"I got kicked off the football team," said Duke.

"For what?"

"NEVER MIND FOR WHAT. I'm gonna EAT your pirate this year." Duke smacked Ted on the forehead and walked back to his table, where Carolina Waltz was sitting, little splotches of Tater Tot ketchup surrounding her mouth.

However, for the first time ever, she wasn't laughing.

She was just looking at Ted.

Ted searched around for an empty table where he could finish his lunch, but he couldn't find one, so he stood in the middle of the cafeteria floor and tried to balance his tray with one hand and eat with the other. Taking a sip of his milk, he wished he had someone to eat lunch with. He just wanted a place to start.

55

XV

A week into the school year, Ted found somebody—a foreign-exchange student named Kettil, who was from Sweden, and whose name actually meant "kettle." It was an appropriate label. Kettil had a stocky midsection and stubby arms and usually looked like he was overheating.

The first time he saw Kettil, Ted felt bad for the Swede, who was standing in the hallway watching the hordes of students rush past. Kettil repeatedly glanced down at a piece of paper in his hand and then back up, until Ted finally walked over to figure out what was going on.

"I'm Ted."

"Kettil."

"Do you need help with something?"

Kettil pointed at the sheet of paper, showing his class schedule.

"You're in Algebra II?"

"Yes please you're welcome."

"Come on. We're in the same class. I'll show you where to go."

"Yes please you're welcome."

"Kettil" and "yes please you're welcome" were pretty much all that Kettil seemed to be able to say in English. This baffled Ted, because wasn't Scandinavia known for its multilingual education system? He had assumed that a high school–age kid would speak at least a little English.

On the third day of their friendship, Kettil sat across from Ted, pointing at different objects in the lunchroom and giving their Swedish translations.

"*Bord*," said Kettil.

"Okay, then. A *bord* is a table," said Ted.

"*Bricka*," said Kettil.

"A *bricka* is a tray."

"*Vägg*," said Kettil.

"The wall is a *vägg*. Got it," said Ted.

It wasn't quite the conversation about girls and movies and those kinds of things that Ted was hoping for with a new friend, but it was something.

During the second week of classes, when Ted walked through the door after school, Debbie called him over for a hug. Ever since he had gotten rid of Scurvy Goonda, he had become just her normal kid enjoying a normal existence at a normal New England high school.

"How was your day, Ted?" said Debbie.

"It was fine, Mom."

"Making friends?"

"Yep. I'm hanging out with a Swede."

"Well, how about bringing your Swede over one of these days? It would be *wonderful* to meet him. Tell him how I love ABBA."

"He doesn't speak much English."

"You can teach him!"

"I'm trying. I think he said he wanted to join the drama club. Either that, or he was saying he wanted some Tater Tots. He's hard to understand."

57

"Oh, and *you* should join the drama club. You could be an actor! I can just see you up on a stage, wearing makeup. You're so *handsome*. You know, I was quite the actress in my day."

"I know. In college you played Elaine in *Arsenic and Old Lace*."

"At Cape Cod Community College I played Elaine in *Arsenic and Old Lace*. People told me I should go to New York. But if I had, I wouldn't have had *you*. Of course, if I hadn't had you, I wouldn't still have all this baby weight."

Ted always felt sorry for his mother when she started talking about her theatrical sojourn, which she remembered almost as fondly as she did the years of her marriage.

"Maybe you'll still go to New York? Eventually?" said Ted.

Debbie smiled sadly at her son.

"I hope I'll still be able to do a lot of things, someday," said Debbie. "Oh, I almost forgot to tell you. That night manager from the supermarket called here today."

"Why?"

"He wouldn't say. He just told me to tell you to call him at the store tonight."

"Okay."

Ted walked toward his room, wondering why in the world Jed would be calling him. As he passed Adeline's room, he saw his sister sitting on the floor scribbling with crayons, furiously switching back and forth between reds and yellows. She hadn't spoken to Ted since Scurvy went away.

"Hi, Adeline?" said Ted. But Adeline just raised her eyes and glared at him.

"Is something wrong?" said Ted.

For the first time in weeks, Adeline said something to him: "Eric is GONE."

"What do you mean he's gone?"

"GONE. GONE!"

"Maybe he's hiding. Were you playing hide-and-seek or some other game?"

"I think I would KNOW if I was playing a game with him. He's just *gone*," said Adeline. Her eyes were getting wet.

"When did you last see him?"

"Last night," said Adeline, sniffling. "He was all sick and covered in those same green bumps that Scurvy had, so I let him sleep in my bed so that he would feel better. When I woke up, he was *gone!*"

"Eric was covered in green bumps?"

"He *caught* them from Scurvy."

"You didn't touch any of my patches, did you?"

"NO I DIDN'T TOUCH ANY OF YOUR STUPID PATCHES. Why would I DO that? Scurvy said that you were going to be able to help Eric, but you didn't do ANYTHING!"

Ted thought about this.

"Adeline, I've never even *seen* Eric," said Ted.

"But Scurvy said you would help," said Adeline.

Ted wasn't sure what to do. Even though Adeline was crying, she didn't want Ted to comfort her, and he wasn't sure what Scurvy had meant by saying he would help Eric. So he just stood there, dumbly leaning against the doorframe.

"I want to draw some more now," said Adeline. "By myself."

Ted went to his bedroom and lay down on his bed, looking up at the glow-in-the-dark stars on the ceiling. He didn't know

59

why he kept them up there. When his father had glued them to the ceiling, he had made sure that every constellation was correct. Ted could still find the North Star in the night sky, and he could point out the fish shape of Piscis Austrinus and talk about how the Greeks thought that the Corona Borealis was the crown of Ariadne.

The constellation Orion was as far away from Ted's bed as possible, in the corner of the room, and he had never looked at it all that much. But tonight as he stared at it, zoning out, he noticed something that he had never seen before. The center star in Orion's belt glowed more brightly than the other stars in the constellation—and all the other stars in the room, for that matter. Not by much, but enough to make Ted get out of bed to take a closer look. He pulled the chair away from his desk and stood on it, so that his head was only a foot or so from the center star.

It was still a basic glow-in-the-dark cutout, but it was made of thicker plastic, and it was larger than its counterparts. Its tips were more defined, and it seemed likely that it had been purchased separately from the other stars, which were clearly part of the same kit. But why would his dad have gone to all that trouble for just one star?

Ted reached up and carefully peeled it off the ceiling. He turned it over in his hands, and when he saw what was on the back, a jolt like he had never felt before shot through his body.

On the star was a single word: *HERE!*

XVI

Ted opened his eyes and saw that it was almost ten-thirty p.m.—he'd fallen asleep right on top of his chemistry textbook. He walked into the kitchen, pulled a yellow phone book out of a drawer, and found the number for the supermarket.

"Stop to Shop," said a voice. "Can I help you?"

"I'm calling for Jed, the night manager, please."

Ted waited a few seconds, and then his old boss's voice clicked on: "You've got Jed, and Jed's got you."

"Hey, Jed. This is Ted Merritt. My mom said you called."

"You bet I did," said Jed, more than a touch of anger in his voice.

"Er," said Ted, "what did you want to talk about?"

"What I want to TALK about is the VANDALISM of the meat section. Your former section if I remember correctly."

Ted paused, completely lost.

"There's something happening in the meat section?" he said.

"OH, COME ON," sneered Jed. "For the last WEEK somebody has been coming here AT NIGHT and ripping apart the meat section. You and I know that you didn't leave here on the best of terms, and that was *your* section, so it seems pretty clear who the prime suspect should be."

"Why don't you ask the current meat guy about what's going on?"

"I have. The attacks always happen when he's away from the section. On break, getting supplies out of the back, that kind of thing."

"Why don't you just check the security cameras to see who is doing it?"

"We have," said Jed, suddenly sounding unsure of himself. "One minute everything is normal, and the next, all the packages are sliced open."

Sliced.

"And we're thinking that maybe you're doing something weird to the cameras."

"Who's 'we'?"

"Well, so far 'we' is me, I guess, but I'm sure if I brought up the issue with the other guys—"

"Jed, I've never been inside the camera room. I stocked meat, that's it."

"You stocked meat, but you're also *crazy*, and if you're acting out some kind of sick revenge thing here, I want it *stopped*."

"What packages are being sliced open?"

"Meat packages."

"But what kind of meat?"

"Bacon."

With that, Ted hung up the phone. Scurvy wasn't gone. He had simply relocated.

XVII

The next day, all over the world, something weird was happening. It was hard to define exactly *what* was different. Some people thought that the air didn't feel the same as it had the day before, while others thought that the sunlight looked odd or that the wind seemed to be blowing in the wrong direction.

In Mongolia, seven-year-old Oochkoo Bat awakened in her drafty room to discover that her best friend, Mandoni—a miniature fire-eating yak—was not sleeping in his normal spot on the closet floor. He was gone. Oochkoo hoped that Mandoni was okay—the yak had been breaking out in green spots for the past week, and though she had tried to hug him and make sure that he was comforted, the yak had still seemed in pain. Not knowing where Mandoni was—or even if her yak was alive—made Oochkoo cry all day.

In Iceland, five-year-old Halldor Gundmondsson pulled open his window blinds to let in the late-summer sunlight, expecting to see his rhinoceros friend, Bjarni, stomping around in his yellow raincoat. The rhinoceros considered himself a fisherman, so Halldor checked the shore when he found the rhinoceros missing. All that was left of the rhino was one of his galoshes, stuck in the crevasse of some volcanic rock.

In the African country of Eritrea, pretty Natsinet Tenolde walked along the dirt streets of her village, searching the tops of houses and the branches of trees for a talking leaf-nosed bat named Gongab. Gongab had been Natsinet's confidant ever since she had lost her mother to illness, but now Gongab was gone, and Natsinet found herself joining other kids from the community who were looking for their own friends. Some of the children were crying, while others were being carried by parents who knew they wouldn't be able to see whatever it was they were searching for, and therefore didn't know quite what to do.

All across the planet, in every country in the world, every single imaginary friend had *vanished*. Young children everywhere were refusing to go to school, screaming that they wanted their friends back and describing how their friends had been sick. Adults frantically telephoned one another or met to try to figure out what was happening. Was this a mass psychosis? Was there something bad in the water supply? Reports of hysterical children were coming in from all over the world, and the grown-ups couldn't seem to wrap their minds around what was happening. *How could all these kids be going nuts at the same time?*

Many of the duller children, sitting in front of their televisions playing shoot-'em-up video games, simply turned up the volume to drown out the voices of kids crying for their friends. But for the kids whose brains cranked and crackled properly, this was a monumental personal crisis.

The worldwide disappearance of imaginary friends was leaving the press, and in particular television newscasters, in a bind. This was clearly a big story, but there wasn't any footage they could broadcast, aside from kids walking around their neighborhoods shouting for lost giants or robots, with the occasional clip of an elementary school girl babbling into a camera about how her jeweled pony was gone. And viewers didn't like to see little kids cry. Confused cops stumbled through interviews, promising to look into the disappearances immediately, though when asked what they would be looking for, they couldn't quite say.

Ted sat on his couch with a red-eyed Adeline next to him, watching a local reporter interview the mother of a six-year-old boy, who was stomping through some hedges in the background:

"And what exactly is he looking for?"

"Well, he has a . . . friend . . . named Flappybappy. And when he woke up this morning, Flappybappy was gone."

"What kind of friend is Flappybappy?"

"Flappybappy is . . . a manatee."

"A manatee."

"One of those elephant things that swim in rivers in Florida. I think he saw something about them on the Discovery Channel, and he's had one ever since."

"But this manatee walks on land."

"That's right. And he always carries doughnuts."

"Were there any indications that . . . Flappybappy might go missing?"

"Well, my son said that he had recently broken out in these bumps, but I don't really know what that means."

Ted felt his sister looking at him. "I didn't have anything to do with this, Adeline," he said.

"EVERYBODY in the whole WORLD lost their friends! And they were all SICK with the same green spots that Scurvy got when YOU started using the patches!"

65

"I'm sure that there were some that had green bumps before I started using the patches."

"There *weren't*," said Adeline. "I can *see* everybody's abstract companions! *You* got Scurvy sick with the bumps, and then Eric caught the disease from Scurvy, and Eric passed it on, and pretty soon *all* of the ab-coms in the whole *world* got sick and it is ALL YOUR FAULT."

"Have you ever read *The Crucible?*" said Ted. He knew that Adeline, being seven years old, had not. "It's a play about witch trials, and in it, one girl starts saying that certain people are witches, and soon enough *all* of her friends are accusing people of being witches. Hysteria is contagious."

"But this is happening ALL OVER THE WORLD."

"Radio, Internet, television—kids are just hearing about it and saying they're missing friends too, to get out of school."

"ERIC THE PLANDA IS GONE AND I'M NOT TRYING TO MISS SCHOOL," said Adeline, hitting the couch with both fists. "IT WAS YOU! YOU GOT THE AB-COMS SICK AND TAKEN AWAY! YOU'RE NOT EVEN MY *BROTHER* ANYMORE! YOU'RE JUST NORMAL AND MEAN!"

Adeline grabbed her schoolbooks and stomped away, and Ted got a terrible feeling in his stomach. What *was* he doing? A month ago, he and Scurvy Goonda were spending every single day together—sleeping in the same bed, even—and now he had somehow become exactly like the people who told him that Scurvy was just the product of something misfiring in his head. But this—hundreds of millions of kids being orphaned by their friends on the same day—this was something real. He was a jerk for refusing to admit it. If this was becoming a normal kid, no thanks.

Ted grabbed his backpack and darted out the front door. He found Adeline at the end of the street, waiting for her school bus with a couple of other second graders, one of whom looked extremely sad.

"What?" said Adeline, seeing him coming.

"You're right," said Ted. "I'm acting toward you the way people act toward me. I'm sorry."

"Okay, Ted. So, now what?"

"I'll try and do something about this. If Scurvy thought that I could stop this from happening in some way—I'll talk to him."

"Scurvy is GONE, Ted."

"Well, maybe not."

The school bus pulled up and the two other seven-year-olds got on. Ted had stood with Adeline many times before to make sure she was safe, and he'd never heard the bus so quiet. She climbed onto the first step and then turned around.

"You PROMISE you're going to do something?" she said.

"I promise to try."

"*Try* doesn't count."

"Okay, Addie," said Ted. "I promise. Get on the bus, and we'll talk more about this later."

Adeline disappeared up the steps and the bus pulled away, leaving Ted holding his backpack, wishing that he hadn't just made an impossible promise. There was no way a problem of this magnitude could be his responsibility, no matter what Scurvy might or might not have told Adeline before stomping

67

away in the middle of the night. Somewhere, there had to be a team of scientists examining data from beeping machines and poring over data readouts, pegging the moment that the disappearances had taken place and working on a quick solution to put everything back the way it was supposed to be. It was ridiculous to think that someone like him could resolve this crisis.

Still, his doctor wouldn't be pleased with what he was about to do.

XVIII

It was almost eleven o'clock, and Ted was glad to have the night alone to himself. It had been an odd day, yet one that was, shockingly, not as awkward as he had anticipated. Many of his classmates must have had younger siblings missing imaginary friends, because the eyes he felt looking at him as he made his way through the hallways weren't of the usual *you're a freak!* variety, but instead were sympathetic, as if his fellow students might finally be considering that his pirate was, or had been, real.

Ted approached Stop to Shop from the road behind the supermarket. He knew that the rear door was always open, and he didn't want to alert Jed to his presence. He pulled the door open just enough so that he could slide inside without risking a squeaking hinge, and bounded behind a water fountain. From there, shuffling close to the ground, he made his way behind the deli display case. It wasn't the best hiding spot because all the food that was usually inside the case had been removed for the night, but it offered an excellent view of his old stomping ground, the meat aisle.

The new meat attendant was a guy Ted had never seen before. He had thin yellow hair and bone-white skin, and he was in the middle of singing to himself. Ted didn't recognize the lyrics to the ditty, which might have been in a foreign language. Before he had been fired, he had heard a rumor that the store might be bringing in a few Czech employees, and this could be one of them.

The possible Czech was drinking steadily from a liter bottle of blue Gatorade. It wouldn't be long before he needed to use the restroom. As expected, once the bottle was empty, the Czech walked toward the break area, leaving the meat aisle unattended.

Something was going to happen.

And then . . . ever so slowly . . . the gray swinging doors that led to the back of the store were pushed open from the inside. A dirty hand emerged and landed with a slap on the tile floor. Then came another hand, and then the rest of a dirty, hairy, ragged body.

"Scurvy," whispered Ted.

Except this Scurvy was gaunt and sick and *covered* in green bumps. He crawled to the base of the meat section, where he paused and slowly removed his sword from its scabbard. With great effort, he swooshed the blade through a row of premium bacon. Plastic packaging erupted into the air, and slabs of raw meat spilled all over the floor.

"Ha-HAR!" said Scurvy, who again attacked the row of bacon. The packaged cold cuts and honey-baked hams now looked like they had been through a war. Ted winced, knowing how irritating it was going to be for the new meat guy to clean up the mess.

"Rarr!" said Scurvy.

Scurvy swung his sword again and again, blade always cutting cleanly through the meats, making small squishing sounds.

"THAT'S fer abandoning me!" said Scurvy, sending more pig wedges cascading to the floor.

"And THAT'S fer gettin' everybody else sick with yer stupid patches!" said Scurvy, and more juices burst in every direction. "Patient ZERO, ya are! Tha great infector!"

Ted was impressed with how accurate Scurvy's assaults were, considering the pirate's weakened condition—in all the years that they had been together, Ted had never seen Scurvy simply go *nuts* with his sword.

"Typhoid Ted! Tha scourge of tha abstract! That's what they should call ya!" said Scurvy, and Ted realized that Scurvy was picturing *him* as he attacked the meat.

"Ho-HO!" said Scurvy, with a final lunge that slit the last remaining undamaged package of bacon in half.

The pirate placed his sword back in its sheath, and then stood quietly for a moment, shoulders heaving, trying to catch his breath. He got down on his knees and began gathering bits of bacon from the floor, shoving as much meat into his pockets as he possibly could, muttering "Oooh, that's a good one" and "Nope, that's turkey bacon" until the *clop clop* sound of approaching footsteps sent him shuffling for the back of the store, pieces of bacon dropping from his greatcoat the entire way.

With one push through the swinging gray doors, Scurvy Goonda was once again gone from Ted's life.

The meat attendant came back from the bathroom just as the doors stopped moving. He stood stock-still in front of the aisle, taking in the scope of the carnage.

"*Hlupák!*" he said.

Had Ted spoken Czech, he would have realized that the

71

meat guy was shouting "Idiot!"—though whether he was shouting it at himself or the meat marauder wasn't altogether clear.

The Czech stomped away muttering under his breath—no doubt heading off to find the night manager—and Ted knew that he didn't have much time if he was going to have a chance to talk to Scurvy. He crawled out from behind the deli cabinet and followed Scurvy's exit path, pushing his way through the gray doors into the back of the store.

A trail of bacon morsels lined the ground where they had fallen from Scurvy's pockets. The more Ted followed the meat, the sicker he felt about where the scraps might be leading him.

It can't be, thought Ted.

At the end of the trail, he leaned over and picked a final glob of quivering pink bacon up from the floor.

Ted was standing in front of the Crusher.

"Scurvy?" said Ted.

He looked down into the guts of the Crusher, where sat twenty or so boxes, fully intact, just waiting for somebody to hit the switch and put them out of their misery. Because the machine wasn't as full as usual, for the first time Ted was able to see just how *deep* the inside chamber really was. Taking in the Crusher's awesome depth, he noticed something peculiar. The places that weren't covered by cardboard seemed to be leaking a bizarre white light. The light looked almost like sunlight, but that didn't make sense, considering it was past midnight and the storage room floor was made of cold cement.

In addition to the light, something else made Ted nervous: several boxes had been splattered with meat juice and bacon gloops, meaning that Scurvy Goonda had likely been inside the Crusher—which was such an act of insanity that Ted could barely wrap his mind around the idea.

"All right, Scurvy," said Ted. "Let's go, olly-olly oxen free. Come on out! I know you're angry at me, but I have a question I need to ask."

Nothing.

"I don't want to come down there!" said Ted, and he really didn't.

He was beginning to think that Scurvy might be hiding in the back right corner of the chamber, where there seemed to be the greatest concentration of bacon gobbets, so he grabbed a mop leaning against a nearby wall, flipped it around, and began poking the boxes with its blunt end.

"C'mon, Scurvy! Come out!"

Ted's mop-poking caused some of the boxes to slide over each other, and more strange light leaked up from the bottom. But still, he didn't see any sign of Scurvy Goonda.

Then, from somewhere else in the storage room, he heard a voice.

"I THINK HE'S BACK HERE," said Jed, who sounded like he was approaching from Ted's left. But when Ted turned to run in the opposite direction, he saw movement and a flash of blue uniforms:

Cops!

Ted scanned the storeroom for a place to hide, but he didn't have any decent choices. He couldn't jump in a trash can because it was full, and the pallets of jumbo soda bottles were too tightly packed to squeeze behind. If he made a dash to hide behind one of the large boxes of diapers or paper towels, the cops were going to spot him and arrest him.

73

He only had one option.

"If you're down there, Scurvy," whispered Ted to himself, "I'm going to kill you."

With that, Ted climbed into the Crusher's central chamber, lowering himself into the heap of cardboard boxes as quietly as he could.

In one way, he felt like he was five years old again and swimming around inside one of those plastic ball pits at the Barnstable County Fair. But he also felt abject terror, because looking up, he could see the inner gears and teeth of the Crusher.

He dug down into the boxes until he thought he was entirely covered. There was more of the light down here than there was above, and he thought he could see where it was coming from—a rectangular sliding panel at the bottom of the bin that had somehow become dislodged, leaving a half-foot gap between the wall and the edge of the steel plate.

Voices filtered down to him from above:

"See anything?" said Jed.

"Nope," said a deep voice, probably a cop. "Thought I heard something, but it might just have been you."

"Whoever did it couldn't have gone far. There are bits of bacon all over the place."

Covered with cardboard as he was, Ted couldn't see that Jed was looking down into the machine. Ted also couldn't see that Jed, having realized that something strange might be going on inside the Crusher, had quickly formed a simple, wicked plan to flush Ted out of the machine.

"WELL, PLENTY OF CARDBOARD THAT NEEDS CRUSHING!" shouted Jed. "BETTER TAKE CARE OF IT!"

And with that, Jed threw the switch.

Ted felt the initial vibrations below his body before he heard the roar of the machine coming to life. He was shocked at how quickly everything happened after that. The bin began rattling furiously, followed by a hydraulic whoosh as the walls started moving in, pressing the cardboard boxes together.

Ted's first instinct was to get out. The obvious way of doing so was to leave the way he'd come in—from above—but an enormous amount of crushing metal was quickly descending upon him from that direction. He could feel the power of the Crusher and all its parts, and he was afraid that if he tried to leap over the wall of the bin, the rapidly lowering metal press might cut him in half.

Which meant, essentially, that there was no way to escape.

Then the survival part of his brain made a decision for him. Instead of warning him to escape by going up, it ordered him to head down. He grabbed the loose panel that was letting in the light, and pulled with the full weight of his body.

To his surprise, the panel slid backward, revealing an empty space underneath the Crusher.

A trapdoor.

Ted slid through the opening feetfirst, barely managing to keep his head out of the way of the metal presses, and snapped the panel shut. Above him, he heard twenty boxes being twisted and smashed into a cardboard brick, followed by the silence of the gears grinding to a halt—making sure that what they had crushed stayed crushed—followed by the sound of the gears turning again, pulling the presses back into their resting positions.

When all of the Crusher's various noises finally stopped,

Ted was just barely able to make out the night manager's muffled voice filtering down to him from above.

"Huh," said Jed. "Thought there might be somebody down there."

"And you turned it *on?*" said one of the cops.

"Well, I was wrong, wasn't I?"

Ted waited until he heard no more voices before he finally allowed himself to exhale and look around—which was difficult, because it was so bright.

He appeared to be in a vent of some kind. The metal walls surrounding him were polished to an almost iridescent shine, which was causing the light to bounce crazily from wall to ceiling to wall, spilling over everything and stinging Ted's eyes.

There was only one way for Ted to go unless he wanted to head back and risk being captured by the cops—toward the end of the tunnel, which was where the light seemed to be coming from. He pressed down on the floor of the vent to make sure it was secure enough to hold his weight, and then he saw something curious: bits of bacon lined the floor of the vent, endlessly stretching out before him in the direction of the light.

"Scurv?" said Ted.

His voice echoed back to him boomingly: SCURV—SCURV—SCURV . . .

Ted started to crawl.

The vent was a few inches wider than his shoulders and a few inches taller than his head. If it was such a tight fit for him, it was likely terribly uncomfortable for Scurvy, who even in his weakened state had a thicker body than Ted. Every few feet, Ted passed another glob of bacon, some of which looked like it had been sitting out for weeks, covered in mold and reeking. Scurvy had apparently made quite a few trips back and forth to the supermarket. It was no wonder that Jed had lost his mind trying to solve the riddle of the bacon vandal.

Suddenly, Ted passed a fresh glob—Scurvy must have just been here.

"Hello?" said Ted.

HELLO—LO—LO said his echo.

He crawled and crawled, but the light at the end of the vent always seemed to be the same distance away. The light was clearly playing tricks on his eyes, so he decided to look only at the floor, which was littered with bacon gloops of various sizes and states of rottenness.

And so it was while he had his head down that he somehow reached the end of the vent—or at least what he presumed to be the end of the vent, because the light was suddenly so overpowering that he couldn't see anything at all. He put his palms down one in front of the other and tried to crawl away from the brightness. And then he started to fall.

Ted felt his stomach leap into his throat and the wind whip through his hair, and he waited for the inevitable impact that would splatter him onto some kind of flat surface below.

But when he looked down, he saw that he was plummeting toward the bright white light. He looked left and then right and saw that the vent was now far wider than it had been in the supermarket. It was as if he had fallen into the world's

77

largest metal-plated well, a fissure so deep that no excavation equipment would ever be able to find him, and his cries for help would never be heard.

But the more Ted looked at the walls around him, the more he started to notice things about the metal vent. It wasn't entirely unbroken—there were small tunnels shooting every which way. The tunnels didn't look quite tall enough to stand up in.

Could I somehow grab on to one of these openings? thought Ted. *No. I'd still be stuck miles beneath the ground with nowhere to go.*

The white light was surging so fast that Ted felt almost relieved to be falling through this giant hole in the world. The wind against his face helped offset some of the hotness seething from the walls surrounding him.

Wait, what's that? thought Ted. Below him, backlit by the white light, a shadow was shooting up toward him.

Ted flapped his arms to get its attention and yelled, "HEY!" as loud as he could, but his words just floated into the air above.

And then the shadow wasn't just a shadow anymore. Ted began to make out hairy arms and legs, but even though the hairy thing was close, it didn't see him until the last possible second. The hairy thing raised its arms and shouted, "WATCH OUT!" but it was too late: both Ted and the hairy thing were moving too fast to change course.

SMACK!

Ted collided with a white-faced saki monkey who was wearing a crisp blue pilot's uniform.

"I *SAID*, 'WATCH OUT!' " said the saki monkey.

The saki monkey was disappointed to see that the crash had ripped the sleeve of his uniform, but the monkey felt better when it saw Ted spiraling toward the middle of the Earth.

"IF I SEE YOU IN MIDDLEMOST," yelled the monkey, "YOU'RE PAYING TO HAVE THIS RETAILORED!"

But the unconscious Ted didn't respond.

XIX

The ThereYouGo Gate, located in the Earth's core, is a principal topic in abstract companion legend. All abstract companions know that the gate is in the center of the world, and they all know that it zips them to Middlemost. These are the two central ideas of the popular campfire song "That Ol' There-YouGo Gate to Middlemost":

> *Oh, ThereYouGo Gate, take me away!*
> *Back to that star where it's pleasant all day!*
> *My best friend has ditched me and I feel like a ghost!*
> *Oh, welcome me back to my home, Middlemost!*

In the last few weeks, countless ab-coms had this song in their heads as they streamed through the ThereYouGo Gate, even though many were returning simply for health reasons. Indeed, when the Greenies plague first hit, all the world's ab-coms who hadn't yet reported to Middlemost received an official dispatch from President Persephone Skeleton:

Attention All
ABSTRACT COMPANIONS!

Got green bumps?

Well, we warned you,
didn't we?
We told you that the humans were planning
to exterminate ALL AB-COMS! But did you
listen? No! And now you're
SICK! And BUMPY!

Come back to your beloved Middlemost
NOW!
We have discovered the antidote! We will
take care of you! If not properly treated, you
will DISAPPEAR PERMANENTLY
into a pool of green sludge!
Do you want that? To be sludgy?

This is the FINAL NOTICE of the call to
arms! Your last day to report to Middlemost
is September 22–which is my birthday,
incidentally. Gifts are strongly
recommended! Come home and be cured!
Come home and join the fight!
TO ARMS!

Your terribly sophisticated leader,
PRESIDENT PERSEPHONE SKELETON

81

Hundreds of thousands of copies of these letters over-
flowed the very large trash cans outside the ThereYouGo

Gate. But Ted didn't see any of them. He was still unconscious.

Odd things flashed through his zonked mind as he plummeted through the ThereYouGo Gate and disappeared in a bright flash of static electricity:

How giraffes sleep less than an hour per night.

How it was impractical that humans only grew two sets of teeth in a lifetime, considering how easy it was to get cavities.

Why the Mona Lisa didn't have any eyebrows.

And then—*PHHZZT!*

XX

SMACK!

Ted's body broke a branch in a massive tree, causing leaves to spray in every direction and snapping him out of his daze just before he hit the ground with a dull thud.

For a long moment, he just lay on his back, looking up at the tree that interrupted his fall.

"What . . . the heck . . . was all . . . of that?" Ted asked the tree, but the tree didn't respond, though it could have if it had wanted to.

High above the tree's branches, he could see a small dark vent that appeared to hover in midair, poking out of the sky like the end of a pipe. A crude catapult built of vines and wooden planks stood near the base of the tree. BACON — HO! had been carved into the side of the catapult. Ted looked back and forth between the vent in the sky and the catapult. Scurvy had often talked about using catapults in sea battles. Had he launched himself with this one?

Ted climbed to his feet and checked in with his body— bending his fingers, shaking out his legs, jogging in place—to make sure everything was in working order. He was definitely battered, but nothing felt broken.

Knowing that he was going to live at least a little while longer, he turned to survey this strange place. To his surprise, it looked a lot like the world he was used to, except that everything just seemed a bit *different*.

He was standing at the top of a hill. Beneath him was a meadow with wild grasses the color of seashells. In the distance he could see the outline of a forest, but the trees seemed too tall to be located next to the low-lying meadow. Edging the forest was a thin strip of pinkish-bluish sand that might have been a desert. Everywhere Ted looked, one type of landscape abruptly stopped and a completely different one began. It was as if Ted were trapped in a terrarium meticulously constructed by ambitious children.

The sky was huge and blue and mottled with white clouds that looked the same as they did back home, but it seemed as though the atmosphere had somehow become confused and had allowed the night to stick around. There were stars everywhere, twinkling bright in the middle of the day and forming constellations that Ted had never seen before. These weren't the same stars he had looked at all his life—or if they were, he definitely wasn't seeing them from the same angle.

On the horizon, he could see what looked like thousands of spotlights, all pointed directly upward, blasting blindingly golden beams out into deep space.

"Hello?" he yelled. "Anybody out there?"

Whoosh! His words hadn't even echoed, but as soon as they left his mouth it was like he'd hit a switch that completely electrified the meadow. Some *things* began racing through the field. He heard the *whap whap whap* of grass rapidly being knocked down, and the somethings sped off in the direction of the pinkish-bluish desert.

"Don't be scared!" yelled Ted. "I'm just lost!"

Then a strange-looking man came floating toward him through the meadow.

"Um—hello there?" said Ted.

The man said nothing.

"I think I took a wrong turn," Ted explained, but the man just kept coming. "I fell from that vent hanging in the sky."

The thought crossed Ted's mind that the man might be deaf, and he briefly considered trying to communicate with him via sign language, but the only sign he remembered from his second-grade class was the one for *I love you*. It seemed inappropriate to make such a sweeping romantic statement to a freaky stranger.

As the man drew closer, Ted noted that he was wearing a well-tailored three-button suit, like something a mortician might wear. His face was handsome and youthful, and his eyes were very, very dark.

85

"Hi?" said Ted when the man was hovering about ten feet away, but this time, the man actually did something. He smiled.

The smile, slick and clearly well-practiced, caused a bolt of fear to shoot up Ted's spine. Ted darted for the meadow, running as fast as he could, but the strange man simply advanced more quickly, easily closing the gap between them and whipping around to confront Ted face to face.

"Well, well, well. I don't think you should be here at all," the man said, his voice deep and smooth as honey.

In the split second before Ted felt a hard blow on the side of his head and the world went black, he caught a second glimpse at the smile. White. Sharp. Fanged.

But then again, vampires always have good teeth.

Part Two

Persephone Skeleton stood in front of a full-length silver mirror combing her hair—or, more precisely, her wig. Over the past three hundred years, she felt she had evolved quite nicely into her fleshless, skinless, featherless appearance. She knew which looks worked for her and which didn't, and she was secretly pleased that her weight had remained consistent. She was, after all, just bones—no skin, no feathers, just bones.

More specifically, she was just cockatoo bones, for Persephone Skeleton was a big, skeletal bird.

"Fabulous!" said Persephone. "Lovely, lovely me. Gorgeous!"

It had taken Persephone a long time to reach her position of power, but here she was at last, looking down upon Ab-Com City from the uppermost room in its tallest building. Each time she crossed her window, she heard the crowd below roaring. From her exalted perch, she could see posters depicting her smiling, government-approved bird-skull image plastered on every building, hanging in every window. Never in the history of Middlemost had a politician won the presidency in such a ridiculous landslide. Pretty soon everything would be ready for her to start making good on some of her promises, and then things were going to get really *exciting*.

She pressed a button on her desk, and a moment later her assistant, Swamster, entered the room wearing a red bathing suit and several gold medals. Swamster was a unique abstract companion—half Olympic swimming champion, half hamster.

"Yes, beloved President Skeleton," said Swamster, his whiskers quivering.

"Come faster next time, Swamster," said Persephone. "The fact that you've been with me for years doesn't mean your job is guaranteed."

"Absolutely, most adored President Skeleton."

"Now, tell me the status of our very special guest," said Persephone.

"He . . . attempted to eat one of the guards."

"What do you mean?"

"Well, just that the guard we sent to retrieve him found him sitting in the middle of a field eating a ton of bacon. The guard approached him, but you see, the guard was a *pig*, and he ended up slaying the guard and then running off with his belly."

"His belly?"

"That's right. His belly. The other guards only found him when he made a campfire to roast up the guard's belly."

"But I trust that the other guards did manage to subdue him?" asked Persephone.

"Oh, they did, they did. Well, eventually they did, and I've been told they tied him to a camel using thick ropes. They should be on their way as we speak."

"Camels are terribly slow."

"Yes, but they are the best thing for our fragile ecosystem."

Persephone leaned toward her assistant, all her bones clacking together as she moved.

"Wait," said Persephone. "What?"

"Nothing, President Skeleton."

"You *talked back* to me."

"That was more of an . . . explanation."

"And now you're doing it again."

"So sorry, President Skeleton."

Persephone paused and Swamster trembled.

"Get out and don't come back until he's arrived," said Persephone.

"Yes, Madam President."

"And shave some of your fur and make me a hat out of it."

Swamster liked his fur, but thought it best not to argue.

"Yes, President Skeleton. Be delighted to. Capital idea. Right away."

Persephone rubbed her eyeholes in frustration and patted the spot where her beak used to be, wondering if it would improve her looks to have somebody's nose chopped off and fastened to her skull.

But then, of course, I would have to have somebody else's face removed to go ALONG with the nose, thought Persephone. *A lone nose simply wouldn't do. And THEN I'd have to have somebody's scalp removed to go with that face, and I'd have to start thinking about what kind of hair would be prettiest with the body, and if*

89

I'm going to do that, I might as well just get a whole skin SUIT to fit me properly.

Persephone really wanted to look good. For Scurvy.

She took another stroll by her window, prompting hurrahs from her fans below, which cheered her up. Her eternal pirate love would be here soon enough, and if he resisted—well, if he resisted, she would have him killed and stuffed and placed above her mantel, which might be almost as satisfying as having him alive and all to herself. Either way, Scurvy *would* be hers. Forever.

11

Ted could feel his brain floating around in his head, bonking against the inside of his skull. He could also feel the heat of a campfire, on the other side of which sat the vampire who had assaulted him. He checked his neck for holes.

"Not to worry," said the vampire. "You're not my blood type. I'm forever an O-positive guy, and you're an AB-negative. Much too bitter for my taste."

Ted pushed himself to a sitting position. He'd been lying in the dirt, and he could taste leaves in his mouth.

"Apologies," said a different voice. "We bet on how many leaves we would be able to cram in your mouth."

"Perhaps you would like to introduce yourself to our humble roundtable?" the vampire suggested.

"My name is Ted," said Ted.

There were murmurs from the group, and money changed hands, most of which was going to the vampire.

"I said that you look just like a Ted," said the vampire. "But my companions bet that you must be a Gustafson or a Zhang."

"Zhang?"

"They're not terribly good wagerers, but you'll soon learn that for yourself," said the vampire.

"Not much elssse to do at night assside from talking and

betting," boomed another voice, whose owner sounded like he was sucking in water and spit as he spoke.

Ted looked at his own feet and saw that he was barefoot.

"What the—" he said, his reaction sending a ripple of laughter through the group. More money changed hands.

"We also bet on how long it would take for you to discover that we threw your shoes into the fire," the vampire explained.

"Why would you do that?" said Ted.

"Because you insisted on staying unconscious," said the vampire.

"You *knocked* me unconscious! Who are you, anyway?"

"I knocked you out only to make sure you came along, but we'll get to that in a moment," said the vampire. "As for your question, may I first refer you to the well-sculpted gentleman?"

"Sculpted?"

"The well-sculpted *Monodon monoceros* to my left—Dr. Narwhal."

"Pleasssed to meet you," said Dr. Narwhal, but Ted was unable to reply, awed as he was by the sheer mass of the Arctic narwhal, who was covered in rolls of fat that spilled over each other and trembled every time Dr. Narwhal moved. In the center of Dr. Narwhal's head was a ten-foot-long tusk that resembled a javelin. From biology class, Ted somehow remembered that the tusk was actually a long tooth, which no doubt accounted for the narwhal's difficulty with pronouncing the letter *s*. Hanging around the narwhal's enormous neck was a stethoscope.

"And to my right," continued the vampire, "you'll see the sensitive artistic genius Vango."

"Can I call you Theo? Agh! Itchy! Sorry!" said Vango. His

92

Dutch accent was thick, and he was scratching at the bandage that covered his left ear.

"But my name is Ted," said Ted.

"Like from Theodore? Bats! In my hair!" said Vango.

"Yes," said Ted.

"But that's so close," said Vango. "Swirls! In my eyes!"

"Please just call me Ted."

"You'll find that Vango often *colors* his sentences with additional details," said the vampire. "He sees the world differently than the rest of us."

"Who are you?" said Ted.

"Ah. I am Dwack," said the vampire. "Member of the eternal undead, and the unofficial tailor for this group."

"He's great at hemming," said Vango. "I should have had him hem my ear."

"He stitched me a nice jacket," said Dr. Narwhal.

"You should wear that jacket more often," said Dwack. "It's slimming and—"

"STOP!" said Ted.

The three turned to look at him.

"You still haven't told me where I am," said Ted.

"Ah, apologies," said Dwack. "You're in Middlemost, the place where we abstract companions are born."

"And the place to which we return when we've been tossed assside," said Dr. Narwhal.

93

III

Scurvy was strapped to a foul-smelling camel, and his back was sore from fighting with Persephone's guards—an Irish athlete holding a hurley, which was an ax-shaped stick used in the sport of hurling, and an Indian man holding a cricket bat.

"Like eating that rope, do ya? Like the way it *tastes*?" said the Hurler, smacking Scurvy on the back of the head.

"Mmmf," said Scurvy.

"*Mmmf* is right," said the Cricketer.

"Trfl ee nfng prrsph," said Scurvy.

"Take off the gag for now," said the Cricketer. "It'll be fun to put it on him again."

The Hurler removed the gag.

"What do you want to say?" said the Hurler.

"Just curious," said Scurvy, spitting out some sand that had been bugging him, "why ya felt tha need tah abduct me while I was *minding me own business* eatin' bacon, and if it might have something tah do with Persephone's recent political victory."

"You are supposed to call her the Most Honorable President Skeleton," said the Hurler.

"Honorable? That bag of bones ain't ever been right in tha noggin!" said Scurvy. "And now she's got all this bleedin' *political power*! What a nightmare."

"And why does she want to see you?" said the Cricketer.

Scurvy paused. "Never ya mind that," he said.

"Fine, then," said the Hurler, moving toward Scurvy with the gag.

"No, *wait*, not tha gag," said Scurvy. "I'll tell ya. Perseph—er, *the Honorable President* or whatever she is, she used tah be me bird."

"Your bird, as in, your lady?" said the Hurler.

"Me bird as in tha bird that used to sit on me shoulder when I was sailing tha high seas. She was me little skeleton cockatoo," said Scurvy.

"She's tall now," said the Hurler.

"Guess she can afford a bit of tha old chop-chop cosmetic surgery," said Scurvy.

"So why does your old pet want to see you?" said the Hurler.

95

"Well," said Scurvy, "I always got tha feeling that me Persephone was a bit *different* than tha birds me mates had, aside from being a skeleton and all. Their birds might sit on yer shoulder and take some food out of yer hand, but ya always got tha sense that they were just *birds*—they'd look out at tha water, they'd squawk, but ya knew they had little brains and ya knew they were gonna be tha same tomorrow as they were today.

"Not my Persephone, though. When I looked into that bird's eye sockets, there was something *strange* there. This is gonna sound mad tah ya, but that bird *loved* me—I'd be willing tah bet me life on it. I used tah be trying tah captain my ship, and she would just sit on me shoulder and *stare* at me. Stare at me like we were on our *honeymoon*, and without *eyeballs* at that."

"Birds do such things, lad," said the Hurler. "I had a bird. I put a mirror in its cage—the thing used to look at itself all day long."

"But it wasn't just tha staring. You know how birds talk? '*Polly want a cracker*,' that kind of stuff?"

"Of course," said the Cricketer.

"Persephone never said anything like that. She'd go like this: '*Squawk! I love you! Squawk! You fulfill me! Squawk! Let's have some fledglings! Squawk! You'll learn to love me!*' I swear to ya."

"Now you're just wasting our time. Help me out, mate," said the Hurler.

The gag went back into Scurvy's mouth.

Scurvy felt the up-and-down motion of the camel underneath him. He examined the sand. He was destined for water, and this landscape was quite unnatural to him.

Despite his predicament, Scurvy wondered where Ted was, how he was doing, how his first month of school had gone. Scurvy hoped he was happy. It used to break his heart watching Ted get beat up every day. Slicing open packages of bacon was one thing, but Scurvy knew that cutting off the head of a high school bully wasn't allowed, as much as he might want to do it. Ab-coms couldn't interfere to that degree. It was against the rules set by the founders of Middlemost thousands of years ago and still adhered to by all ab-coms.

More than anything, Scurvy was angry at himself for not telling Ted things he should have told him much earlier. Like not telling Ted how important he was. He hoped that all the ab-coms hadn't yet been called back from Earth, because if they had, terrible things were in store.

IV

Ted was awakened at the crack of dawn by Vango, who was brushing his cheek with a horsehair paintbrush, a contented look on his face, murmuring something that sounded like "pretty as a picture," though in the fog of half sleep, Ted couldn't be entirely sure.

"Good morning, sweet Theo," said Vango. "Sweet like a macaroon!"

"Time to leave!" said Dwack.

Ted had slept fitfully, dreaming of the Crusher and claustrophobic tunnels. A nervous feeling washed over him.

"I'll stay here," said Ted. "You go on ahead."

Dwack and Dr. Narwhal just looked at Ted while Vango removed a canvas painting from its easel and slipped it into a bag. Ted caught a glimpse of the picture, which appeared to be a portrait of him with his eyes closed. Had Vango been painting him while he was sleeping?

"You don't know anything about where you are," Dwack said to Ted.

"True. But where are you *going*?" said Ted.

"We just have to keep moving because, technically, what we're doing here is illegal," said Dwack.

"WOULD SOMEBODY PLEASE TELL ME WHAT IS GOING ON?" screamed Ted, his voice echoing above the forest.

V

Ted had picked an unfortunate time to shout, for at the same time he was demanding to be told what was going on, one of President Skeleton's hot-air surveillance balloons was floating high above. A three-eyed emu named Ewd, who was operating the balloon, heard his voice echoing all around her.

"What the—" said Ewd, whose job was to search for abcoms who, through either insanity or suicidal tendencies, had decided *not* to obey the presidential recall decree. The emu leaned over the side of her basket, batted her telescope into position using the side of her head, and peered through the eyehole, looking straight down at the forest below.

A thousand feet below her, she caught glimpses of a narwhal shuffling ponderously across the forest floor, an artist cleaning his teeth with a paintbrush, and a vampire arguing with a teenage boy.

The emu pressed the button on her talkie-talkie.

"I've located four deserters," said Ewd. "Request permission to blow them up." The emu glanced at her bag of TNT, which she had been itching to use ever since she'd gotten her surveillance job.

"What do the deserters look like?" came the static-drenched response.

"Hmm . . . a narwhal, a vampire, an impressionist artist, and a teenage boy."

"*Early* impressionist?" came the response.

"Hard to tell from here," said Ewd. "Maybe postimpressionist, but that's just a gut feeling based on the way the guy is dressed, his palette, his choices of color."

The emu was proud of her art-history knowledge, having been the ab-com for a New York City child whose parents forced high-level cultural lessons on him as a toddler.

"Anything strange about the teenage boy?"

"Looks like he and the vampire have something going on together. Again, request permission to explode them, boom."

"Request denied. We'll send out a recon team. Seems worth following them if there's a chance that they might lead us to an ACORN cell. Keep an eye on them until we get there."

99

"Fine, fine," said Ewd. "I never get to do anything combustible. Out."

Ewd put down her talkie-talkie and let the wind push her hot-air balloon along. As a bird that couldn't fly, she liked having this perspective on the world, looking down on everything, imagining what it would be like to blow everything up, wondering how high the resulting clouds of smoke would rise. *Would they drift all the way up here?* she thought, disappointed that she couldn't obliterate the deserters and find out right away. She had been told that her impatience was one of the reasons that she wasn't chosen for a higher position in the Presidential Guard. It would be best to show everybody that she *could* control her impulses. For now.

Six years ago, when she was living a wilder lifestyle, she

would have blown the deserters sky-high and danced over their ashes. She had definitely matured.

"*Ack!* Where are they?" said Ewd, once again craning her neck over the side of the basket. If she'd lost sight of them, her bosses were going to be quite miffed. She swung the telescope around. Still nothing. The deserters had deserted.

"Crud!" said Ewd out loud. "I'm always messing things up." She sighed and then stuck her head in her bag of TNT, hiding from the world and all her mistakes.

VI

"Sit," said Dwack. "This will be your crash course in Middle-most."

Ted sat and watched as Dwack poked seven dots in the sand—two at the top, three close together in the middle, and two more at the bottom. Looking at the pattern of the dots, Ted instantly recognized what they were.

"Orion," said Ted.

"Very good," said Dwack. "This is the constellation Orion as seen from Earth, and *this*"—Dwack circled the center star in Orion's belt—"is Middlemost."

Ted's mind flashed to the glow-in-the-dark star on his ceiling, and the HERE! message. *Oh geez*.

"How did it get that name?" he asked.

"It is the middle star—or rather, the middle *object*, because as you can tell, where we are now isn't exactly a star—in the middle of a famous constellation. You reach it by falling through the vent at the middle of the Earth, and when you're here, it means you are halfway between being a working abstract companion and just being gone. If you look at this place the way we look at it, it is pretty much the center of everything—Middlemost."

"But we don't know how much longer we'll be staying," said Dr. Narwhal.

"I don't understand," said Ted.

"I'm sorry, but there isn't time to explain it right now," said Dwack. "We need to keep moving. Persephone Skeleton has eyes everywhere."

"That's weird. My friend Scurvy Goonda used to have a cockatoo named Persephone Skeleton," remarked Ted.

Dwack, Dr. Narwhal, and Vango looked at Ted.

"Scurvy Gordon?" said Dr. Narwhal.

"Well, yeah. I mean, I called him Scurvy Goonda because when I was little, I couldn't say 'Gordon.' You know Scurvy?"

"When Persephone was running for office, all of her profiles mentioned her true love, Scurvy Gordon."

"But Persephone is a *bird*."

"Kids request strange friendsss," said Dr. Narwhal.

"What does that mean, *request*?" said Ted. "I thought I created Scurvy."

"In a manner of speaking, you did," said Dwack. "But he still had to go through one of the factories."

"What are the factories?" said Ted.

"Again, there isn't time to explain that now," said Dwack.

"Can you tell me who created you?" said Ted.

"A little girl," sighed Dwack, "who spent too much time staring at a box of Count Chocula. The girl's mother said that Count Chocula was a vampire based on Dracula, but she couldn't say, 'Drac,' so she said, 'Dwack.' And here I am."

"Who made you?" Ted asked Dr. Narwhal.

"A boy in Greenland named Nuka whossse brother died because there was no physsssician in his village," said Dr. Narwhal. "He needed a new friend and he got me."

"And you?" Ted asked Vango.

"A Brazilian boy whose parents had a print of one of Van Gogh's self-portraits hanging on the wall," said Vango. "Which is why, in a pinch, I can speak some Portuguese. *Boa vinda!*"

VII

Aren't you tired of being kicked around?
Join the Ab-Com army!
Do your part for Middlemost!

The new ad campaign was going fantastically well. The government had employed the best PR company in Middlemost, and the concepts the company was developing were incredible—images of elephant seals and chimeras battling humans, slaying little kids, butchering adults, doing all the things that ab-coms had been thinking about for years but had never had the guts to try. But now everybody was talking about the importance of this vengeful mission, and Persephone Skeleton was hearing them loud and clear.

And so was Persephone's boss.

Each day, new hordes of ab-coms were lining up at the free clinics, receiving shots to cure their bodies of the Greenies. There wasn't enough room in Middlemost to handle all the refugees, who were building ramshackle cities out of trash and cardboard. Sure, Persephone could give them tents and food, but the overcrowding kept everybody nice and angry. All Persephone had to do was channel that anger.

"SWAMSTER!" shouted Persephone.

Swamster ran into her chambers, whiskers twitching.

"I'm sorry, President Skeleton," said Swamster. "I was just chewing up some cardboard from a roll of toilet paper. My teeth have been getting so long and I—"

104

"Enough!" said Persephone. "How long until my darling, dearest Scurvy arrives?"

"I've only been told he is en route, President Skeleton," said Swamster, still a bit flustered. He had really enjoyed chewing that cardboard roll, feeling his teeth getting shorter, knowing that his smile would be improved.

"Excellent," said Persephone. "When he gets here, be sure to bring my boyfriend to my quarters."

"Of course," said Swamster. "Oh. And I learned something *else* that you might like to know."

"Yes?" said Persephone.

"It seems that, well, one of our lookouts spotted a group of deserters running through the woods."

"There are hundreds of deserters."

"Thousands, actually. We're estimating."

"I don't care about one tiny group," said Persephone.

"Of course not, Madam President," said Swamster. "But our lookout thought that one of them might be a *boy* rather than an ab-com."

Persephone thought about this.

"A boy boy?" she asked.

"A boy boy."

"How would the lookout know?" said Persephone.

"Well, as you *of course* know, very few kids have teenage boys as their ab-coms. Little girls are absolutely *loath* to dream up teenage males as friends, and young boys are more prone to think about ninjas or lions or—"

"—or pirates," said Persephone.

"Right. And with all the yelling this boy was apparently

doing, which is what males his age in the other world seem to do, our lookout thought that *perhaps* he might be . . . real."

Persephone paused, rolling this over in her brain.

"How did he get here?" she said.

"He must have fallen through the ThereYouGo Gate," said Swamster.

"Well then," said Persephone. "In the interest of national security, I'd like to make *two* decrees."

"I have my notepad out."

"Seal up *all* the vents leading to the ThereYouGo Gate *aside* from the one we'll be using to make our attack."

"Seal up the vents! Very good, President Skeleton. And your second request?"

"Eradicate the boy. I can't have a human finding out about our plan."

Swamster wrote *eradicate boy* in his notepad. He looked down at the command.

"May I say something?" said Swamster.

"If it's brief."

"It's just that getting rid of the boy in the way you seem to be suggesting seems a bit callous, President Skeleton. Couldn't we capture him but let him go? I do it all the time with moths and fireflies, though they always yell at me afterward."

Persephone stared at Swamster.

"You think I'm being harsh?" said Persephone.

"We could just as easily send him back to where he came from. No doubt he simply got lost."

"Hmm. Since those are your feelings," said Persephone, "I'd like *you* to track the boy down. And kill him yourself."

Swamster's blood went cold.

"But, President Skeleton, I *couldn't*."

"You're either with me," Persephone explained, "or you are against me."

"Of course I'm with you," said Swamster. "You know how I feel about the plan. I love working here. It's just—"

"There's a war coming. Do your part. Find the boy. Goodbye."

"But—"

"Don't you want a promotion?"

More than anything else in the world, Swamster wanted a promotion. It was why he'd taken the job so many years ago.

"President Skeleton," he said. "Of course I would like a promotion."

"Then do your duty for our glorious cause."

Swamster nodded quickly and exited the room. He would do anything for a promotion.

VIII

Vango and Dr. Narwhal were walking ahead of Ted and Dwack, checking to make sure that the road was clear. The group had exited the forest moments before and was now making its way into an odd landscape of towering red-rock mesas, boulders piled on top of boulders, and Joshua trees that seemed to be twisting painfully as they reached toward the sky.

Dwack, paying the scenery no mind, was explaining important things to Ted:

"President Skeleton got into office on an antihuman campaign," said Dwack. "There were a lot of sad ab-coms in Middlemost, and she played to their emotions."

"What were they sad about?"

Dwack shook his head. "You're lucky I'm a good vampire, because many undead I know would drink your blood and throw away your husk for a comment like that."

"What did I say?"

"Don't you have a best friend?"

Ted thought about this.

"I haven't had a real friend since Scurvy left," he said. It was strange to admit it out loud. "Aside from maybe Kettil. But he doesn't understand English."

"Did this Scurvy *leave*, or did you get rid of him?"

"I used a medicine patch that made Scurvy sick," said Ted, quietly. "He broke out in all these green bumps."

"The Greenies. Of course. President Skeleton is giving away shots of the antidote to the virus as a recruiting tool for her army. Vango, Dr. Narwhal, and I were only spared the infection because we left Earth years ago. Let me ask you a question: how many years were you and Scurvy together?"

"Seven."

"*Seven years*, and then—poof!—goodbye. If you were Scurvy, how would you feel about that?"

"The doctor said he was just a figment in my head."

"And now, being here, you know that isn't true," said Dwack. "The girl who discarded me also took medication. I remember it clearly—it was an antidepressant her parents put her on because she spent all her time talking to me."

"What happened?"

"She turned her attention to other things, and after being ignored for a few weeks, I got the point. I left, and came here. We had spent two years together, and she didn't even say goodbye."

"That's terrible."

"But that's just the thing—it's not terrible. It's *normal*. Or perhaps it's both. Every ab-com who lives here in Middlemost was tossed aside. Needless to say, some friends are quite bitter. Understandably so, no?"

"Okay."

"President Skeleton tapped into that bitterness. Her campaign focused on the terrible things humans had done to ab-coms, and the general population *lapped it up*. The rallies were huge, and some of the slogans—my word, if humans knew what was being said about them. But as Persephone Skeleton's popularity increased, all of a sudden her message became *Let's get BACK at the humans*. Of course, not everybody here wants violence, but those of us who don't have to stick together, because we're seen as antigovernment and antipatriotic."

"Which is what you, Dr. Narwhal, and Vango are."

"Dissenters, yes. That's why we're looking for ACORN."

"What's ACORN?"

"The Abstract Companion Organization for Resistance Now—A.C.O.R.N. Up until now, abstract companions have never been allowed to physically touch humans other than the people to whom they were assigned. But at the moment, President Skeleton is in the process of changing that law."

"Dwack?"

"Yes?"

"Where are Dr. Narwhal and Vango?"

Dwack stopped and looked around, scanning the rocky landscape. Dr. Narwhal and Vango *had* disappeared.

"Don't yell for them," said Dwack. "If there are unsavory characters out there, the last thing we want to do is let them know where we are. . . ."

"They might already know where we are," said Ted.

"Why do you say that?"

"Look up."

Dwack looked up.

Dozens of ab-coms were standing on the colossal boulders surrounding them, but Dwack could only make out their silhouettes, because he was staring into the sun. In the middle of the silhouettes, he could see a large squiggling bag, which, if he had to guess, probably had Dr. Narwhal inside. Next to the large bag was a smaller bag that wasn't moving much at all. Vango wasn't struggling.

"A well-planned ambush," whispered Dwack. "I can probably fight off five of them. How many do you think you can take?"

"None," whispered Ted. "I'm a terrible fighter."

"Well," said Dwack, "perhaps we should surrender, then."

111

IX

"Ladies, gentlemen, and creatures—all you giant slugs and snails and the like—of the Senate!" said a proboscis monkey wearing a sequined jacket. "If you've got hands, please put them together and welcome the beautiful, newly elected PRESIDENT PERSEPHONE SKELETON, BECAUSE SHE IS HERE TONIGHT!"

The Senate chamber erupted into applause as Persephone entered and walked to the raised podium where the president traditionally addressed the Senate. A freshly painted portrait of her hung on the wall behind her head, and in front of her, the hall was filled with 750 senators hailing from all over Middlemost. They had come together to welcome their new leader. And to cast today's crucial vote.

Persephone looked over her audience with her empty eye sockets, at the adoring faces of her government colleagues as they waited for her to speak, and at the few individuals who seemed dismayed by her new leadership role. She stared at these dissenters.

Mental note: Have all the non-adorers killed.

Another mental note: As soon as possible.

"Senators of Middlemost!" shrieked Persephone. "Today we write a new page in the history of Middlemost. Too long have we allowed ourselves to be pushed around and tossed aside by the humans who claimed to be our *friends*!"

Cheers from the Senate!

"My human pushed me down the laundry chute!" said a senator.

"Mine tried to eat me!" said an admittedly delicious-looking turkey senator.

"You're my only friend now, President Skeleton!"

"I *am* your friend, and I hear you loud and very clear!" said Persephone. "Too long have we been *stuck* with a self-imposed nonviolence law that has *denied* us the right to strike back against those who would exile and discard us! And that is why I ask you to vote today to repeal that law, and to join me on the first step toward a world in which there will be no more humans to banish us at will!"

Roars of agreement!

"Humans are *so* two thousand years ago!" said a senator.

"It's all been downhill since the ancient Greeks!" said another.

113

"Allow me to be candid and practical for a moment," said Persephone. "There's no more space in Middlemost. We're running out of food. We're running out of materials to build cities. Billions of ab-coms have come here since humans first figured out how to walk upright, and because of the call to arms, there are billions more of us here as we speak.

"Now think about *Earth*. What's going on there? Wars. Global warming. Climate change. Droughts. Famine. The humans don't *deserve* what's left of the world they have. They're heading for a meltdown. Disease! Species extinction! The melting of the ice caps! But *we* could save the Earth, friends. *We* have lived there, and we know how precious it is. *We* could restore *balance*! The Earth *needs* us, we need a new home, and all that is standing in our way are the humans who threw each and every one of us away like *garbage!*"

Cries of "Hear! Hear!" and "Garbage, indeed!" rang out from the senators.

"Southern California is mine!"

"I get the Croatian coastline!"

"I'll take all of England, except for Essex!"

"Now, now, let's not divide up the world *before* it is ours," said Persephone. "First things first—as you know, an eighty-five-percent vote is necessary to overturn the nonviolence law. I propose that we make a *statement* today, and overturn it with one hundred percent of the vote. A vote for a fight is a vote *for* the future—"

"HAVE YOU LOST YOUR MIND, PERSEPHONE?" boomed a voice from the back of the chamber.

Persephone paused, astounded.

"Who? Said? That?" she asked.

"*I* did," said the voice, which was now getting closer. Persephone saw an ancient double-pouched kangaroo bouncing ponderously down the red-carpeted center aisle of the chamber, his multicolored tail dragging behind.

"Senator Thip-Thap," said Persephone. He was her old mentor.

"You've disappointed me, Persephone," said Senator Thip-Thap.

When Persephone had first arrived in Middlemost, she'd had a difficult time adjusting to her new environment. She was lonely. Senator Thip-Thap took her in and gave her a home and friendship during her first couple of centuries there. She served as a clerk in his office, learning the basics of government, before starting her political career in earnest. She knew that she owed much of her success to Senator Thip-Thap—who was now staring at her, shaking angrily.

"You should be ashamed of yourself!" said Senator Thip-Thap. "Spewing a message of violence. It got you into office because you earned the votes of fools, but it must *stop here*."

Nervous chattering from the audience.

"Your colleagues seem to disagree," said Persephone.

"Yes, you were cast aside," said Senator Thip-Thap, turning to the Senate chamber. "*All* of you were cast aside! But we've seen what violence does to humans, and we *know* that it is always a mistake! And now you want to take up arms against them? You want to *eradicate* them from their own world?"

Senator Thip-Thap slammed his cane into the ground.

"The humans who abandoned you were CHILDREN!" he exploded. "Children who didn't know any better because they were *young*. I *implore* you—forget this madness, and find another way to preserve Middlemost *without* violence."

115

There was silence in the Senate chamber.

"It's rude to interrupt your president when she is speaking," said Persephone. "Would the officer of the court please have Senator Thip-Thap taken to a comfortable place where he can *lie down*? He's quite old, and not quite sane."

"Of course, President Skeleton," said the court proboscis monkey, lumbering toward Senator Thip-Thap, who stared at Persephone.

"And you wonder why nobody loves you," said Senator Thip-Thap.

"I HAVE THE LOVE OF A *WORLD*," she snapped. "*Out* with this shoddy antique!"

The court monkey grabbed Senator Thip-Thap and dragged him out of the Senate chamber while the rest of the audience looked on, giving their silent consent. As soon as the monkey was out of the room, Persephone straightened her body, cracked her bones, and spoke sweetly into the microphone.

"Now then," she said. "Let us get this vote under way. I trust there won't be any more distractions, aside from my beauty. As I was saying . . ."

X

Being inside a thick sack, Ted only knew that he'd been placed on a wagon of some kind, and he could feel Vango, Dr. Narwhal, and Dwack beside him. Their mouths were taped shut and their wrists bound with heavy ropes.

When the wagon stopped, Ted detected a flurry of activity outside the sack.

"Move!" said a rough voice as Ted was yanked off the wagon and carried by several pairs of hands. Behind him, he heard labored grunting and guessed that the kidnappers were attempting to lift Dr. Narwhal.

"Set his flippers free and make him walk," said another voice. "If he doesn't move, we'll have to roll him."

Suddenly Ted was dropped roughly onto the ground, and his sack was untied and swiftly removed. He opened his eyes and saw that he was in a wide tunnel constructed entirely of bending, arching trees. Everywhere he looked, other tree-tunnels connected to this main corridor.

Dwack, Vango, and Dr. Narwhal sat beside him.

And standing in front of him was the most beautiful girl he'd ever seen.

"*Mon Dieu!*" she said. "You are a ragtag lot. And you *stink!*"

XI

After the vote, Persephone departed the Senate chamber for her high-rise apartment, feeling great about herself. It was almost unprecedented to see a *unanimous* yes vote, and the invasion was *going* to happen. She just needed to hammer out some final details. But that meeting wasn't for another couple of weeks, so she had some time to relax . . . and get married.

Persephone looked through the window at the Ab-Com City skyline. Though she knew she should move into the stodgy Presidential Palace on the outskirts of the city, she preferred living in this apartment, her home, which she had been in ever since she had started earning enough money from bribes and kickbacks to have the type of life she had fantasized about during her sailing days.

When she met her Scurvy.

Persephone sat down on her feather bed—made from specific birds whose plumage had made her jealous—and removed her wig. It had been a long day, and she needed to rest if she was going to see Scurvy soon. He was the love of her life, and she wanted to look gorgeous.

"SWAMSTER," she yelled. "BRING MY BATH SALTS!"

But Swamster didn't respond.

"Oh yes," said Persephone to herself. "I sent him to kill that boy."

Persephone flopped back on her bed and rubbed her eye-holes with the delicate bones that formed her wings. She looked at the ceiling, where years before she had commissioned an artist to paint a portrait of Scurvy, just the way she'd remembered him. Masculine. Dashing. Perfect.

"Ah, *mi amor*," said Persephone.

She had first met Scurvy on a pirate ship, where she had been the ab-com of a cabin girl named Grace, who had helped her mother cook, clean, and sew for the sailors. Grace had spent her entire life on the boat and saw plenty of scrap bones that sailors tossed her way after they were done eating. The cabin girl was terribly lonely, and she reconstructed these bones in her imagination to make a friend—her cockatoo, Persephone Skeleton.

One day, the ship stopped in Port Royal, Jamaica, to pick up supplies and replace crew members who had been lost at sea or killed in battle. A sailor came aboard with his young son Myles, who had dreamed of being a pirate since he was old enough to stare out at the boats coming into port. Myles had inherited an abstract companion to match his obsession—Scurvy Gordon. Myles the cabin boy met Grace the cabin girl, and from that day on, Scurvy and Persephone were inseparable.

During the days, Persephone sat on Scurvy's shoulder as he captained his ship up and down the coast of the Americas, one of her eyes on the ocean, looking for ships, the other focused on Scurvy's face. She had never seen such a handsome man. In battles, Persephone fought alongside Scurvy, clawing and pecking the eyes of rival sailors and buccaneers. During long days at sea, she entertained Scurvy with her songs: CAW CAW! And

119

Scurvy always smiled and sang along, yelling his own CAW CAWs at the sea.

With Grace's help, Persephone gradually learned some proper English, though at first she was limited mainly to nautical terms and curse words: *CAW CAW! TURN STARBOARD, YA RUM BUCKET!* But at night, Scurvy had her sleep on a perch in his personal quarters belowdecks, and it was here that Persephone eventually said the things she really wanted to say:

CAW CAW! I LOVE YOU, SCURVY!

All day long, she would sit on Scurvy's shoulder and tell him again and again how she felt inside: *CAW CAW! LET'S BUILD A NEST TOGETHER! CAW CAW!*

But Scurvy never seemed to take her declarations seriously, and it almost seemed like he was confused by what she was saying. Confused by her *love!* Over time, Persephone could see that he was starting to shut her out completely. He stopped letting her sleep in his quarters and instead kept her in a cage in the galley. He stopped having her ride on his shoulder as he captained the ship.

Eventually, he stopped visiting her altogether, and Grace lost interest in her as well. She was never let out of her cage, nobody came to play with her, nobody came to talk to her. Stuck below the ship's deck, she didn't even know if it was morning or night. Persephone became bitter. Scurvy had cut Persephone out of his life completely—just because she loved him.

Then came the night the ship went down. She had been asleep in her cage—she liked to sleep, because sometimes she dreamed that Scurvy loved her back—when all of a sudden she heard a pounding above deck. She heard the shouts of men fighting and the booms of cannons being fired at close range, and shortly afterward came the crackle of the wooden ship burning.

She watched the fire scorch through the ceiling and begin to creep down the walls.

CAW CAW! she yelled.

She watched the flames leap along the floor.

CAW CAW CAW! she pleaded, begging *anybody* to save her.

She watched the blaze consume the oak stand beneath her and lick the bars of her cage.

CAW? she said, realizing that nobody was going to save her.

GRACE? SCURVY? She looked at the stairs leading down to the galley, willing her love to rush into the room and save her.

But he didn't. And the ship sank.

And that was that.

XII

Ted was looking at the beautiful girl—staring at her, to be precise. The girl's skin had a porcelain, polished quality to it, as if she were a statue. He guessed that she was about his age, and considering that she was wearing a pink leotard and a tutu, he guessed that she was a ballerina.

A yellow elk wearing a bowler hat stood next to her. The elk didn't speak, and it seemed entirely deferential to the incomprehensibly beautiful ballerina.

"So," said the ballerina. "It's probably a good time for at least *one* of you to tell me what you were doing creeping around when my guards picked you up."

"I am Dwack," said Dwack. "And these are my associates, Dr. Narwhal, Vango, and Ted, a human who took a bit of a wrong turn from his own world."

"Human," said the ballerina, looking at Ted. "Interesting."

The ballerina let her pretty porcelain eyes remain on Ted for a moment longer than any lovely girl had ever looked at him before.

"Go on," she said.

"And had your men—or your mammalia," said Dwack, nodding at the dapper elk, "taken the time to question us about where we were going, they would have found that we were searching for ACORN."

Dwack paused.

"Which," he continued, "considering that you are hiding in a tree cave, I'd imagine you'd know something about."

The ballerina narrowed her eyes.

"How do I know you're not spies?" she said.

"Simple," said Dwack. "Look at Vango."

Even sitting in place, Vango was trembling visibly, and his eye was twitching. He looked completely out of his mind.

"He needs to paint every day," said Dwack, "or else he has, let's say, an *episode*. Now, do you believe that the Presidential Guard would let such a loose cannon join its spies?"

The ballerina was studying Vango. He clearly creeped her out, though she was holding her head high and keeping her face quiet, trying not to betray a reaction.

"Perhaps not," said the ballerina. "But what of the rest of you?"

123

"I have nothing ill to say about Dr. Narwhal," said Dwack. "And as for myself, I find our current administration a bit . . . *gauche*. They have no style. I would never be a part of such a flair-free bunch."

"And what about the near-man?" said the ballerina.

Ted's face warmed uncomfortably. A *near-man*? What was with the hyphen?

"He's just lost," said Dwack. "But you can question him yourself, if you have any concerns."

"Well?" said the ballerina. "How do I know you're not working for President Skeleton?"

Ted thought about this.

"Back in my world I have a family I love," he said. "I have

a little sister, Adeline, who I would never allow anyone to hurt."

The ballerina thought about this, and then she smiled.

"Very good. My name is Joelle-Michelle Athenais-Benedicte de la Valliere. If you were looking for ACORN, you have found it."

Part Three

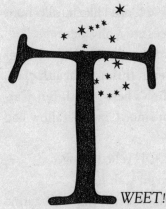

WEET!

Carolina Waltz didn't even *like* football. TWEET, the whistle blew, and a pile of fat grunting guys moved six feet. And then *TWEET*, the whistle blew again, the referee put down the ball, and the nonsense started all over again.

But still, she cheered when the rest of the crowd cheered, and when her friends commented on which players they thought were cute, she responded in the way that she knew she was supposed to: *Oh, he is so NOT!* or maybe she would give an *Oh, I TOTALLY know what you MEAN*. More and more, she found herself talking like a bleached blonde from one of those fake reality shows that had nothing to do with the way she lived on Cape Cod. The guys liked it when she played the stupid girl, and her friends thought "mean beauty queen" was her true personality.

Somehow, she had reached a point where every day she felt like she was playing a role in somebody else's movie.

CRUNCH! Down on the field, male bodies crashed into each other, and when the whistle stopped the action, one of the players was rolling around on the ground holding his knee, badly injured. It all just didn't seem worth it to Carolina.

"Ow," said her friend Shelly. "That looked like it *really* hurt. We learned in health class that knees are really *important*."

Imagine that! Knees are important! thought Carolina. It boggled her mind that Shelly had to learn this from health class. Shelly *thought* that she was Carolina's best friend. But Carolina didn't have a best friend. Not since Czarina Tallow had left her.

"KILL 'EM, JIMMY! WOO-HOO!" yelled Bridget.

Who cares about any of this? thought Carolina.

Her mother used to joke about the Russian empress Czarina Tallow being Carolina's imaginary friend, but Carolina never really thought of Czarina like that. It wasn't like Czarina would walk down the hallways with her in high school or anything— Czarina liked to spend her days in the garden writing letters back home to Russia rather than be cooped up inside—but when Carolina got home at the end of the day, Czarina would be there.

"You look zo lovely," Czarina would say.

And Carolina would thank her politely.

Of course, in public and in front of her parents, Carolina had kept secret the fact that Czarina was still hanging around. If she was at her mother's house, and her mom heard her talking to Czarina in her bedroom, Carolina would pretend like she was on the phone. If she was hanging out with her father on a summer weekend, and he noticed her lips moving while she was talking to Czarina on the beach—Czarina sitting modestly on a blanket, holding a parasol—Carolina would simply act like she was singing to herself.

"OH MY GOD, TOUCHDOWN! YAH!" yelled Shelly, and because the rest of the crowd was suddenly standing, Carolina got up on her feet.

Carolina wasn't quite sure why Czarina had first appeared. When she was little, instead of Dr. Seuss books or stories about Matilda, her mother used to read Carolina Russian novels like *The Brothers Karamazov* and *War and Peace*. Carolina's mother had earned a master's degree in Russian literature at Brown University, and she hoped to inspire the same love for great books in her daughter that she had.

And then one day when she got back from kindergarten, Carolina found a Russian noblewoman sitting on her bed.

"You are an enchanting girl!" the noblewoman had said.

"I am? But, I mean, who *are* you?"

"I am Czarina Tallow of Russia."

Carolina recognized this name—her mother had shown her how to rearrange the letters in her own name into "Czarina Tallow." She called it an anagram.

"EXTRA POINT! YAH!" yelled Bridget.

For half of Carolina's life, Czarina Tallow had been her secret, and she was fine with that. They were different—Czarina wore lace gloves and a crown; Carolina wore a tank top and jeans. Czarina came from a big family; Carolina was an only child. Czarina adored gold and gemstones; Carolina didn't care much for jewelry. But they got along famously, and Carolina hoped that Czarina would be a part of her life forever.

127

Then, a few weeks ago, Carolina came home from her job as a summer lifeguard, and Czarina was sick. She wouldn't let Carolina see her face. The next day, she was gone. She hadn't left a letter behind, which was terribly unlike her.

That's when Carolina started hearing from her friends about how their younger siblings and cousins were crying that their so-called imaginary friends had vanished. There were even reports on the television about how kids were searching for them. Bespectacled experts swamped the talk shows to try to explain what was going on. With all the reports and all the theories, the one thing Carolina could come up with was . . . Ted Merritt.

"FUMBLE!" shouted Bridget. "Are you even *watching* this, Carolina?"

"Fumble!" said Carolina. "Woo!" That seemed to satisfy Bridget, who turned her attention back to the game.

Even though she didn't really know him, she had always felt like she and Ted shared a mutual secret. And he seemed interesting—always wearing long-sleeved shirts, silently hustling from class to class, like he was constantly in his head. She couldn't help but wonder what went on up there.

Plus, she thought he was cute.

But they were in *completely* different social circles, and in hers it was a *rule* that you didn't speak to Ted Merritt unless you were making fun of him.

The night she'd seen him wrestling on the ground with nothing, she had laughed at him as loud as any of her friends, and she remembered the way he'd looked at her, like she was really hurting him. Carolina still felt terrible about it all.

"GO, JOE! GO, JOE! GO, JOE!" shouted Shelly, yelling at a football player on the sidelines. "I LOVE YOU, JOE!"

"Love you back, Wendy!" said Joe, pointing to Shelly.

"Shelly!" yelled Shelly. "My name is Shelly! We make out, remember?"

"We sure do, Wendy!"

Carolina had been looking for a chance to apologize to Ted at school, but she hadn't seen him around in a few days.

"You need to get into the *game*, Carolina," said Bridget. "Come on, your turn to start the wave."

Carolina knew that if she didn't, her "friends" would gossip about why she was acting *weird*. So she rose out of her seat and threw her arms in the air.

"WOO, FOOTBALL!"

11

For the first time in centuries, Persephone was nervous. She didn't even know she could *get* nervous, but she could have sworn she was *sweating,* and without sweat glands! Butterflies flapped where her stomach would have been. She looked in the mirror on the wall and dragged a cylinder of ColorBoom! brand red lipstick across the bony protrusion that was all that remained of her beak.

"Mirror, mirror on the wall," she started, just for the heck of it, when all of a sudden the mirror fell to the ground with a bang, shattering into thousands of pieces.

Her interim assistant, Bugslush—a honey possum with an Australian accent and a stuttering problem—had been called up from her cleaning crew to work for Persephone in Swamster's absence, and he was still getting used to the job. Jittery by nature, he was simultaneously terrified of the president and eternally grateful for his promotion.

Bugslush had taken the job against the advice of everyone he'd talked to about it. His background was in chemistry, but he wanted to get into politics, and this was his big chance.

"D-*drat,*" said Bugslush. "Th-thousands of ap-pologies, President Skeleton. I d-didn't *know* that I was shutting the d-door so hard. I'll have that m-mirror replaced *im-mediately. I'M SO STUPID!*"

130

"Exactly," said Persephone. "Now, do calm down, Bugslush."

Bugslush began arranging the two place settings the president had requested.

President Skeleton had told Bugslush that tonight was a special night, and she wanted it to be perfect. Normally she didn't have dinner because food fell through her empty rib cage and splattered on the floor.

"So what I need you to do is this," she had said. "I need you to reach into my chest cavity, in between my rib bones, and attach a plastic bag to the top of my spine so that it will catch the dinner and drinks that I consume."

"Er," Bugslush had said. "O-k-kay."

It seemed like a lot to ask on his first day on the job, but he did what she told him to do. Reaching into the president's bony chest, he fastened a tall trash bag to the top vertebra of her spine, leaving the mouth of the bag wide open to make sure it caught everything.

131

"There you go," Bugslush had said.

"Very good," President Skeleton had replied. "Now zip me up."

For the occasion, Persephone had picked out a blue silk dress, which would hide the plastic bag. She knew that Scurvy liked the color blue.

She applied some mascara to the upper edges of her eye sockets. She was going for a dramatic look.

"Oh," she said. "Do you have a tissue?"

Bugslush looked around for a handkerchief and then remembered that, in a moment of weakness, he had taken some handkerchiefs off a table and chewed them into bits because he was making a new nest in his bedroom. It was a stupid, irrational decision, but what was done was done, and he didn't see the point of admitting his mistake. Better to blame somebody else.

"I d-don't," said Bugslush nervously. "I think . . . S-s-swamster might have s-stolen them."

"That doesn't surprise me," said Persephone. She wiped the excess mascara away with a dinner napkin.

Bugslush walked around the dinner table, spraying down the ham, adjusting the piles of fruit, straightening the stacks of bacon, and lighting the candelabra. He watched Persephone out of the corner of his eye as she applied blush to her cheekbones and perfume behind the holes in her skull that were all she had for ears. Her mind seemed to be somewhere else.

"I'm d-done arranging the t-table, President Skeleton," said Bugslush.

"That's nice," said Persephone, rearranging the straps of her dress.

"Is there anything else you n-need before I bring in Mr. G-goonda?"

"Uh-huh."

"W-what would you like?"

"What?"

"W-what would you like?"

"Uh-huh."

Bugslush paused. It seemed he could say anything, and President Skeleton would simply respond with an "Uh-huh" or "What?" This Scurvy fellow seemed to have taken hold of her brain.

"Swamster?" said Persephone.

"It's B-bugslush, President Skeleton," said Bugslush. "You sent Swamster into the f-field, remember?"

"Bugslush, can I ask you something?"

"Of c-course."

"How do I look tonight?" Persephone asked, almost demurely.

Bugslush could tell, as he looked Persephone over, that she was very nervous. She wanted so badly to look pretty for her date.

Persephone had on a blond wig whose nylon bangs fell down over half of her face, making her look like an old-time movie star; mascara was slathered on the rims of her eye sockets, crimson rouge was painted on her cheekbones, lipstick surrounded her scorched beak. A prom dress hung loosely from her gnarled shoulders down to the floor, and her feet were jammed into high heels. An odd musky perfume filled the room. She was a complete disaster in every way.

133

Bugslush's heart broke for a moment, because he knew that—before the power and the politics—Persephone had once been *good*. Not good-looking. But much more normal, and maybe even nice.

"P-president Skeleton," said Bugslush. "You look b-beautiful."

Persephone smiled, which just looked like her opening her mouth slightly, because she didn't have cheek muscles.

"Thank you, Bugslush," said Persephone.

"Shall I b-bring in our guest?"

"Please do," said Persephone. "And, Bugslush?"

"Y-yes?"

"If you ever take that long to compliment me again, I will turn your pelt into a vomit bag."

Bugslush started to shake.

"Yes, President Skeleton."

"Am I clear?"

"Very clear, President Skeleton," said Bugslush. "Vomit bag."

"Excellent," said Persephone. "Now, please fetch my special guest, if you would be so kind."

134

III

ACORN's tree-tunnel hideout wound on and on, chock-ablock with thousands of ab-coms of all sizes, shapes, colors, lack of colors, textures, feathers, tails, spots, smells, and demeanors. There was a shark stroking its beard while doing tricks with a leather whip. There was a movie-theater attendant spraying an enormous Bermuda spider with melted butter. There was a tired bison eating gravestones. A six-legged coyote was kicking a living soccer ball that was shouting in pain every time a foot whacked into its side. A grumpy orchid kept having its leaves stepped on, a zebra biathlete was adjusting its skis, and a mule was balancing a vase on its head while mumbling about a modeling career. Ted had never seen such a menagerie of misfits.

Joelle-Michelle led Ted and his cohorts through the tunnel. Watching her—ballet slippers, tights, pale skin, and long legs—was liquefying Ted's brain. Each time she leaped in the air or randomly spun in place, Ted malfunctioned. He couldn't stop looking.

From this point on, Ted thought, *I will be fully devoted to the worship of Joelle-Michelle Athenais-Benedicte de la Valliere, the ballerina. She has left me no other choice.*

"Is this all of ACORN?" asked Dwack, floating along as he was led down another tunnel.

Ted noted that the worried look on the vampire's face matched the look on the faces of Vango and Dr. Narwhal. It was hard to believe that these bizarre creatures had the abilities to fight a war. Could it be that all the intelligent ab-coms had simply obeyed the call to arms and joined President Skeleton's forces, leaving ACORN to the outcasts and degenerates?

"Yes, this is ACORN," Joelle-Michelle said to Dwack. "Were you expecting something else?"

"Everybody seems a little freaky," said Vango.

"Then you will fit in *perfectly*, won't you?" said Joelle-Michelle.

"It looksss like a lot of them are having some problemsss," chuckled Dr. Narwhal, pointing his horn at an Egyptian mummy whose head was wrapped completely in sparkling bandages and who was stumbling around blindly.

136

Joelle-Michelle strode up to Dr. Narwhal until she was belly to belly with the arctic beast. She took a long moment to stare Dr. Narwhal down, and then suddenly her arms shot forward so quickly that all Ted saw was a flash of very attractive elbow.

The next thing anybody knew, the teenage ballerina figurine had Dr. Narwhal's spiral horn in her hands and was pulling his massive head down so that she could look at him over the tip of her nose.

"Now you listen to me, you can opener," said Joelle-Michelle. "I *run* ACORN, and if you don't think that my troops are up to your standards, that's fine with me. You can leave and be hunted down by Persephone's army and be processed into bars of soap. But if you want to be a part of

ACORN and try to create a better Middlemost, then you *will not* talk poorly about anybody who is putting his or her or its life on the line. AM I CLEAR?"

"I think you wrenched my ssspine," said Dr. Narwhal.

"Answer. The. Question," said Joelle-Michelle.

"You are ever so clear, Mademoissselle Joelle-Michelle," said Dr. Narwhal. Joelle-Michelle let him go.

Then she pointed at Vango.

"I hear you loud and clear too," said Vango. "As loud as the screaming in my head!"

Joelle-Michelle merely raised an eyebrow at Dwack.

"Not one critical word will cross my fangs," said Dwack.

"Excellente!" said Joelle-Michelle, who pivoted to look at Ted. "And I can't imagine that I'll have any problems with you."

"None. *Vive l'ACORN*," he said (because he'd heard somebody say something like that in a war movie).

Joelle-Michelle smiled.

"You speak French?" she said. Ted had never seen eyes her color before.

"Oh, yes," lied Ted. "I love to speak French."

Joelle-Michelle studied Ted and then cocked her head.

"Je sais que vous mentez à moi," said Joelle-Michelle, which if Ted spoke French, he would have known meant "I know you are lying to me."

"Oui," said Ted, which meant "yes" and was the only French he knew aside from *vive*.

"Bien sûr," said Joelle-Michelle, and Ted knew that she had pegged him as a fake. When the group started moving

137

again, Ted walked at the back of the pack, behind Dr. Narwhal. He never knew how to act around girls.

"ACORN, as you know, is overwhelmingly outmanned by President Skeleton's army," said Joelle-Michelle, waltz-stepping the group deeper into the tunnel. Ted felt pressure on his eardrums—they must be far underground. "But each day ACORN grows. We are the ab-coms who do not think our friends should be punished for relinquishing us. We are the companions who believe Middlemost should be a place of peace, not a place where we are drafted into wars under threat of arrest. We believe that everybody should be treated for the loathsome Greenies, not only those who join Persephone's army."

"I haven't yet seen anybody here who is ill," said Dwack.

Joelle-Michelle raised a flawlessly arched eyebrow at him.

"It's a perfectly acceptable observation," said Dwack.

"Come here," said Joelle-Michelle. "All of you."

Joelle-Michelle led the group to a door guarded by a Russian cosmonaut.

"Monsieur cosmonaut, please open the observation window," said Joelle-Michelle.

The cosmonaut slid the heavy door into the tunnel wall, revealing a transparent door underneath. A mustard-colored light leaked into the hallway, and through the foggy glass Ted could see dark shapes moving slowly around inside the room.

"Now step closer," said Joelle-Michelle, and Ted, Dwack, Vango, and Dr. Narwhal did what she said.

Pushing their faces against the glass, they could see that the dark shapes were actually abstract companions, all with the same sort of stumbling gait, as if they weren't quite sure where they were going.

"What's wrong with them?" said Ted.

"They're in the latter stages of the Greenies," Joelle-Michelle explained. "The disease spreads and spreads, eating away at its host until there is nothing left—just a pool of sludge on the ground."

"Who are these poor beings?" said Dwack.

"These companions are steadfast believers in ACORN who refused to receive help from President Skeleton's army. We haven't been able to do anything for them."

"Somebody's got to *cure* them," said Ted, thinking of Scurvy. Was *this* what his pirate looked like now?

"That's where you four come in," said Joelle-Michelle.

"What do you mean?" said Dwack.

"Well, we have a job that nobody else wants to do," said Joelle-Michelle. "And you're the new guys. C'*est à vous!* Right, Ted?"

"Right," said Ted, absolutely not recognizing that she had just said, "It's your turn!"

"Come," said Joelle-Michelle, "let me show you something."

She led the group deeper into the tree tunnel, eventually stopping outside a thick oak door.

"Inside this room is perhaps the only chance we have against President Skeleton's army," said Joelle-Michelle. "You'll need to put on those protective coats."

With her toe, Joelle-Michelle pointed to a row of suits hanging from small branches poking out of the wall. When

139

everybody was fully covered, she nodded and pushed open the oak door.

Ted's visor was blasted by steam. The air was thick and hot, and ab-coms were rushing around in all directions.

Joelle-Michelle led the group to a steel vat in the center of the room. It was filled with bubbling purple liquid. Workers wearing protective suits were mixing the liquid with long metal poles while a mechanical claw above dropped gray rectangular cartridges and shiny silver discs into the vat.

Video games.

"We call this VIDGA solution," said Joelle-Michelle, yelling to be heard over the industrial noises. "For almost a year, we had been searching for an anti-imagination serum to use against President Skeleton's forces in case Persephone came to power.

"And then our scientists had an epiphany. What saps imagination the most? Video games. The first batch that they melted down was worthless—it didn't do anything. But then one of our particularly gifted scientists pointed out that *some* video games make you think—puzzle-solving games and graphic-design games and music-composition games and so forth. This scientist suggested we melt down a batch consisting only of shoot-'em-ups and games that focus on the most brain-dead entertainment. Alas, that scientist was splashed with the solution during the melting process, and—POP!— he exploded into a cloud of purple sludge, proving his theory but ending his life. Only games that kill imagination can be used to make VIDGA, but a little bit of that solution is enough to cause any ab-com to explode."

Ted looked down at the burbling liquid.

"So, what do you do with it?" he said.

"We use it to coat our weapons," said Joelle-Michelle. "As you'll find out. You see, there's a Greenies antidote, and we know where it's being made. Which reminds me, I have a badminton racket for you."

"What?"

"You'll understand soon."

141

IV

If Persephone's chest had still contained a heart, it would have been pumping furiously. But alas, since that wasn't an option, her foot was nervously banging out a steady rhythm—*BaBUMP-BaBUMP-BaBUMP!*

"Pretty bird," chanted Persephone to herself. "Pretty bird. Pretty bird. He will find you pretty. Hello, Scurvy. Hello, *Scurvy*. Hel-LO, Scur-VY."

Persephone was sitting at one end of a long table filled with all kinds of food—everything she remembered that Scurvy liked. Tapioca. Crab legs. Shepherd's pie. Beef tartare. And piles and piles of bacon covering specially ordered golden plates, cooked to every degree of crispiness and floppy-fattiness. Persephone even had bacon made from bulls and frogs and horses and social workers—all in the hopes of making her adorable Scurvy happy. She had heard that the way to a man's heart was through his stomach, and if Scurvy didn't love her, well then, she would feed him his own heart.

Persephone listened to the sound of her own bones clattering. She was second-guessing her blue dress. Was it too forward? She really should have gone with something more demure—after all, she didn't want Scurvy *knowing* that she had been thinking about him for the past three hundred years. Might seem a touch desperate.

"Oh," she said, panicking. "I need to change, I need to change."

But then the doorknob turned.

Persephone almost fainted.

The doorknob turned some more and then returned to its original position.

Persephone felt like she was a teenager.

The doorknob attempted to turn again and then shook back and forth a bit.

"Er, P-p-president Skeleton," said Bugslush. "I think I might have accidentally l-locked myself out. And I don't have a k-k-key."

Persephone sighed. Even though her knees were weak from all this anxiety, she pulled herself to her feet and walked across the floor to the locked door, her high heels clopping all the way. She took a deep breath into her nonexistent lungs and turned the knob.

Bugslush strode confidently inside, masking his mistake, and bowed toward the invited guest.

"President Skelet-ton," said Bugslush. "May I introduce Mr. Sc-sc-scurvy Gordon?"

"I prefer Goonda these days," said a voice from the other side of the doorway. And with that, Scurvy walked into the room. His shabby clothes had been pressed, his boots had been shined to a blinding polish, his beard had been trimmed, his eyebrows had been tamed, his fingernails had been clipped, his skin had been exfoliated, and his tricorne hat had been cleaned and hammered back into its original shape.

Inside, Persephone swooned.

Scurvy had been groomed against his will by Persephone's

143

personal staff of well-compensated beauticians, but despite the aggressive makeover, he had to admit that on the whole, he enjoyed the spiffing up. He felt particularly handsome tonight.

"Scurvy!" said Persephone, her eye sockets transfixed on her eternal love.

"Good gravy," said Scurvy, looking at Persephone. "Yer so *tall*."

Persephone twisted her jawbone into a sort of smile.

"Power makes everybody seem taller," said Persephone.

"Strange tah hear ya talkin'," said Scurvy.

"I've worked on my diction since . . . the boat," said Persephone.

"Oh," said Scurvy.

"You still have your hat," said Persephone, all excited and girlish.

144

"Three hundred years and counting. Har!" said Scurvy, trying to make his voice sound normal. He couldn't believe that this was the bird who used to creep him out by staring at him sixteen hours a day, sitting on his shoulder three inches away.

"And your *dreadful* Greenies have been cured, I see," said Persephone.

"Yer doctors gave me an antidote," said Scurvy. A white-coated physician had given him a shot, and within a few minutes, all the bumps had disappeared, and his strength was returning. "Brand-new me."

"You're just the same as I remember you," said Persephone, leaning in closer.

Scurvy realized that he had been paid a compliment, and that Persephone was expecting him to offer one in return.

"And you," said Scurvy, "are more . . . *colorful* than ever. Ya got all dressed up."

Persephone curtsied modestly.

"It's a special occasion," she said. "Come and join me at the table."

And that's when Scurvy looked at what they were having for dinner.

Stretching out on the table in front of Scurvy was a fantasy that played out nightly behind his eyelids, when he was in bed and just letting his mind wander. He had never seen so much bacon—it was as though the bounty of the supermarket meat rack had tripled in size and been dumped onto enormous gold platters. The plates of bacon were topped with bacon bits and sugarcoated bacon candies, and there were glasses of pureed bacon to wash down the rest of the bacon. It was a meal sent from heaven.

"B-bacon, Mr. Goonda?" said Bugslush.

"Holy crow," said Scurvy as Bugslush placed a two-foot-long slab on his plate.

145

The honey possum picked up a silver gravy boat.

"Some bacon s-sauce for your b-bacon?" said Bugslush.

"Please," said Scurvy, and Bugslush poured a long stream of greasy sauce over Scurvy's slab of bacon.

"May I bring anything for y-you, President Skeleton?" said Bugslush.

"That will be all, Bugslush," said Persephone. "Mr. Goonda and I have much to talk about."

With a bow, Bugslush left the room, thrilled to be dismissed.

As soon as the door shut behind Bugslush, Persephone picked up a large glass of scarlet wine and swirled the liquid with small rotations of her bony wrist. She looked at Scurvy, studying him. It had been so long. She took a drink, but to Scurvy it didn't look like she was really tasting the *vino*—it simply went down the hatch, and a strange plunking sound came from her torso, as though the liquid was thunking into . . . a plastic bag?

"Here you are," said Persephone, coyly. "Here. You. Are. Indeed."

But Scurvy already knew he was definitely *here*, and even though there was more bacon around than he had ever seen in any one place, he didn't like the way that this heavily accessorized skeleton was looking at him. There was something going on behind those empty eyes. He put his head down and took a huge bite of his bacon slab, hoping that when he looked up again, she would be gone.

"You know," said Persephone. "I forgave you for not saving me all those years ago. After all, the boat was on fire, and you probably weren't able to come down into the galley, even to save a devoted friend."

"Right, the sinkin'," said Scurvy. "I remember that night. I *attempted* tah get downstairs and grab yer cage, because a captain *never* lets any of his crew perish. But ya should have seen tha fight on deck—two of tha king's ships and mercenaries galore."

"Hmm . . . sounds rough," said Persephone. "Not as bad as being trapped alone in a burning cage, but still . . . quite bad."

"I tried, Persephone. I tried tah get through tha fire, but I was tossed overboard in tha fight. I was meant tah go down with that ship."

"Then *prove* that you tried, Scurvy!" said Persephone. She knew it was an unfair request, but she had been waiting to talk about this for three hundred years. The possibility that Scurvy *hadn't* abandoned her was overwhelming. If she was going to completely reverse her thinking after three hundred years, she was going to need evidence.

Scurvy rolled up the legs of his pants, exposing calf muscles covered everywhere in coarse black hair. That is, everywhere except in two odd spots—blotches of exposed scar tissue.

"See these?" said Scurvy, pointing at the hairless patches of skin.

"I do," said Persephone.

"I have them because I was attacked by an ab-com from the other boat when I was trying to run downstairs tah get ya. I couldn't get there, Persephone. I've carried these scars fer three centuries."

Persephone considered this.

"I see," she said. She wasn't sure if Scurvy was telling the truth—he could have received those scars anywhere.

"You swear that you got attacked that very day."

"I swear tah ya. Tha reason I got tha scars is that I was trying so hard tah get tah ya before ya were hurt that I wasn't payin' as much attention tah my fightin' as I shoulda been."

Persephone noticed that Scurvy had stopped eating the bacon. That was the clincher—he never stopped eating except to make an important point.

And now she loved him more than ever.

"Oh, my darling," she said, and drank the rest of her glass of wine, which splashed audibly into her trash bag.

"Scurvy," she continued. "The reason I invited you here tonight is . . . it's because I want to be with you."

As soon as those words came out of Persephone's beak,

147

Scurvy realized he had made a mistake. In lying about how he had tried to rescue Persephone—when in reality he had been far too busy fighting to worry about some creepy skeleton bird—he had inadvertently given her the impression that he was valiantly looking out for her. The truth was, he'd gotten the burns on his legs when he'd been cooking bacon naked and dropped the pan.

"Er," said Scurvy. "What does that mean, exactly? That ya want to be *with* me."

"It means that I want you in my life," said Persephone.

"Well, that's great! I mean, we're doing that right now, aren't we? Technically, I'm *in* yer life—if I'm sitting across tha table from ya, I'm occupying *space* in yer life, ya might say, so we're right where we need tah be."

"That's not exactly what I mean, Scurvy," said Persephone. "I want *you*. Always. Here and everywhere else we might go."

"But, Persephone, you were my *bird*!"

"I *used* to be your bird, but now I want to be your wife," said Persephone, twirling a wing bone in the curls of her blond wig. "Say yes, my darling. Or else, my darling."

V

Swamster was not built for the outdoors. All around him, filling up the transport trucks, were members of President Skeleton's elite guard: a Bazlook that looked like a sloth with a tiny head on an enormous body, a Bradook that had the appearance of a blond furball with tiny eyes poking out, a snaggletoothed Krumsplat that had the appearance of a rabid porcupine and moved along by hurling itself high into the air, splatting to the ground, and then repeating the process.

"Ye look uncomfortable with that crossbow," the Bazlook told Swamster.

"I'm more accustomed to finger-sandwich platters," Swamster explained.

"Well," said the Bradook, "you better get used to it, because it's going to be a busy hunting day."

Swamster had never hunted for anything in his life, aside from *just* the right swimsuit to disguise the bit of extra around his waist.

The caravan approached a road that cut through a field of spotlights pointed at the sky, and the Krumsplat handed around sunglasses—looking at the beams could damage the eyes. The spotlights had been designed by the first inhabitants of Middlemost, who figured if they could make their world look like a star, all potential invaders would leave them alone for fear of being burned up. The spotlights had worked wonders ever since.

"How much longer until we reach the place where the boy was seen?" said Swamster.

"Soon," said the Krumsplat.

"Let's say that we do find the boy," said Swamster. "We kill him, let him know who's boss, kill him, that kind of thing. Are we supposed to just leave his body lying out, or can we at least send it back to Earth so that his family can bury him properly?"

"President Skeleton said I should eat it," said the Bazlook. "And she told me to make sure you have a bite, to toughen you up."

"Eat the boy. Excellent. Can't wait."

VI

Scurvy scowled.

The truth was, he was simply not a one-woman kind of pirate—something that wasn't all that unusual among men of his seafaring occupation. And he truly wasn't a one-woman pirate if the woman in question happened to be a skeleton cockatoo. His world travels had revealed to him that there were many, many ab-com women. Before he had even met Persephone, he had been married three times.

Scurvy had taken his first wife, Sofia, while he was haunting the islands of the Mediterranean, bouncing from the Islas Baleares to Corsica to Crete, and living a sailor's life. Sofia stayed with him for as long as she could stand the claustrophobic ship holds and the savage confrontations that were a part of Scurvy's everyday pirate existence, until the day finally came when she left him for a watchmaker from Constantinople, whom she had married secretly, claiming that her marriage to Scurvy had never been legal, due to the fact that a barnacle and not a priest had performed the ceremony.

For his second marriage, he had picked a tall, mysterious woman from Casablanca named Amal—a woman so mysterious that she never removed the veil that covered most of her face. But he was mesmerized by her striking eyes—she had to be an unimaginable beauty under those alluring veils, he was sure of it.

Amal was more patient with Scurvy's lifestyle than Sofia had been, and she would wait for him in Morocco while he was away at sea for months and years. Whenever he made his way back to northern Africa, she was always standing at the end of the dock, veils blowing in the Atlantic winds, meeting his ship as it pulled into port.

Eventually, Scurvy discovered that Amal wore a veil because she was a bearded woman in the circus, but he got over this minor detail quickly—he wasn't a picky man. He and Amal spent their nights talking about beard maintenance, and because of her tips Scurvy's mane had been silky smooth for three centuries.

His third wife had been Cindy, whom he had left on Antarctica because she so thoroughly aggravated him. She was probably annoying the penguins there today. He didn't like thinking about Cindy, because it wasn't usually his style to leave women at the bottom of the world, and he still felt guilty about the whole situation.

Between wives, there had been girlfriends—more than Scurvy could count—at ports across all seven continents. But as Persephone sat across the table from him, he *knew* that she was thinking that he was a soul mate or some such thing . . . which was simply not the case. She was a cockatoo who had creeped him out three hundred years ago, someone he hadn't really thought about until he got the recall notice, and there was no good way to tell her as much. She didn't seem like the understanding, oh-well-we-can-still-be-friends type.

"Look, Persephone," he said. "There are some things that ya should know."

152

Abruptly, Persephone picked up a silver bell near her plate and rang it several times.

"What's that for?" said Scurvy.

"It's for something I think we both want," said Persephone.

"I haven't seen ya since the late sixteen hundreds," said Scurvy. "Why do ya think ya know what I want?"

"Because I know *you*."

"I'm not sure that's true, me birdie."

"Well, if I'm wrong, I have ways of making you change," said Persephone. "Change is *good*, Scurvy."

A few seconds later, Bugslush entered the room carrying a velvet pillow. On top of the pillow was a gold ring. He brought it over to Scurvy and got down on one knee. Scurvy's blood ran cold.

"Bugslush," said Persephone. "I think you have something to ask Mr. Goonda."

153

Bugslush cleared his throat.

"President Skeleton," said Bugslush, "wishes to ask for your hand in m-m-marriage."

"Refuse me," said Persephone, "and it's the gallows, my Scurvy-Durvy Bo-Burvy. I will hang you very, very high."

VII

Ted crouched behind a rock next to Dwack, near a road that dead-ended at a factory far in the distance. Dwack had explained that because of its remote location, the road was used frequently by individuals who wanted to get around on their own terms, far away from the eye of the government, which was why ACORN knew about it. They had provided Ted with an excellent map of where he, Dwack, Vango, and Dr. Narwhal should set up their ambush.

Though *whom* exactly they would be ambushing, Joelle-Michelle wouldn't say.

Erka erka erka! came a strange sound from down the road. Joelle-Michelle had made Vango the lookout, which required him to alert the others of oncoming transports with a birdcall. Joelle-Michelle had allowed Vango to choose the alarm himself, and he eventually picked *erka erka erka* after being discouraged from going with his first choice of *gobble gobble*.

Erka erka erka!

The bird call was the signal for Dr. Narwhal to station himself by the side of the road. He had been provided with a broken bicycle to make it seem as though he had simply been cycling along the abandoned road when all of a sudden his tire malfunctioned. Ted thought it more than dubious that Dr. Narwhal would have the proper center of gravity to permit bicycle riding.

The idea was that an approaching truck would slow down at the sight of a stranded arctic moon whale standing on the side of a dusty highway, and it was Dr. Narwhal's job to wander directly into the middle of the road and make sure that the truck stopped. As soon as that happened, Ted and Dwack would storm the truck.

ERKA ERKA ERKA! came a louder Vango call. Ted felt nervous sweat starting to drip down his face.

ACORN had been watching a certain truck for the past week as it shuttled back and forth from the factory to Ab-Com City. But though its spies had not yet risked getting close enough to the truck to actually determine who was piloting the vehicle, they had learned what the truck contained.

Thousands upon thousands of doses of Greenies antidote!

ACORN would continue to monitor the foursome's activities with powerful binoculars from a safe position more than a mile away. After Dr. Narwhal stopped the truck, Ted and Dwack would launch a mini-attack that would flush the guards out of the truck.

155

This would most likely result in them being killed, therein proving their loyalty to ACORN's noble mission.

Hopefully, in the process of being ripped apart or blown into bits or eaten alive, Ted and Dwack would be able to draw *all* of the truck's guards out into the open. Thus, ACORN would know exactly how many soldiers to send to attack the truck again further down the road.

"Wait," Ted had said when Joelle-Michelle had first explained the plan to him. "You're saying that, almost certainly, we're going to be killed."

"*Absolument*," Joelle-Michelle confirmed.

"But I don't want to be killed," Ted had replied.

"Quite understandable," said Joelle-Michelle. "But all of us who have joined ACORN must do many unpleasant things, unfortunately."

"Joelle-Michelle, I am up for awful tasks. Just assign me any one that doesn't involve me being ripped to shreds."

Joelle-Michelle considered this request.

"*Non*. I think we'll just stick with having you flush the guards out of the truck. It would mean so much to me."

And with that, Ted Merritt began to understand why guys do stupid things for pretty girls.

ERKA! ERKA! ERKA!

The huge truck bearing the presidential seal was now close enough that Ted could see it from his hiding spot as it kicked up clouds of dust and barreled over potholes. He looked down at the VIDGA-dipped badminton racket Joelle-Michelle had given him to use as a weapon. If dying was what it took to impress her, then he would go down fighting.

Ted watched Dr. Narwhal bravely take a few steps toward the center of the road, waving his flipper to get the driver's attention.

"Hellooooo," said Dr. Narwhal.

An otter head with a rooster crest poked out of the stopped truck.

"What are you doing here?" said the rooster-otter.

"Out for an innocent bike ride, and I'm afraid I've got a flat tire," said Dr. Narwhal.

"You're not supposed to be out here. This is a restricted road."

"It is? Oh, darn. I never noticed. I'm positively addicted

to my exercissse," said Dr. Narwhal. "I'm Dr. Narwhal, by the way."

"They call me Scozzbottle."

"Well then, Scozzbottle," said Dr. Narwhal. "Mind giving me a lift?"

Scozzbottle eyed Dr. Narwhal curiously. Behind his rock, Ted's hand was shaking as he gripped his badminton racket.

"You're not allowed to go in our direction," said Scozzbottle.

"YOU KNOW," said a deep voice from inside the truck. "WE HAVE A BIKE PUMP IN DA BACK. I BROUGHT IT IN CASE WE WANTED TO PLAY BASKETBALL."

"There should be some duct tape in the tool kit," said another gruff, rumbling voice. "Might work as a patch."

Scozzbottle stared at Dr. Narwhal.

"I'd be ever ssso grateful for your help," Dr. Narwhal said politely.

157

"All right," said Scozzbottle.

With that, the three largest ab-coms Ted had ever seen emerged from the truck. Scozzbottle lumbered toward Dr. Narwhal's bicycle, followed by a goat made of stone and sod, and a hyena with spots made of orange and yellow flames leaping from his pelt.

"That's Fyrena, and that's Wockgrass," said Scozzbottle, introducing his coworkers.

"HELLO," said Fyrena.

"Howdy," said Wockgrass.

Fyrena walked over to Dr. Narwhal's bike, holding the roll of duct tape.

"BIG HOLE IN DA TIRE," Fyrena snarled.

"I know," said Dr. Narwhal. "I mussst have run over something sharp."

"You should get a bigger bike," grunted Wockgrass. "This one's frame ain't meant to hold somebody your size."

"Too true," said Dr. Narwhal. "I keep hoping that if I use the bike enough, I'll lossse weight, and then I won't have to get a new one."

"That's called a circle of denial," said Scozzbottle, astutely.

Dr. Narwhal flicked his eyes toward the rocks where Ted and Dwack were hiding, silently telling them, *NOW!*

Dwack looked at Ted and nodded: *It's time.*

Ted shook his head at Dwack in response: *I'm not sure it's time.* His hands were shaking on his badminton racket. The three Presidential Guards surrounding Dr. Narwhal's bicycle were so *huge.*

Then Dwack took a terrific leap and soared right at them.

"Hey there!" yelled Dwack, and the moment Fyrena looked up, Dwack was on him, slashing with the VIDGA solution–covered cane that Joelle-Michelle had given him—and missing completely.

When he saw Dwack plummeting toward him, Fyrena rolled out of the way, Dwack tumbled to the ground, and the chaos began. Fyrena propelled himself at Dwack, whacking the vampire's cane aside with an enormous paw and sending it banging to the ground, and then Dwack and Fyrena were rolling around on top of each other, punching and spitting and hacking and gouging.

"An AMBUSH! You dirty—" said Scozzbottle, but he didn't have the time to finish his sentence before Dr. Narwhal tackled him and began slapping Scozzbottle with his flippers again and again, making terrific *thwack* sounds that rang out across the empty road. Wockgrass leaped onto Dr. Narwhal's back and sunk his teeth into Dr. Narwhal's aquatic hide, provoking Dr. Narwhal to yell, "Ted!"

But Ted was paralyzed by thoughts about what he should have been doing, and he couldn't move. He imagined slashing through the fray on the back of a huge horse and using the badminton racket to swat back the balls of flames that were leaping from Fyrena. He pictured himself flipping Scozzbottle over his shoulder like a judo champion, tossing him into a cage with his cohorts, and delivering them to Joelle-Michelle tied with a bow. He pictured Joelle-Michelle handing him a trophy and—

"Ted! Get down here and *help*!" said Dwack, holding Fyrena's neck, dodging the flames pouring from the cat's mouth.

"Come on, Vango!" yelled Dr. Narwhal.

"No chance!" yelled Vango. "I was just supposed to be lookout. *'Erka erka,'* remember?"

Ted watched Dwack grab on to one of Fyrena's scalding spots and cry out in pain.

Oh geez, thought Ted, shifting his weight from foot to foot, waiting for his body to tell him what to do. He watched Scozzbottle pick up the cane Dwack had dropped and advance toward Dr. Narwhal, grinning.

It was the same grin Duke had on his face every time he beat up Ted. And as Ted looked at that grin, something exploded inside him. He grabbed his badminton racket and charged.

"GET AWAY FROM THEM," yelled Ted, rearing back with

159

his badminton racket and swinging it with all his might into Wockgrass's stone body.

POP!

The goat disappeared in a mist of purplish muck that splattered on Ted's body and face. It smelled a bit like mayonnaise.

"My eyes!" said Ted, momentarily blinded. Dwack and Dr. Narwhal glanced over from their fights to see if he was okay, and that moment of distraction was all the remaining Presidential Guards needed.

"Bloodsucker!" said Fyrena, swinging his massive paw against Dwack's face and knocking him out.

"Hey, big guy!" said Scozzbottle, whacking Dr. Narwhal on the base of the neck. Dr. Narwhal crumpled in an unconscious heap.

Blinded by the purple muck, Ted could hear the sounds of the fights around him ending, and he was afraid. He flailed with his badminton racket but hit nothing. He heard footsteps approaching.

"Stand BACK!" said Ted, pointing his badminton racket in the direction of the footsteps.

"Oh, I don't think I'll be doing that," said Scozzbottle.

Still blinded by the purple muck, Ted smelled Scozzbottle's oily fur, and then he felt Fyrena wrapping a smoking, smoldering paw around his mouth and nose.

Good night.

VIII

Carolina Waltz walked through the empty supermarket aisles searching for Ted Merritt. She was starting to worry about what might have happened to him. Not only did she want to apologize and tell him that she never really thought that he was crazy, she also wanted to ask him if he knew where Czarina Tallow might have gone. *Has Ted dropped out of school?* she wondered. *Is he working at the supermarket full-time?* She didn't know where he could have gone, and the Stop to Shop seemed as good a place as any to look for him.

She turned down another aisle and nearly tripped over a man who was sitting on a skateboard in front of a soup display. The man wore headphones and was singing along to a disco song.

Carolina tapped his shoulder, and he looked up at her with watery red eyes.

"Well there," he said, and winked. "Pretty-pretty."

A creepy feeling ran all over Carolina's skin.

"Um, hi," said Carolina. "I was wondering if you could help me find somebody."

"I think you just found him."

"Uh, no," said Carolina, pressing on. "His name is Ted Merritt. He used to work here."

"'Used to' is right."

"What does that mean?"

"Come over here and I'll tell you," he said.

She didn't want to get any closer to the man, but she lowered her ear so he could whisper whatever he had to say. His breath smelled like onion soup.

"Curly hair," he said. "Looks like you take care of it."

"Tell me what you were going to say," said Carolina.

"If you ever asked the night manager about it, he'd say that Ted was fired and never came back."

"Okay."

"But he did, once. He came back last week, and Jed chased him into the Crusher and hit the switch. I saw it myself. It wouldn't surprise me if he's still stuck in the gears. But you didn't hear that from me, curly-curly."

"Can you point out this Crusher for me?" Carolina had a sick feeling in her stomach.

162

"Ain't supposed to be in the back if you ain't an employee."

Carolina got an idea.

"If you tell me where it is," she said, "I'll wait for you back there."

He grinned, and Carolina could see bits of something—fish skin?—stuck in his teeth.

"Go back through those swinging doors marked 'Authorized Personnel Only,'" he said. "Hang a left, and you'll see it—ugly metal thing filled with cardboard."

"Thanks."

"I'll meet you behind it, as soon as I finish this shelf."

Carolina walked away, breathing deeply to prevent herself from dry heaving. She pushed her way through the swinging doors, looked to make sure nobody was around, hung a quick left, and there it was—the Crusher.

Carolina could see straight to the bottom of the Crusher, which appeared to be made of overlapping sheets of steel. Those jaws, the idea of Ted caught in them . . . And then she spotted something that made her heart sink.

In the back corner of the Crusher, there was a gap between the wall and one of the steel plates. A small amount of light seemed to be pouring through this crack, and hanging over the lip of the fissure was something that looked like *meat*.

It can't be, thought Carolina.

She climbed down into the Crusher and crawled over to the steel panel until she was nose to slab with the meat.

Is this a cut of Ted's thigh, a piece of his shoulder? thought Carolina. *Or could it be . . . bacon?* She wrapped her fingers around the edge of the panel and slid it open, revealing a narrow compartment underneath.

"Huh?" said Carolina.

She lowered herself into the slot.

It appeared that she was in a vent of some sort, and at the end of the narrow passage, she could make out a faint light.

"Where are you, pretty?" she heard the creepy guy say above her. "Breaking promises gets you a bad reputation."

Carolina slid the steel panel closed above her.

There was just enough light coming from the end of the passage for her to see where she was going. She could hear muffled sounds up ahead—hammers and drills.

"I'm coming, Ted," she said to herself, and followed the light.

163

THUD! THUD! THUD!

   KA-SHOOM! KA-SHOOM!

   RRR-CLUNK! RRR-CLUNK!

A bottle was placed against Ted's lips.

"Drink," he heard Dr. Narwhal saying. He did what he was told, drinking deeply of whatever had been offered. The liquid burned his throat and shot him to a sitting position, making him spit and hack.

"What is that?" yelled Ted.

"Vango's persssonal tonic," said Dr. Narwhal.

FZZZ-BOOM! FZZZ-BOOM!

Looking around, Ted saw that they were in an office of some kind. There were a desk, a bookshelf, a halogen lamp, and a thick metal door.

"What happened?" said Ted.

"It seems that we are being kept prisoner," said Dwack.

"Where are we?"

"Ever wondered where ab-coms come from?" said Dwack.

Ted walked to a long window that was built into the wall behind him. Below was some sort of a chaotic workshop. There were tubes everywhere, clear gelatinous cylinders that hung down from the ceiling over conveyor belts and workstations like tentacles. Ted could see what looked like light blue clouds moving down through the tubes. When the clouds reached the ends of the tubes, they were shot into enormous steel vats. Then workers in yellow suits marked WATCH-OUT! examined them and took furious notes on serious-looking clipboards.

Dwack pointed to one of the clear tentacles hanging from the ceiling.

"*Those*," said Dwack, "are idea tubes. You can't tell from here, but see the way they punch out through the ceiling? They extend to the edge of the atmosphere. Factories like this use the tubes to capture kids' ideas that have floated out into space. That's what those little blue clouds are."

"Ideas?"

"Those light blue clouds are their ideas for friends," said Dwack. "When kids generate ideas, the ideas fly from their brains—there is nothing in the universe that moves faster than the ideas of children, not even light—and those ideas find their way here, like flocks of geese."

"What do those guys in the suits do?"

"They read the orders and start the building process. Their WATCHOUT! suits are standard protective equipment."

On the factory floor, some of the vats were filled with what looked like sculpting clay, others with various parts of ab-coms—hooves, antlers, legs, bodies, hats, coats, wigs, and paws. A WATCHOUT! worker stared down at an order and then sifted through the spare parts inside a vat until he found a raccoon tail and a baseball helmet. The worker placed these pieces on a conveyor belt, where they glided toward another group of workers, one of whom shook his head and put the pieces aside, dissatisfied for some reason.

"Where do the spare parts come from?" said Ted.

"That's a bit of a morbid topic. Look over there," said Dwack, pointing to a queue of depressed-looking abstract companions who were lined up outside a steel door, where two WATCHOUT! workers seemed to be collecting the ab-coms' personal information on their serious-looking clipboards.

"Everybody in the line looks miserable," said Ted.

Ted watched an old robot hug a fat ninja, hang its head, and walk heavily through the steel door. It looked like it was going off to meet a firing squad.

"Many ab-coms have a hard time adjusting to their new lives in Middlemost without their friends. For these individuals, there's a donation program, you could call it—they give themselves to future generations."

Moments later, a different WATCHOUT! worker emerged from the back room, pushing a wheelbarrow full of robot parts.

"Is that . . . ?"

"I'm afraid so," said Dwack. "You'd be surprised how many companions choose that way out. It keeps the population down to some degree, but I've always found it all a bit distasteful."

The remains of the robot coasted along the conveyor belt to the WATCHOUT! worker who had put aside the baseball helmet and the raccoon tail. The worker nodded. Putting everything together with sculpting clay, he quickly assembled a baseball-playing robot raccoon, after which he placed the new abstract companion on another conveyor belt, which dead-ended above a tank of viscous maroon liquid.

"Activator solution," explained Dwack.

"What's it made of?" said Ted.

"There's some sunshine in there, some chocolate, some music, a little bit of campfire, some old stories, some snow, a little bit of the ocean. If it brings imagination to life, it goes in the pot."

The robot raccoon splashed down into the maroon solution. A mechanical arm fastened a lid on top of the tank, which immediately started to vibrate rapidly—VZZZZ. After a few seconds, the shaking abruptly stopped, the liquid drained from the tank, the mechanical arm removed the lid, and the whole vat FLIPPED on its edge, dumping the hacking and sputtering robot raccoon onto an inflatable cushion surrounded by padded walls.

"It's alive," said Ted.

"That's how it happens," said Dwack.

A pair of WATCHOUT! workers came out with sponges and towels to clean the new ab-com, which was blinking into the light, trying to figure out what had just happened. The WATCHOUT! workers scooped up the robot raccoon and carried it on a gurney to the end of the thickest tentacle-tube in the room.

167

And then . . . *SLURP!* The robot raccoon was sucked into the wide tube and disappeared.

"That tube would normally take the new ab-com to a vent like the one you passed through, and from there it would be delivered to Earth," said Dwack. "But because of the call to arms, I'm not sure where all the new companions are going. Directly into the army, if I had to guess."

"Wait a minute," said Ted. "When Scurvy Goonda showed up in my life, he'd already had *tons* of experiences before me. How is that possible if he was created for me here?"

"Lots of kids want pirates as their ab-coms," explained Dwack. "If there is a perfectly adequate one out in the world—like Scurvy, for instance—they're often used again and again. Whenever Scurvy was cast off by one child, he would probably just find another. He must have liked his job. But at some point, he was made here, the same as everybody else."

And then came a voice from behind Ted and Dwack.

"Ah . . . er . . . AHEM. You're in trouble. I think. I mean, I know that you are. I think that I know. Ahem."

Ted, Dwack, Vango, and Dr. Narwhal turned around and saw a swimsuit-wearing Swamster standing in the doorway, chewing nervously on a piece of cardboard.

Dwack recognized the intruder as a Swamster because he had known others—visiting Denmark, he had once met an entire team of water polo Swamsters—but there was something *different* about this one. Behind his gold medals, *this* Swamster didn't seem the least bit confident.

"You should really, uh, well I'm not sure what you should do," said Swamster. "Hold on. I need to think about it."

"Who are you?" said Dr. Narwhal.

"I'm your worst . . . nightmare?" Swamster said, and then slumped his shoulders, not quite sure his prisoners would believe him.

They didn't.

"Bah-hah-hah!" laughed Vango.

"Har-har-har!" laughed Dr. Narwhal.

When Ted saw Dwack smile, he couldn't stop himself from chuckling, and pretty soon, everybody was laughing at the Swamster.

Who suddenly looked terribly sad.

"Fine then, laugh," said Swamster. "It's not just me here, you know, but I figured I'd introduce myself to you first to be polite. But clearly you don't care about any of that. So, GUARDS!"

X

"Okay, my lovely-bubbly," said Persephone, "which of these invitations do you like?"

Scurvy was wearing a cable-knit sweater and sensible khaki pants, and he was holding a martini glass. His hair was parted neatly on the side, and his beard had been deloused. A fire roared in the hearth, and the den was filled with tasteful leather furniture. Taxidermied animal heads hung on the wall.

Persephone had taken Scurvy on a weekend out to the country—or rather, out to this exclusive spa and lodge located in the forest just outside Ab-Com City. Persephone liked to come here periodically to relax and have her bones bleached and lengthened.

Scurvy stared down at three sample wedding invitations. All of them looked ridiculously fancy—one the color of crushed eggshells and made of velvet; another effervescent, with an almost gauzy feel to it; the third wrapped in a pink bow, with different cards for "directions," "response," and "reception."

He couldn't believe he was getting married again. But it was marry or die, and he had been in relationships that felt like death before, so he decided to cut his losses and make Persephone an honest skeleton.

"I don't know, honey," said Scurvy.

"I want your pet name for me to be Ploopsie," said Persephone.

"Of course ya do," said Scurvy. "As I was saying, I'm not sure *which* of them tah choose. They're all so *magnificent*."

Scurvy looked around the room, searching for possible escape paths. Persephone had stationed her guards outside all the main doorways, but he thought that if he could tie Persephone to a chair, he might be able to extinguish the fire in the fireplace and crawl up and out through the chimney, like a reverse Santa.

"Magnificent like me?" said Persephone.

Scurvy paused.

"Exactly like ya, Pooprie," said Scurvy, lying.

"Ploopsie."

"Rightie-o."

Persephone was content. Everything was working out exactly the way she wanted. She had her man. She was planning her wedding. She was about to attack Earth. Life was beautiful.

171

"We'll take the sea-green invitations," said Persephone to the wedding planner standing on the other side of the table.

"An excellent choice, President Skeleton," said the planner. "Very elegant."

"But still fun!" said Persephone.

"*Very* fun. I'll have them printed up *immediately*. I love brief engagements—looks like the pressure is on for yours truly!"

Scurvy didn't like the planner, who was organizing the wedding and everything else that would make Persephone's life easier until the big day. He was the one who had purchased Scurvy's new cable-knit sweater.

The planner skittered away with the invitations. Scurvy watched him scoot past Persephone's guards, and Scurvy considered snapping a leg off the table and using it as a club as he made a break for freedom. If that didn't work, he could use it to beat himself unconscious. Maybe Persephone wouldn't marry him if he was in a coma?

Persephone exhaled and put her wing bones around Scurvy's shoulders. She pecked him with her beak, which was the way she kissed. Scurvy could feel his upper lip starting to bleed through his mustache.

"The invitations are perfect," said Persephone.

She waited.

"And so . . . are you?" said Scurvy.

Persephone smiled. Scurvy noticed a loose floorboard near the hearth. Could he dig his way out of here?

"Can you believe it?" she said. "After *three hundred years* we're finally getting *married!*"

"I really *can't* believe it," said Scurvy. "But don't ya think that maybe we should wait a wee bit longer? Have some time tah, uh, *enjoy* our engagement? Maybe take some time off, go on one of them luxury cruises instead of waging war against humankind."

"Oh, Scurvy, you're so *silly*," said Persephone. "We're both just two silly kids in love."

Persephone patted Scurvy on his bottom and giggled.

"So what should we look at next?" said Persephone. "The silverware or the centerpiece arrangements?"

Scurvy looked around, sweating. The walls of the room didn't seem *too* thick. Could he get enough space to work up a good head of steam? Could he then just crash through the wall and keep on running?

"Let's go with tha centerpieces," he said.

"FLORAL CENTERPIECES!" screeched Persephone.

With a staff of assistants carrying dozens of flower arrange-ments, the wedding planner breezed into the room, smiling hugely.

"It's flower time for our blushing bridal rose!" said the planner.

"This is so much *fun!*" said Persephone. "Isn't it, Scurby-Durby Bo-Burby?"

"Yes, Ploppy," said Scurvy.

"Ploopsie," said Persephone.

"Now, as you can see, this is a gorgeous *variety* of blooms," said the planner. "Peonies, sweet peas, orange-tipped leucaden-drons."

Scurvy wondered if it would be possible to recontract the Greenies and melt into a puddle of sludge. Would it really be so bad?

173

Promotion, promotion, promotion, thought Swamster to himself. *Just get through this*.

"Tell me, Swamster," said Dwack. "Do you have some sort of plan for us, or are you going to just lead us around in circles?"

"There is a plan," said Swamster.

Promotion, promotion, promotion.

They were standing in front of the room in which the robot had been torn apart. A small sign hung in the middle of the door:

174

WARNING

PROCESSING ROOM

IT WILL BE MESSY INSIDE

Two WATCHOUT! workers opened the door, and the Baz-look and Krumsplat pushed their prisoners through. CLANG! The door closed behind them.

"Well," said Dwack. "This is rather unfortunate."

The processing room was filled with racks and pulleys and machines with sharp teeth. The floor was covered with puddles of sticky ooze, and hacksaws and ominous-looking instruments hung on the wall, all within reach of a dozen or so WATCHOUT! workers who awaited their next victims.

"Hello, everybody," said Swamster to the WATCHOUT! workers. "This is Ted, and these are Dwack, Vango, and Dr. Narwhal. President Skeleton has asked that you process and recycle them, starting with the boy."

"Whoa, whoa, whoa," said Ted. "I'm not even from Middlemost. You can't recycle me."

"You're quite incorrect. I have orders from President Skeleton to recycle you into"—Swamster checked his notes—"place mats for the president's wedding to Mr. Scurvy Gordon."

"She's marrying *Scurvy?*" said Ted.

"Ah, but alas, I'm afraid you're not invited," said the lead WATCHOUT! worker, removing her hood. "*C'est la vie.*"

It was Joelle-Michelle. The rest of the WATCHOUT! workers removed their suits.

They were all members of ACORN.

175

XII

As Carolina hit the ThereYouGo Gate, there came the brief sensation of being squeezed, and—SMACK—she landed on a catering table piled high with sandwiches.

Am I dead? she first thought. But then she breathed deeply and grabbed a very real-seeming peach that had rolled next to her. In the middle of the sky, high above where she lay sprawled, she could see what looked like a vent surrounded by construction scaffolding and ladders.

All at once, a bunch of weirdos rushed over and surrounded her. All of them were dressed in construction-work uniforms, and some appeared to be in the middle of eating lunch, holding half-eaten sandwiches.

"Well," said Carolina, "I guess I'm in hell."

"Nope. Just Middlemost," said a short weirdo.

"Middlemost?" said Carolina. "Is that like purgatory or something?"

The weirdos looked at each other.

"Not sure about that purgatory," said a weirdo wearing a plaid suit, pointing to the hole in the sky. "We're just here to close up that vent."

"But that vent is how I got here, wherever here is," said Carolina.

All she got in response were mumbles: *Not our problem.*

Shouldn't have fallen through the vent in the first place. Take it up with management.

"President Skeleton was the one who told us to close the vent," said the plaid weirdo. "If you have a complaint, you need an appointment to talk to her."

"Fine. I'll make an appointment," said Carolina. "Where does your president live anyway?"

"Ab-Com City, of course. We have a crew that's *supposed* to head back there tonight. But we're a little short-staffed, so we might not make it out of here on schedule."

"Hey, I can swing a hammer," said Carolina. "And my father taught me how to weld. Being pretty doesn't mean I'm unskilled."

"We weren't even thinking that you were pretty."

"Just give me a tool belt and let's get to work."

"But it's sandwich time."

"Then I'll start, and you can catch up when you're done. I really need to talk to this skeleton person."

"She's not really a person."

"Whatever she is. We need to chat."

The tallest weirdo pointed to the vent, and Carolina picked up a blowtorch.

"By the way, you haven't seen a guy named Ted Merritt around, have you? Or a Czarina Tallow? A Russian empress?"

The weirdos shook their various heads.

Carolina started to climb the scaffolding. "Give me twenty minutes and I'll have this hole closed."

177

XIII

Joelle-Michelle's original plan had indeed panned out—backward.

She hadn't foreseen Fyrena and Scozzbottle simply knocking the new guys unconscious, loading them in their truck, and then taking off the way they'd come.

Once Joelle-Michelle and her fighters followed the truck to the processing factory, they subdued a pair of dozing guards, and from there, it was a simple matter of eluding factory employees and collecting WATCHOUT! suits. Joelle-Michelle had felt bad about having sent Ted off to be killed—she was relieved to see that he had merely been clobbered stupid.

When they gathered in the processing room to figure out what to do next—hoping to also convince some of the depressed individuals who were having themselves processed to join ACORN instead—all of a sudden the new recruits walked in, guided by a nervous Swamster, who kept saying how he never wanted to be out in the field in the first place.

"Boddah you?" Brother Dezo now said to the hog-tied Krumsplat and Bazlook. Brother Dezo was a Hawaiian musician who spoke pidgin English and served as Joelle-Michelle's second-in-charge. Dezo carried a ukulele and had a voice like an angel.

"Bind and gag the Swamster," said Joelle-Michelle. "We'll take him with us."

"Oh thank you, thank you," said Swamster. "I really am a decent—"

"I could change my mind," said Joelle-Michelle.

Swamster clammed up.

"As for the Bazlook and the Krumsplat—what do you think, Brother Dezo?"

"Dey probably come after us da moment we were gone," said Brother Dezo. "Pop den?"

"Pop, *s'il vous plaît,*" said Joelle-Michelle.

With that, Brother Dezo stepped forward and swung his ukulele two times: *POP! POP!*

The Bazlook and the Krumsplat exploded into puddles of purple muck. Brother Dezo deftly stepped out of the way to avoid the spray—he'd done this before.

179

"And that is that. Is everybody all right?" asked Joelle-Michelle crisply of her new recruits.

"I think we're exceptional," said Dwack.

"Ted," said Joelle-Michelle. "I wanted to tell you that I saw you fight. You were brave."

Ted's heart leaped.

"Dr. Narwhal, are you well enough to carry Swamster?" said Joelle-Michelle.

"Indeed I am," said Dr. Narwhal. "I'll squeeze him nice and tight."

"*Merveilleux!* Onward!" Joelle-Michelle pirouetted, did a ballerina flutter kick, and started to march forward.

Ted wedged himself somewhere in the middle of the pack,

happy to be surrounded and protected by thick, heavily armed bodies. There was no ambush waiting on the other side of the door—only a line of depressed abstract companions waiting to end their lives.

"No need to have yourselves ripped apart!" said Joelle-Michelle. "There is a place for you in ACORN. *Viens avec moi! Come with me!*"

And that was all it took to convince these lost souls. Nobody disobeyed Joelle-Michelle, and the desperate ab-coms followed her and the rest of ACORN as they weaved their way through the processing factory. If they encountered a WATCHOUT! worker, they gave the worker the choice of joining ACORN or being *popped*. Most preferred to join—working in a processing factory was a terrible job anyway.

The group passed numerous exits as it made its way through the factory corridors. Joelle-Michelle seemed to be looking for something but nobody asked what. Finally, she motioned for one of the new WATCHOUT! recruits to come and talk to her.

The WATCHOUT! worker led everybody to a door secured by a scary-looking combination lock. The sign on the door read:

KEEP OUT!
AUTHORIZED PERSONNEL ONLY!
EVEN IF YOU ARE AUTHORIZED,
YOU PROBABLY STILL SHOULDN'T
COME IN!

The WATCHOUT! worker punched in a code, and the door unlocked with a loud CLICK. Joelle-Michelle turned to her followers.

"This is it," she whispered. "When we get inside, each of you need to do your part. The fate of ACORN depends on *you*!"

Joelle-Michelle pushed open the door and an alarm exploded like a thousand fire engines.

WHOOOOOOP! WHOOOOOP!

"Everybody, inside, NOW!" said Joelle-Michelle, hustling her battalion through the door. "Get inside and grab what you can!"

Running through the door with the rest of ACORN, Ted stole a glimpse at Joelle-Michelle. He would follow her anywhere.

"Stop staring at me, Ted," snapped Joelle-Michelle.

Geez. She was *incredible*.

Part Four

Adeline's third-grade teacher, Miss Hitchings, was wearing a beaded necklace. A tattoo of dolphins circled her wrist. Her unkempt hair was sun-bleached from the summer vacation she had taken to India. She carried around a backpack covered in patches from various countries. Her kids loved her.

And so had Adeline, until recently.

Debbie sat across from Miss Hitchings. It was the first time in days she had stopped crying. Her cheeks felt like they were covered in salt.

"Mrs. Merritt," said Miss Hitchings, "thank you for coming in. I know this must be a difficult time."

"People have been nice," said Debbie, feeling the tears coming on again. "Organizing searches and putting up flyers and those kinds of things."

"My book club searched the beaches last night. The whole community is with you."

"Thank you."

"I wanted you to come in because since Ted's disappearance, Adeline hasn't, well, she hasn't talked."

"You mean in class?"

"She doesn't say a word even when I call on her. At recess, she sits by herself drawing pictures in the dirt. Her old friends don't try to get her to play anymore. She hasn't talked at *all*. She's just . . . alone."

Debbie nodded. She knew this.

"All day long, she draws in her notebook," said Miss Hitchings. "And at the end of the day, she rips out the pictures and throws them away. I saved some."

Miss Hitchings slid some crumpled sheets of white lined paper across the table—pictures of a little girl, clearly Adeline, standing with her older brother and a panda that had a tree growing out of its head. Words like *quiet* and *bye* were scribbled on some of the pages.

"She draws these same things at home," said Debbie.

"Do you know what they mean?"

"Adeline's imaginary friend disappeared when everybody else's did," said Debbie.

"It's incredible," said Miss Hitchings. "My kids tell me theirs are still gone."

"Adeline got into a fight with Ted before he disappeared. She blamed him for her friend disappearing—I still don't quite understand why—and then Ted was gone too. I think Adeline might believe that what she said caused Ted to vanish."

"So she isn't talking anymore—"

"Because she might be afraid of saying something else wrong."

Miss Hitchings leaned back in her chair and exhaled.

"I did take her to a psychiatrist," said Debbie.

"What did he suggest?"

"He prescribed her medication."

"What did you do?"

"I told him we'd no longer be needing his services."

WHOOOOOOP! WHOOOOOP!

The alarm was deafening, and ACORN's longer-eared soldiers howled in pain. Ted clasped his hands against the sides of his head and tried to concentrate on moving forward into the AUTHORIZED PERSONNEL ONLY room.

As soon as Ted passed through the door, he forgot about the noise.

"Yow-za," said Ted.

The room was split straight down the middle, divided into two distinct operations. The right side of the room was dominated by a conveyor belt carrying small glass bottles. A tank filled with an iridescent silver liquid was suspended above the belt. The belt would stop and start as nozzles squirted the silver liquid into the bottles, which then traveled to the end of the belt and fell neatly into cardboard crates. These crates were stamped with huge letters that left no doubt what was inside:

Greenies Antidote
Time to Feel Good!

The cure.

Though he knew how important the antidote was, Ted was

more interested in another conveyor belt. The one that was carrying Ab-Com Patches.

"Oh man," said Ted.

Thoughts started to come together in Ted's head.

If this place—a processing factory controlled by President Skeleton—was where the Ab-Com Patches were being manufactured, it meant that whatever was *in* the patches was also being controlled by President Skeleton.

It was after Ted started using the patches that all the ab-coms in the world got sick.

And if President Skeleton and Scurvy were now getting *married*, it probably meant that President Skeleton knew that Scurvy had been living on Cape Cod. She *wanted* him back in Middlemost, and there would have been no better way to get him to return than by giving Ted the patch directly and making Scurvy sick.

187

The patches were contaminated with the Greenies, which made all the ab-coms in the world ill, said Ted to himself. *Persephone Skeleton planted the disease.*

"Ted!" yelled Joelle-Michelle above the sound of the alarm. "Grab as many of the boxes of the antidote as you can! We need to get *out*!"

All around Ted, ACORN soldiers were fighting through the blaring alarm and grabbing for the boxes of antidote. But then came a whole other kind of yowling noise: the sound of Presidential Guards storming into the room, all horns and claws and bad intentions.

"Put down the boxes!" yelled Joelle-Michelle. "The guards are coming! To arms!"

The ACORN soldiers might have been a motley crew, but

they had been well trained by Joelle-Michelle. As soon as she shouted, the soldiers whipped around and charged the oncoming Presidential Guards. The guards and ACORN came together in a tremendous clatter of bones and swords and steel and flesh and anything else that could be smashed together. But ACORN had a secret weapon that the Presidential Guards didn't.

POP-POP-POP!

With each cut from a butter knife or blow from an ACORN boomerang or spatula or field hockey stick, Presidential Guards exploded into clouds of muck that turned the air purple and splattered the ACORN soldiers, who kept slicing through the detonations and the backup guards slipping and tumbling into the room. ACORN had done this before.

188 Strangely enough, Ted Merritt wasn't paying attention to any of it.

"Ted, grab your badminton racket!" said Joelle-Michelle, who was kicking her way through the exploding Presidential Guards—the outsides of her pointe shoes were painted in the VIDGA solution. "We need you, *now!*"

But Ted was transfixed by the spot where the Ab-Com Patches were sitting on the belt that rolled a vat filled with the "medical" powder that was stuffed inside them. Ted's eyes climbed to a glass cylinder that was connected to the vat by a series of pipes and capillaries, but it was what was *inside* that cylinder that made Ted walk toward it.

"Eric?" said Ted.

Ted had never seen Eric the Planda before, but from Adeline's descriptions and her pictures, he was certain this was Adeline's friend. The planda was sitting inside the cylinder with his arms wrapped around his knees. His eyes were half shut, like he was having a difficult time staying awake.

Much of the planda's fur had fallen out, and the bonsai tree growing out of his head was dead. From head to toe, he was *covered* in green bumps. It seemed the sick creature was being used to contaminate the powder that was then being packed into the Ab-Com Patches.

"Eric! Hey, *Eric*!"

The planda's eyelids fluttered.

"It's *you*, Eric, isn't it?" said Ted.

The planda rotated his head toward Ted.

"ERIC!"

Ted leaped up on the conveyor belt and charged toward Eric, shouting, "I'm coming, Eric! I'll be right there!"

"Nah you ain't!" said a Presidential Guard who popped up in front of Ted, ferociously swinging a hockey stick at Ted's head. Instinctively, Ted stepped out of the way and smacked the hockey player with his badminton racket.

"Take *that*!" shouted Ted, and the hockey player exploded into purple muck.

Presidential Guards leaped at him from all sides, and he cut them all down—*POP-POP-POP!* One feathered samurai managed to cut Ted's T-shirt sleeve, but the samurai burst into sludge a moment later.

Ted sprinted and jumped onto the powder vat, which teetered back and forth under his weight. He gripped the edge of the vat and tried to pull himself up, but a tiny clown grabbed on to his feet and began to pull him down toward a crowd of Presidential Guards.

"Let me go!" yelled Ted.

"No go," said the wicked clown, climbing up Ted's legs. "No go a-ro-ro-ro!"

POP! Brother Dezo's ukulele smashed into the evil clown, who burst into purple.

"He bad clown!" said Brother Dezo. "He get da haad rub!"

His legs free, Ted climbed to the top of the vat and from there made another leap to the glass cylinder that held Eric. The planda, who was pressed against the glass, looked into Ted's eyes—he had been through a lot.

"All right, buddy," said Ted, balancing his weight on one of the pipes leading down to the vat. "Stand back as much as you can. I'm not quite sure how I'm going to do this."

Ted flipped his badminton racket around and smacked the butt of it into the glass cylinder.

Nothing happened.

"Come on!" said Ted. He tried again and again with the racket's hilt—*wham! wham!* Nothing happened. Eric began pushing on the glass where Ted had struck it.

"I *will* get you out," said Ted. His brain started to whir, and he began thinking of all the things he could use to free Eric. *If only I had a sledgehammer or a laser or one of those cartoon holes I could stick on the glass.*

Below him, snarling Presidential Guards were climbing up the vat, crawling over each other and getting steadily closer.

Come on, THINK! Ted told himself. He imagined himself swinging down on a vine from the top of the room to knock the cylinder off its platform, or maybe freezing the glass to make it shatter more easily.

And then all of a sudden the pain came, a white-hot burning sensation in his forearm. At first he thought that he'd been cut, or splattered with chemicals, but when he looked down at his arm, he saw that his birthmark seemed to glow.

The skin on his forearm, normally a dull brown, had taken on a reddish tint, and the three circles that sat in the middle of the birthmarked skin—usually a triangle of pale dots—were throwing off three burning colors: green, blue, and orange.

Could I get Eric out if I had a cutter made from the hardest diamonds on Earth?

His arm got hotter.

Or if a guy who got into the Guinness World Records *book for eating glass suddenly showed up?*

His birthmark changed colors again, so he closed his eyes. He needed to *think*. He couldn't allow himself to be distracted.

Then he was hit by a strange thought.

What if I had an opera singer who could hit one of those extremely high-pitched notes?

The sizzling sensation in his arm stopped. Ted opened his eyes and saw that his forearm and hand were completely missing.

Missing, as in they were *gone*. Ted was a one-and-a-half-armed man.

Then he spotted it. His arm was floating down toward the ground, his hand opening and closing the entire time, as if pleased with its newfound freedom. The limb made its way to a hovering position about four feet above the floor, where it stopped and appeared to think for a moment. Though it had no eyes, it seemed to turn and look at Ted.

"Hey, get back on my elbow!" hissed Ted.

His hand didn't respond. Instead, all at once, the arm started to work in a flurry of activity, as if it were plucking atoms out of the air and rapidly assembling them into a human figure, working from the ground up. The fingers were a blur and the wrist kept snapping back and forth as it flew through its strange building process.

First a pair of small feet wedged into tiny heels.

Then plump legs attached to a round torso covered in a white dress from which two robust arms sprouted.

Next a thick neck, a couple of chins, and then a round Scandinavian face topped by a pair of thick golden braids.

And finally, the hand rested, clearly exhausted.

And the woman opened her mouth, and . . . *"LA-LA-LA-LA-LAAAAA!"*

The notes rang out above the blaring alarm and the sounds of fighting below, grinding the battle to a halt as *everybody* in the room put hands to ears, or whatever body parts were used for listening.

The glass cylinder started to tremble.

The opera singer pushed her voice up into the next octave.

Eric had curled up into a ball inside the cylinder. Ignoring his stinging eardrums, Ted used his one remaining arm to climb away from the cylinder as the opera singer took a final breath.

"LAAAAAA-LA!"

BOOM!

The cylinder shattered into a blizzard of glass splinters. Ted managed to swing his body underneath the powder vat to get out of the way, but the guards weren't so fortunate. Glass showered down on them, and when they hit the ground, ACORN attacked them with arrows and clubs and other weaponry.

Hanging underneath the vat, Ted looked at the opera singer, who looked back at him, apparently confused about how she'd gotten here and what she was doing.

192

"Uh," explained Ted.

The opera singer winked and walked away. Ted's hand floated back toward him and nonchalantly reattached itself to his elbow. His birthmark returned to its normal color and the skin cooled to the same temperature as the rest of his body.

Ted dropped down to the conveyor belt and looked up at where the glass cylinder had been moments before. Eric was curled into a ball, unscathed.

ACORN soldiers took advantage of the bedlam to dispatch what was left of the Presidential Guard. Within moments, ACORN stood victorious amid an ocean of purple muck.

"Eric!" yelled Ted, and the planda looked up from his fetal position. Seeing that everything was safe, Eric climbed down, toddled over to Ted, and put his thick arms around him.

"Very nice to see you, Eric," said Ted.

193

Ted turned away from the planda to help ACORN fighters with the boxes of antidote, when he suddenly became aware that nobody else in the room was moving.

Everybody was staring at Ted. Dwack and Dr. Narwhal were scratched and breathing hard and covered in purple muck, but alive. Even Vango looked like he'd seen some action—he was trembling and suffering from post-conflict trauma, but his hands were stained purple, and Ted could see that the sharp handles of his paintbrushes were coated in muck.

"Is something wrong?" said Ted.

"Ted," said Joelle-Michelle, purple stains up and down her ballet tights, "where did that opera singer come from?"

"I, my hand, it built her," said Ted. "I was thinking of ways to get Eric out of the cylinder—by the way, this is my sister's friend—and the singer, she was my idea."

Eric waved a paw at the group.

"Your arm made an opera singer?" said Joelle-Michelle.

"This is all new to me," said Ted.

Joelle-Michelle nodded. She looked at Ted's torn shirt-sleeve, causing him to reflexively hold his arm against his body. He didn't want her to see his birthmark, especially after all the weirdness of a few moments ago.

"Why do you hide your arm?" said Joelle-Michelle.

Ted stammered and flushed. "I have a birthmark. I usually keep it covered."

"May I see it?"

"Kind of a rude question after what I just told you."

"We French are famous for being spectacularly rude," said Joelle-Michelle, walking over. Ted wanted to resist, but his brain short-circuited. She smelled like vanilla. He extended his arm.

194

Joelle-Michelle lightly traced her finger from the bend of Ted's elbow to the top of his wrist, pausing to look at the three pale circles in the triangle pattern. She stared him in the eye.

"You were born with this?" she said.

"It's hereditary. My father had one too," said Ted.

Joelle-Michelle looked sideways at Brother Dezo, who raised an eyebrow. She turned to the rest of the ACORN fighters.

"*Compagnons*," she said. "Gather as many boxes as you can and get outside. Brother Dezo, find a furnace and incinerate the Ab-Com Patches. Our backup should be here by now."

The room was suddenly a flurry of activity, with boxes of antidote being stacked and then hustled out the exit and mounds of Ab-Com Patches being destroyed. A group of the larger ACORN fighters went to work dislodging the entire tank of antidote, rocking it back and forth on its hinges until it broke off with a loud *snap*. Grunting and groaning, they heaved the tank out the door.

"Wait," said Ted to Joelle-Michelle, who had also turned her attention to collecting bottles of antidote. "Why did you ask me about the opera singer and my birthmark? Do you know why my arm popped off?"

Joelle-Michelle paused, and leaned close to Ted's ear.

"Because you are more important than you could ever imagine," she whispered.

195

III

Scurvy was pacing back and forth. He hadn't touched the set of red bootee pajamas that Persephone had laid out for him. There was only one bed in the room, and he knew that she wanted to pillow talk and snuggle.

"Cursed bootee pajamas!" said Scurvy. He picked a piece of candied bacon off a silver tray sitting on the nightstand, popped it into his mouth, and felt it plunk down into his belly. Since Persephone had claimed ownership of him, he wasn't getting that same bacon *thrill* anymore.

"Ya okay in there?" said Scurvy to the closed bathroom door. His plan was to enter the bathroom as soon as Persephone exited and spend the rest of the night in there, thus avoiding snuggling.

"Just freshening up," lied Persephone. In reality, she was dumping the contents of the plastic bag Bugslush had installed in her empty stomach cavity into the sink.

"Oh, there's no need fer that," said Scurvy. "Ya seem plenty fresh."

Scurvy winced. He'd meant *It's useless to even try to fix yourself!* But it might have come across as *You're perfect the way you are!*

"Flattery will get you everywhere," said Persephone through the door.

With that, Persephone stepped out of the bathroom, and Scurvy's eyes almost started to bleed.

She was still wearing her makeup—smeared lipstick, heavy foundation, false eyelashes over empty sockets—but she had replaced her presidential outfit with a silk nightgown that sagged from her bony shoulders, revealing frail wing bones and twiggy legs. She had doused herself in meat-scented perfume, and while the trick almost worked, Scurvy couldn't lie to himself: when he looked at Persephone, all he saw was a tattered cockatoo skeleton.

She curtsied.

"Do you like it?" she said.

"Ya look . . . great?" said Scurvy, lying.

"Kiss me on the forehead," she ordered, and Scurvy did so. Her skull was hard and cold.

"Now come and join me near the window for tea," she said. "We have more wedding details to discuss."

197

"Yep. Sure thing. I'm just gonna use tha facilities," said Scurvy. "Be right out."

"Don't be long!"

"Course not," said Scurvy. "Can't wait tah talk and talk and talk until tha end of time."

Scurvy winked at Persephone and glided into the bathroom. As soon as he shut the door, he searched the wall for a way *out*. He spotted a window high up—it would have to do. He stood on the toilet, climbed onto the sink, and unlatched the window, which opened with a satisfying *whoosh*.

"Are you okay in there, Scurvy-Burvy?" said Persephone.

"Brushing me chompers," said Scurvy, leaping from the sink to the window and squirming his way out. He silently cursed his belly—he'd put on more weight than he had realized.

"Come on!" said Scurvy, talking to his gut.

Don't expect too much of me, his gut replied.

"I *expect* ya tah suck up and squeeze me through this window," said Scurvy.

Do you know how much meat you put in me every day? said his gut. *Where am I supposed to put it all?*

"Scurvy?" came Persephone's voice from the other room.

"Coming, me fancy fiancée," Scurvy said before turning his attention back to his belly.

"Please help me out here," he whispered to his midsection. "You know I can't take her anymore."

You'll be nicer to me? asked his stomach.

"I promise I'll treat ya good from now on."

Against its better judgment, Scurvy's belly decided to believe him and sucked up into his torso, allowing him to squeeze out the small window. He tumbled to the hard ground outside, climbed to his feet, and started to run—anywhere.

He hadn't even made it out of the yard when he felt a knife at his throat.

"You have no place to go, Mr. Goonda," said a voice in the dark.

"Marriage is a sacred commitment," said another voice. "Them vows, they're not to be taken lightly."

A horde of Presidential Guards stepped out of the night. Scurvy was completely surrounded.

"Might be less embarrassing for you if you went back the way you came," said a third voice.

Scurvy let the guards walk him back to the lodge.

"Give an old pirate a boost, then?" said Scurvy, and the guards helped him up to the window and shoved him through.

"You almost done in there, Scurvy-Lurvy?" said Persephone through the door. "I can't wait to see you in your bootee jam-jams!"

"Yer Scurvy-Lurvy is going tah sleep in tha bathtub," said Scurvy, removing his boots. "Better for me back tah sleep on a slightly curved surface."

"But our tea."

"I'm not much in tha mood fer tea."

"You never used to sleep in the bathtub."

"Over tha centuries, people change."

There was silence from the bedroom.

"Fine," said Persephone, pouting. "I'm going to have my tea all by myself. I'll see you in the morning. And every morning."

"Of course ya will, me dove," said Scurvy, lowering his body into the tub. Through the door, he heard Persephone's bones rattle as she tossed and turned. It was going to be an uncomfortable night.

199

IV

Ted volunteered to enter the quarantine area first. Because he wasn't an abstract companion, he wasn't afraid of the Greenies—and besides, if he was the one who started the plague with his Ab-Com Patch, it was his responsibility to end it. He carried five boxes of antidote in his arms and a camel pack of antidote on his back.

Once ACORN had made it safely back to the caves, Dr. Narwhal conducted an experiment on a rugby player afflicted with the Greenies. After dosing himself with antidote just to be safe, Dr. Narwhal gave the rugby player a tenth of a drop to see if that was enough to provide a cure, but when that didn't work, he increased the dosage to half a drop. Still nothing. Another four-tenths of a drop added up to a full drop, at which point the antidote started to have a noticeable effect— the green bumps faded, and the rugby player rumbled away happily.

"One drop each," Dr. Narwhal told Ted after the experiment.

As Ted prepared to enter the quarantine area, he felt the eyes of ACORN on his back. Word of his birthmark had apparently spread, and his fellow ACORN fighters suddenly seemed to have a strange respect for him. They listened to him intently when he spoke, held doors for him, and in general treated him like . . . a leader?

"I'm not sure what you'll see in there," said Joelle-Michelle. "Cure as many as you can."

"I will. But later you have to tell me what the heck is going on."

Ted entered the quarantine area.

The room was bigger than it looked from the other side of the door, and the air inside was hazy and stale. Through the vapor, Ted could see figures moving at half speed and shapes lying on the ground.

"Hello," said Ted. "I'm Ted."

Ted felt everything and everyone in the cavernous room turn toward him.

"I have the antidote for all of you," said Ted, opening the first box of bottles. "Everything is going to be okay."

The first wave of sick ab-coms made their way over to Ted.

A man-sized piranha wearing a knitted scarf walked up to Ted and opened its gaping, tooth-filled mouth. Ted reached forward with an eyedropper of antidote and *drip*!

He put a single drop on the piranha's tongue.

"It will take a second to start working," said Ted.

"*Obrigado,*" said the piranha, which meant "thank you" in Portuguese.

An elegantly dressed woman stepped up to Ted. Her posture was ramrod straight, and she held a parasol over her shoulder.

"Young man," the woman said. It was clearly an effort for her to speak. "I am Czarina Tallow. Vat do I do?"

"Hello, Czarina. Just open your mouth, please."

Drip. Ted placed a drop of antidote on her tongue.

"You'll feel it working in a moment," said Ted.

201

"Thank you zo much. Is zere anything I can do to help you?" said Czarina.

"Please take a few bottles of the antidote and give it to anybody who is too weak to stand in line," said Ted. "Just a drop each."

The Czarina got to work. Each time Ted cured somebody, he gave the ab-com a dropper of antidote, and soon everybody was curing everybody else. As the ill regained their strength, Ted realized how many members of ACORN there might be.

When he ran out of antidote, he knocked on the quarantine door. Hordes of healthy ab-coms followed Ted through it, hugging ACORN friends they hadn't thought they'd see again. Joelle-Michelle looked around at her new troops and smiled.

"Need more antidote?" said Joelle-Michelle.

"As much as you have," said Ted.

"We have tanks of it," said Joelle-Michelle. "Our scientists reverse-engineered the formula."

"Does that mean this might almost be a fair fight?"

"*Je ne sais pas.* We're outnumbered ten thousand to one, so it will be difficult," said Joelle-Michelle. "But we might be able to win."

"How?"

"We have you," Joelle-Michelle said. She picked up several boxes of antidote. "Tonight you and I will talk in private about everything."

Ted watched her pirouette into the quarantine room. He felt a bit like pirouetting himself.

V

"Faster!" yelled the plaid weirdo. "We've got three more vents to do today, and you are slacking!"

Carolina was standing at the top of a twenty-story scaffolding tower, stretching to reach an enormous vent. But even standing on her toes and holding the blowtorch high above her head, Carolina couldn't quite reach the vent. It didn't help that the work crew had attached a long, thick chain to her ankle so she couldn't escape.

"I can't reach it," she yelled down to the ground.

The members of the work crew grumbled and looked back and forth at each other. They had been eating and drinking while watching Carolina do all the work, and nobody wanted to climb the towering scaffolding.

"Sure you can!" said a tango dancer. "Just, uh, stand on those end posts."

"If I stand on one of the end posts, I'll fall," said Carolina.

"I'll catch ya!" said a tiny pixie.

"Even if I *could* balance on the end post," said Carolina, "I couldn't hold the steel plate *and* keep my balance. *Somebody* needs to help me."

The members of the work crew shuffled around and shook their heads, irritated that they actually had to *do* something. And then, all at once, each crew member brought his hand—or whatever he used for a hand—to his nose, or whatever he used for a nose.

It was an abstract-companion version of "Not It."

The plaid one looked around and saw that the other crew members were holding something against their noses. He was it.

"AW, COME ON!" said the weirdo—whose name was Whamburt—as he threw his fedora to the ground. Unsteadily, he began to ascend the scaffolding, hiccuping and cursing. When he reached the top, Carolina gave him instructions.

"Since you're taller than me, I'm going to give you the steel plate. Then I'm going to weld the bottom part shut, give you the blowtorch, and you'll weld the top."

"Let's just do it and get back to the ground," said Whamburt. "I hate heights."

204

A few moments later, Carolina was soldering the bottom of the vent shut while Whamburt held the steel plate with his shaking hands.

"So," said Carolina, "why are you covering all these vents?"

"To make sure nothing comes in and nothing goes out," said the weirdo. "President Skeleton only wants one vent open for the attack."

"What attack?"

"Er. Nothing you need to worry about. Though your friends back home might. Here, give me that blowtorch. You're not doing it right."

Carolina handed him the blowtorch.

"C'mon, what did you mean, attack? Where is this vent?"

Whamburt flinched. He knew that he had said too much.

"Never mind. You'll see it when we get there. OH NO! AGH!"

Whamburt had somehow set himself on fire and was batting himself wildly, trying to put out the flames. "HELP! I'M SMOLDERING!" he yelled.

"Stop, drop, and roll!" said Carolina.

"HELP!"

"Stop!" said Carolina.

"WHAT NEXT?" said Whamburt, flames leaping high off his head.

"Drop!" said Carolina.

Whamburt collapsed onto his side.

"WHAT NOW?"

"Roll!" said Carolina. "Roll until the flames go out!"

Carolina watched as Whamburt, following her instructions, rolled off the platform and plummeted to the ground. She hadn't been entirely wrong: the fall did put out the flames, but it also resulted in the weirdo splatting in front of the rest of the work crew.

Everybody looked up at her.

"Murderer!" said the tango dancer.

"No, no, no!" said Carolina. "He accidentally set himself on—"

"Murderer!" yelled another worker. "*She* set Whamburt on fire and pushed him!"

"No, I *swear* I didn't do anything like that," said Carolina. "He was—"

"MURDERER!" yelled the crew, and a sharp pull on her chain sent Carolina tumbling off the platform. She felt her body picking up speed and saw the strange sky whirling above her. Her final thoughts ran through her brain—flashes of her family, and a sharp pang of regret about Ted Merritt.

205

And then she fell into the arms of the tiny pixie. He was much stronger than he looked.

"Murderer!" said the pixie.

The other workers descended upon Carolina angrily, winding the chain around her body and heaving her into the back of a dark, tool-filled cart. *I am having,* thought Carolina, *a really odd day.*

VI

There was an energy coursing through the ACORN tree caves. Hundreds of newly cured abstract companions were in the midst of turning the quarantine cavern into barracks. Others were in the boiler room melting bad video games into VIDGA solution and dipping their armaments in it. Meanwhile, Ted sat around a small fire with Dwack, Vango, and Dr. Narwhal, eating baked beans—ACORN had amassed storerooms of canned goods for fighters who needed to eat. Dwack had found a few bags of blood in the first-aid room. He was sucking on them while everybody else gobbled up dinner.

"What comes next?" said Vango.

"I have a feeling that we'll know soon," said Dwack, wiping some blood off his chin.

Nearby, Ted noticed a female golfer flipping through a crumpled newspaper. He thought he saw the word *Scurvy* in a headline.

"Excuse me," said Ted. "Could I take a look at that when you're done?"

"Sure," said the golfer, handing over most of the newspaper but keeping the funny pages for herself.

Ted looked at the name of the paper:

THE MIDDLEMOST MOSTEST

The front page contained a pair of stories about vents being sealed up throughout Middlemost and a raid made on a processing factory by ACORN "terrorists." Ted flipped past advertisements and long articles detailing the might of President Skeleton's army and the sheer number of troops it would be sending to Earth. From the newspaper's perspective, victory was already assured.

Finally, in the Lifestyle section, Ted found the headline he was looking for.

PRESIDENT SKELETON AND SCURVY GOONDA STILL MADLY IN LOVE

Underneath the headline was a full-color picture of Scurvy sitting on a white couch next to a heavily accessorized bird skeleton. He wore a smile that Ted had never seen him use before. It was a sheepish, forced, creepy grin, as though Scurvy had been given several different instructions on how to smile and had just combined them all together in the most awkward possible way.

Ted was glad to see that Scurvy looked healthy and robust—indeed, he looked fatter than Ted had ever seen him before—but all that was left of the old Scurvy were his boots and his tricorne hat. The rest of him had been groomed, trimmed, plucked, styled, and moisturized. His greatcoat had been replaced with a gauzy, preppy button-down shirt, and instead of his normal striped trousers, he was wearing slacks embroidered with pictures of happy little whales.

"*That's* your pirate?" said Vango.

"Looksss like they're in love," said Dr. Narwhal.

Ted looked at Scurvy's eyes in the photograph and knew they were pleading for help. He scanned the article.

President Skeleton and Mr. Goonda met when he was a pirate sea captain and she was his lovely, trusty bird, sitting faithfully upon his shoulder.

"I loved him from the first moment I saw him," says President Skeleton. "And he loved me too. Isn't that right, Scurvy?"

"That's . . . right," confirms Mr. Goonda.

"We could just never be together because of certain circumstances," says President Skeleton. "But we always wished we could, isn't that right, Scurvy?"

"That's right . . . too," says Mr. Goonda. "Ha-ha . . . ha."

Now that they are together and true love reigns, President Skeleton and Mr. Goonda hope to spend the next few centuries making up for lost time. But first, a wedding that is sure to be the grandest Middlemost has ever seen.

"Everybody is invited!" says President Skeleton. "It's the perfect way to welcome a new era and introduce Middlemost to my true love. Right, Scurvy?"

"Yer my bird," Mr. Goonda tells President Skeleton, smiling sweetly. "I just hope nobody tries tah save me BEFORE we get married. Not that anybody would, because tha guards are always around—aside from when they're changing shifts at 12:30 and 5:30 every afternoon. And it would probably be too dirty tah BREAK INTO A BUILDING through one of those man-sized water pipes that every building is connected tah. Because I *really* want this wedding tah happen."

"I know you do, Lurvy-Burvy," says President Skeleton, giving Mr. Goonda a delicate peck on his nose.

Clearly, love is in the air.

209

"We've got to save him! He's being forced into this marriage," Ted explained. "That's *not* my Scurvy."

"Ted, Scurvy's nuptials are the least of our problems," said Dr. Narwhal.

"I'll determine the importance of our problems," said Joelle-Michelle, standing behind the fire. She turned to Ted.

"Walk with me," she said.

"Is it possible to go aboveground?" said Ted, crumpling up the newspaper. "I need some air."

"Come," said Joelle-Michelle. She offered Ted her hand. "I know a place."

VII

With the wedding less than a week away, Persephone made the tough decision to move out of her apartment high above Ab-Com City and into the Presidential Palace. She had avoided this arrangement throughout her short term in office because she found the palace too drafty, and she could never quite warm up her bones while she was there. It was a strange-looking structure. Constructed of porous rock, it stood three stories tall and was formed in a square around a large central courtyard that was filled with citrus trees and flowering bushes.

"Cut *everything* down," yelled Persephone from her balcony overlooking the courtyard. She had assembled a landscaping crew to rid the courtyard of all the plants prior to the wedding, but a tree-hugging type was refusing to cut down the redwood in the center of the courtyard.

"Just *do it!*" shouted Persephone. Chairs for thousands of guests needed to be set up! A dance floor needed to be installed! Where would the wedding band set up if there were lavender gardens and water lily ponds in the way? Couldn't the landscapers see the *stress* Persephone was under? Did she need to have them all killed?

"Use a flamethrower!" she yelled. "Use an atomic bomb! I don't care! Just get *rid* of those *plants!*"

She stalked off the balcony and went back inside her

bedroom, puffing loudly from her nonexistent lungs. "Worthless! Bugslush!"

Bugslush rushed, shaking, into the room, his skinny possum tail dragging behind him.

"Y-y-y-y-y-y—" said Bugslush.

"The word is 'yes,'" said Persephone. "Say it!"

"Y-y-y-y-y—"

"Oh forget it!" said Persephone. "Just bring in another three space heaters *immediately*—big ones that have some power. It's *freezing* in here."

"Y-y-y—"

"Away!" said Persephone, sending Bugslush hustling out of the room. She looked down at her feet.

"Scurvy!" she yelled.

No response.

"Scurvy!" she yelled. "My foot massage!"

She stepped back out onto her balcony. Beneath her, the landscaping crew toiled in the courtyard.

"Have you seen my Scurvy?" Persephone asked the landscapers, who shook their heads silently.

I can't plan this wedding ALONE! thought Persephone. *Doesn't he know how much this MATTERS to me?* She wished she had tear ducts so she could cry. Planning a wedding *and* an invasion—it was all so *much*.

Scurvy was also making plans. Just a few minutes before, he had made another escape attempt, this time by hiding in the truck the landscapers were using to haul away the foliage, ducking under a bushel of hydrangeas to cover his head. But the truck had barely rolled out of the palace driveway before it was besieged by guards who poked and stabbed the enormous pile of dead plants. Scurvy was jabbed in the ribs and he caught the end of a pole in the eye.

"ALL RIGHT," said Scurvy. "I'm coming out, I'm coming out!"

He wiped the dirt and leaves off his body and stepped out of the truck holding his hands above his head.

"Yar gotta stop dis," said one of the guards, picking leaves out of Scurvy's hair. "Yar lucky we like yar—if we told Persephone yar keep tryin' to run, she wouldn't be so forgivin'."

"Why haven't you turned me in?" said Scurvy.

"None of us would want tar marry Persephone either," said the guard.

"I appreciate yer understanding," said Scurvy.

"Let's get yar spiffed up and back dere den," said the guard.

A pair of guards whisked Scurvy away to the palace basement, where a brigade of dalmatians rinsed him with a fire hose. He was then delivered to a stylist, who tamed and blow-dried his hair, after which he was hustled to a menswear specialist, who outfitted him in a stylish seersucker suit. A few moments later, he was delivered to Persephone's bedroom, all spick-and-span and perfect husband material.

"*There* you are," said Persephone.

"No, there *ya* are," said Scurvy. "Always, always there. Right there in front of me, everywhere I go."

"I was *calling* for you," said Persephone, dangling her bony legs in the air. "My feet *hurt* and I've been under so much *pressure.*"

"I know, Poppy," said Scurvy.

"Ploopsie."

"Popsie."

213

"Start with the left one," said Persephone.

Scurvy bit the inside of his cheek and sat down on the bed. Persephone put her feet in his lap. Scurvy popped out the rocks and clumps of dirt that were stuck between the bones, and then began to rub them down, trying to make himself believe that he was rolling Cuban cigars instead of massaging Persephone's revolting talons.

"Mmm," said Persephone, "that feels *wonderful!*"

"But ya don't have any nerve endings," said Scurvy.

"I know, but I can *imagine*," said Persephone.

KNOCK-KNOCK!

"Bring the space heaters in and leave!" said Persephone. The door opened, but it wasn't Bugslush.

"I'm sorry for interrupting, President Skeleton," said a guardsman. "But one of the work crews is here with a prisoner. They're saying she's a murderer."

"And why am I supposed to deal with this?" said Persephone. "I'm sure the work crew has its own notion of justice and can punish the prisoner accordingly."

The guard nervously shifted his weight from foot to foot, to foot to foot. He had four feet.

"It's just that the prisoner is . . . human, President Skeleton."

"Human, as in, from Earth?" said Persephone.

"Precisely, yes," said the guard. "Specifically, she says she is from Falmouth, which is a town somewhere on a peninsula called Cape Cod."

Scurvy stopped massaging Persephone's bones.

"Bring the prisoner in," said Persephone.

The door closed and reopened.

"G-got th-the s-space h-heaters!" said Bugslush, out of breath, dragging the heavy radiators behind him.

"Not now, Bugslush!" said Persephone.

The guard shuffled the shackled girl into the room. She was obviously scared, but she held her head high and kept her posture straight.

Scurvy took one look at the prisoner and flipped Persephone's feet off his lap, sending the president somersaulting on the bed.

"Carolina Waltz!" he shouted, thunderstruck. "*Here* is a monster if ever I've known one. Tha meanest girl in New England, this 'un."

"H-how do you know me?" said Carolina, looking at the strange man who was wearing a seersucker suit and a pirate hat.

"Yes, how do you know *her*?" said Persephone.

"This lass was tha tormentor of me Ted!" said Scurvy.

"Oh my," said Carolina, stunned. "You're Ted's pirate."

"She was all Ted ever wanted, this one," said Scurvy, "and she treated him like something she'd just as soon scrape off shoes. Oh, tha gallows are too good for Miss Carolina Waltz, head executioner of Falmouth High School!"

"Well then," said Persephone. "There doesn't seem to be a question of what we should do with her."

"No!" said Carolina. "Please, pirate—"

"It's Sir Scurvy Goonda tah you!" said Scurvy.

"I'm sorry, Sir Scurvy Goonda, sir," said Carolina. "The reason I came here, wherever I am, is because I was looking for Ted because I wanted to apologize to him."

"A convenient yarn, considering yer current predicament," said Scurvy. "Ya and I both know Ted is back on tha Cape, just as ya and I both know that there is no room fer remorse in tha roach nest where your heart is supposed to be."

It had been a long time since Persephone had seen Scurvy deal with a prisoner in such a manner. He was thrilling.

"PLEASE, Scurvy, sir," said Carolina, babbling and on the verge of falling apart. "I came here because Ted has *vanished*. He's not at school or anywhere in Falmouth. I went looking for him at the supermarket, and a disgusting man told me he was crushed in this machine they have that compacts cardboard, and I took a look inside it and found a passage and I ended up here and I think he might have come here too, and everything happened because I wanted to tell him I was sorry."

Scurvy looked at Carolina for a long time.

"Space h-heater?" said Bugslush, interrupting the silence.

"Out, Bugslush!" said Persephone, sending the honey possum scurrying from the room.

"Persephone," said Scurvy. "May I speak tah the prisoner alone fer a moment?"

"You may not—" started Persephone, but a look from Scurvy cut her short. "Oh, all right. But be quick about it. My right foot awaits."

Persephone left the room with her guard. The door shut behind them.

Scurvy stared at Carolina.

"Ya think Ted might have gone through tha tunnel in tha Crusher as well?"

"The gross man in the soup aisle told me it was the last place he was seen," sniffled Carolina. "I crawled and crawled. Incidentally, there was a lot of rotting bacon down there."

Ted could have followed the bacon.

"Huh," said Scurvy. "Me Ted's in Middlemost."

"I think so," said Carolina.

Scurvy smiled.

"Why are you smiling?" said Carolina.

"Because," said Scurvy. "It means he's exactly where he needs tah be."

217

VIII

Joelle-Michelle tiptoed her way through crowded caves as Ted attempted to keep pace, squeezing past the teeming hordes of abcoms who were trying to find places to eat or converse or sleep for the night. He was smeared with slime and had been showered with sprinkles when he smacked into an enormous frozen yogurt. By the time Joelle-Michelle found the staircase she was looking for, he looked like he had rolled around on the ground at a petting zoo and then been attacked by a dessert truck.

When Joelle-Michelle finally turned to look at him, she couldn't stop laughing. She, of course, was spotless.

"Your style is so *creative*," she said. "And slime is good for the skin, I hear."

"I got some in my mouth," said Ted.

"*Bon appétit!*" said Joelle-Michelle, walking up the staircase. "*Suivez-moi!* Follow me!"

Ted looked at her legs and forgot he was covered in glop. He followed those legs.

At the top of the steps, they emerged from the caves and were in a simple garden with a walkway, a few rosebushes, and a stone bench. Willow trees surrounded the garden, closing it in, though there was no canopy above to hide the night sky. Ted looked up and saw the same unfamiliar stars he had stared at the day he'd arrived.

"Here," said Joelle-Michelle, handing him some leaves. "Clean your face."

Ted wiped down his face as Joelle-Michelle sat on the bench. The garden was blissfully silent.

"This is my favorite place in Middlemost," said Joelle-Michelle. "The circle of trees was already here when we found it. I just had a few rosebushes put in. It didn't need anything else."

"It's really nice," said Ted.

"It's quiet," said Joelle-Michelle. "I come here when I don't know what else to do."

Ted couldn't imagine Joelle-Michelle not knowing what to do.

"I'm going to unpin my hair," she said, reaching back to undo her ponytail. "Having it back so tight all the time, it gives me headaches."

"A ballerina's cross to bear," said Ted, without having the faintest idea what he was talking about.

219

"That and weighing ninety-five pounds, wearing tights, and being considered over-the-hill at age twenty-five," said Joelle-Michelle.

"So you'll have another decade of peak performance."

"I'm a hundred and twenty years old, Ted."

"Wow. I mean, you must have taken excellent care of yourself."

"Thank you for saying that," said Joelle-Michelle. "But it's simply how I was made. Eternally a teenage ballerina."

"Who made you?" said Ted.

"*Wished* for me is a better term, I think," said Joelle-Michelle. "It was a French girl named Maryse. She had never been to a ballet, but there was an art gallery near the tiny apartment in

Paris she shared with her poor mother. She would look at the ballerina figurines in the front window, and one day she wished for me."

"Why did you have to come to Middlemost?" said Ted.

"She didn't need me anymore," said Joelle-Michelle. "One Christmas an uncle bought her a pair of ballet slippers, and she could *be* her dream. So I came here."

"Did she become a dancer?" asked Ted.

"I have no idea," said Joelle-Michelle. "I wish I did. I cared very much about that little girl."

Joelle-Michelle was staring down at her slippers. Ted didn't know what he should say. The quiet of the garden felt overwhelming.

"Ted," said Joelle-Michelle, "do you know why we're sitting here?"

"You wanted to talk to me," said Ted.

"*Oui*, of course, there is that," said Joelle-Michelle. "But you must have a suspicion *why*."

"It has something to do with what happened at the factory," said Ted. "The opera singer."

Joelle-Michelle nodded.

"May I see your arm?" she said.

He held out his left arm.

Joelle-Michelle took his wrist in her hand and ran her finger over the birthmark.

"I've never seen one up close before," said Joelle-Michelle. "You keep this hidden?"

"It's ugly."

Joelle-Michelle looked at Ted.

"It makes you insecure, this mark?" she said.

"Sometimes."

"You're too handsome to be insecure. Don't worry about this."

Handsome. *Handsome?*

Ted croaked out, "But what is it?"

"It isn't a birthmark," said Joelle-Michelle. "Well, it *is*, in a way, but it's more that this mark is hereditary, meaning it has been passed down through the years. Through the ages, really. You come from a bloodline that is very important to all of us, Ted," said Joelle-Michelle.

She paused to think about what she would say next. "Has anybody told you the story about the caveman who founded Middlemost?"

"No."

"The story is that thousands of years ago, a depressed woolly mammoth ab-com who had been rejected by his caveman tried to end his life by throwing himself into a volcano. But the mammoth didn't realize that the volcano was *extinct,* and he fell straight to the middle of the Earth, passed through the fold in space that we know as the ThereYouGo Gate, and ended up here. His caveman felt so bad about what happened that he threw himself into the volcano after his mammoth—and he too ended up here."

"Sounds familiar."

"The caveman tried to get his mammoth to go back through the hole. But the mammoth's feelings had been badly hurt, and it refused to go. So the caveman decided to make things as happy as he could for his friend. He imagined green fields and blue oceans, and they appeared. He imagined deserts and cities. He thought about how content his mammoth had made him before he chose to get rid of it, and he decided that all humans should have abstract companions. He thought of tubes that would be able to suck up children's thoughts that had floated out into space. He dreamed up the processing factories so that kids could have abstract companions, creating the system we have today. He made all these things just by thinking about them. When he was done, he created a herd of mammoths to keep his mammoth company."

"Geez, that must have been one happy mammoth."

"That's just the thing," said Joelle-Michelle. "The mammoth was *so* pleased with his friends and his oceans and his fields that he tried to embrace his caveman, but in the process ended up trampling him to death."

"Yikes," said Ted. He hadn't been expecting that.

"Mammoths are big," said Joelle-Michelle.

"I've seen them at the Museum of Science," said Ted.

"So the mammoth reluctantly returned to Earth. The caveman had two sons—both of whom had the same birthmark as their father—and the mammoth told *their* abstract companions about Middlemost. Those kids had kids, and the pattern kept repeating itself until there were enough abstract companions to populate Middlemost.

"That's when the vents were created, to stabilize the passageways, because so many abstract companions were coming to Middlemost. At first they were placed in out-of-the-way spots, but when people started building factories and supermarkets, they could be placed almost anywhere."

Ted thought about this.

"So I have caveman blood," said Ted.

"It's quite a heritage," laughed Joelle-Michelle.

"Does this mean I can create things?"

"You created the opera singer."

"But I don't know *how*," said Ted. "I was under pressure and I was trying to think of a way to get Eric out of the glass cylinder, and it just *happened*."

"All that matters is that the ability is in you," said Joelle-Michelle. "But we don't have much time, so we might have to figure out a way of using it on a more consistent basis."

"So we can stop President Skeleton."

"Ah, but even President Skeleton reports to a superior," said Joelle-Michelle.

"What does that mean?"

"There are other people who have the birthmark, Ted," said Joelle-Michelle, "and they're not all as kind as you."

Joelle-Michelle put her hand on his birthmark and ran her palm over his forearm. After years of hiding it, Ted found it bizarre to think that it might make him special in some way.

223

"Who is President Skeleton's superior?" said Ted.

Joelle-Michelle paused.

"His name isn't very intimidating," she said.

"What's his name?"

"It's Lloyd," said Joelle-Michelle. "Lloyd Munch."

"Munch?"

"I think it's Danish."

Ted thought about the name.

"You're right," he said. "That's not very intimidating."

"He's a terrible person."

"Person as in human?" said Ted.

"You didn't think you were the only human to have ever come here, did you?"

"I just assumed."

"Members of your bloodline have an instinct to seek out Middlemost," said Joelle-Michelle. "Your ancestors created this place. It's your home too."

Joelle-Michelle scooched closer to Ted on the bench.

"Right," said Ted, nervously. "Then, uh, welcome to my home, I guess."

"It's a beautiful home, and that's why we're defending it," said Joelle-Michelle. "Tell me, have you never met a French girl before?"

Ted's throat was bone dry. He felt faint.

"Ho, brah!" said Brother Dezo, walking up the steps into the garden. "Da Swamster geev us da stink eye. Need Joelle-Michelle."

"Of course," said Joelle-Michelle, getting up from the bench. "We will continue this conversation later, yes?"

"Hhhhh," said Ted, which was the only noise he could push out of his throat.

"Very good," said Joelle-Michelle, disappearing with Brother Dezo.

Ted sat on the bench and thought that if he were back on Cape Cod, he would probably be getting beat up right about now.

IX

Swamster was sitting on a hard wooden chair chained to a table, squinting under the hot white lights. This was ACORN's interrogation room, and a cop was standing across from him, shouting into his face and occasionally slamming the table. The cop wore a pink uniform and carried a fancy umbrella instead of a nightstick.

The cop slammed the umbrella down on the table—
WHAP!

"We *know* that you served as Persephone's—"

"President Skeleton's—"

"*Persephone's* personal attaché for many, many years," said the cop. "We know that you rarely leave her apartment building, and we know that when you did go into the field, you were in the company of two Presidential Guards. How can you possibly claim that you're innocent?"

"Well, you see," said Swamster, "I didn't actually want to leave the apartment building. I *did* want a promotion, but I'm really better suited to the service sector and—"

WHAP! WHAP! WHAP! The umbrella came down on the table three more times.

"Enough!" said the cop. "Persephone's wedding is taking place at the Presidential Palace."

"The president *loathes* the palace," said Swamster. "Much

too massive. She always said she wanted something more intimate."

"Nevertheless, we need to know how to get into the palace," said the cop. "We need to know where the guards are going to be, where the bride will be entering from, where—"

"But I haven't been involved in the planning," said Swamster. "If I had, I would have picked a far more tasteful venue."

The cop held the umbrella an inch from Swamster's face.

"I'm going to leave this room," said the cop. "And when I get back, you're going to have answers for me—or prepare to POP!"

Swamster nodded nervously. He didn't want to pop—it sounded unpleasant and unhygienic.

The cop left the room.

226

ACORN was just as awful as the president had said they were. Granted, Persephone was trying to wipe out ACORN, but what else was she going to do? He didn't understand why ACORN *wouldn't* want to take over the Earth. Progress was always about *expansion*.

Of course, Swamster *had* loved the little boy who had been his friend. His name was James. He was from Chicago and wanted to be an Olympic swimmer, which was why he had outfitted Swamster in the swimsuit and all the gold medals, though Swamster sometimes felt bad that he hadn't actually earned any of them. What if James was hurt during the invasion?

Still, ACORN shouldn't heartlessly ruin Persephone's wedding. Even if ACORN disagreed with her political position, Persephone had waited so long for some measure of personal happiness, and to strike during her special day—well, it was just a lousy thing to do.

Though she might be curt with him from time to time, Swamster really did miss Persephone.

Swamster looked at the table. It was bolted to the floor, but the table leg to which he was chained looked like it was made of pine. He had always enjoyed the taste of pine, and it had been days and days since he had last filed down his teeth.

Swamster dropped to his knees and started chewing. He worked furiously, quickly turning the leg into a pile of shavings. Within moments, he was completely through the wood. The chain was still attached to him, but he was free!

Behind him, the doorknob started to turn. He pressed himself against the wall behind the door. When the cop walked into the room, Swamster grabbed for the cop's umbrella.

"What the—?" the cop said.

"Ha!" said Swamster, and with a quick thump, he brought the umbrella down on his interrogator's head. *POP!* The officer exploded into a spray of purple muck that smothered Swamster, sticking to his fur and drenching his swimsuit.

Swamster hadn't expected that.

His first instinct was to yell, and then perhaps look for some soda water to get out the stains, but he knew that if he shouted, more ACORN soldiers would come. So he wiped the purple muck out of his eyes and looked down at the umbrella.

"Fashionable umbrella," he said.

Swamster poked his head out into the corridor. It was teeming with abstract companions—a veritable shoving and shifting horde. There was no way anybody was going to notice Swamster. He slung the chain around his neck as if it were a piece of jewelry and kept the umbrella at his side, taking care not to let it touch him. And with that, he stepped out into

227

the hallway, shutting the door of the interrogation room behind him.

Hugging the wall, he followed the EXIT signs, steadily making his way down the passageway. Each time he was bumped, he positioned the umbrella away from the bumper. Every time he needed to step over somebody, he lifted the umbrella into the air, keeping it away from their heads so they didn't explode.

As he scurried along, he noticed that the ACORN fighters appeared genuinely *happy*—they were talking to each other and laughing and generally seemed like they believed in their silly cause. How could they take this side of the fight instead of following somebody as brilliant and fearsome as President Skeleton?

Up ahead, Swamster saw light filtering in through the exit to the cave. His heart was beating fast—he couldn't wait to get back to the president and settle back into his assistant position. She would *have* to be impressed that he had returned from behind enemy lines, and the amount of information he had in his head—she would probably give him a *huge* promotion.

Swamster was picturing himself back in his warm room chewing on a nice cardboard toilet paper tube, when suddenly— *POP!*

While daydreaming, Swamster had let his umbrella poke a fireman, who burst into a purple mist that covered the nearby ab-coms.

"Oh, I'm quite sorry—" *POP!*

He had accidentally jabbed a cat with butterfly wings, which detonated above him, splashing more ab-coms.

Suddenly all eyes turned on Swamster.

"It's the Swamster!" somebody yelled, and Swamster

instantly was mobbed by ACORN fighters. But the tree-cave exit was close.

Swamster closed his eyes and swung the umbrella in front of him, pushing himself toward what he *hoped* was the exit.

"I'm coming, President Skeleton!" yelled Swamster, slashing his way forward. "I'm still your LOYAL ASSISTANT!"

Swamster felt goop spattering on his face, and he wasn't quite sure what he was doing, but with each step forward he whirled and whipped the umbrella until he thought his arms would detach. Then came a moment when he was just swinging the umbrella through empty air, and everything was quiet around him.

He opened his eyes and saw that he was standing in an enormous purple puddle. He wiped off his umbrella on the cave wall, walked out into the sunshine of Middlemost, and vowed that as soon as he got home, he was never going outside again. Ever.

229

Part Five

For over a month now, children had been missing their ab-coms. After realizing that nothing happened when they tried to think up new friends, many of these kids attempted to fill the voids in their lives by befriending inanimate objects.

In Mongolia, young Oochkoo Bat's fire-eating yak, Mandoni, had not returned to its normal spot in the closet. Lonely and not quite knowing what else to do, Oochkoo tried to play games with an enormous boulder that sat in her backyard, but when Oochkoo wanted to play hide-and-seek, the rock would never participate. And when she wanted the rock's opinion on how to dress her dolls, it just stood there, like it didn't care about Oochkoo at all.

In Iceland, little Halldor Gundmondsson waited and waited for his fisherman rhinoceros, Bjarni, to come home. But as Halldor walked the shore in the weeks following the beast's disappearance, he never found a trace of his friend. Eventually, Halldor stopped going outside altogether—he knew he would just be disappointed if he did—and simply sat in his room every day, rolling a wooden hat rack around on the floor, even though the hat rack would have much preferred to be left alone, holding hats.

In Eritrea, tiny Natsinet Tenolde tried to invent a replacement for Gongab, her leaf-nosed bat, but no matter what she dreamed up—lizards or dugongs or dorcas gazelles—nothing ever appeared. Eventually, disappointment overtook her. She stopped using her imagination and, for the first time, started to notice the problems around her. Sick people. Broken houses. Failed crops. Without her imagination, there was nothing to take her away from her surroundings, and she just got sadder and sadder.

Across the world, the mass disappearance of ab-coms had zapped the personalities of happy kids. Many of these children plopped down in front of their televisions or video game systems, and spent their afternoons changing channels and tapping buttons. Lots of kids stopped reading—with their imaginations deteriorating from lack of exercise, readers could no longer visualize stories like they could before. They stopped adventuring through forests near their houses or deserts near their tents or snowbanks near their igloos, because they no longer wondered what they might find.

On Cape Cod, Adeline Merritt was eating a pizza-flavored Hot Pocket and staring at the ocean. She could feel tomato sauce on her chin, but she didn't care. It was almost autumn now, but out here on the porch, the breeze was still warm, and the leaves on the trees hadn't changed color.

Weeks ago, she had stopped expecting a boat to sail up in front of her house and Scurvy Goonda to emerge from it with

232

Ted and Eric. Nobody was coming home. It was all her fault. She had been mean to Ted and blamed him for everything. Then he had disappeared and hadn't come back, and it was all because of her.

She looked down at the blank page on her drawing pad. For weeks, she had sat with the pad in front of her, picked up a crayon, and then . . . nothing. Her whole life, ideas had popped into her head and she would *have* to draw—her family or a boat she had seen on Nantucket Sound or a picture of Eric on the beach. Something. But now, no matter how hard she tried to imagine something to draw, all she could visualize was pudding.

"I miss Ted," she told the kitchen mop that had been her friend since Ted and Eric had gone missing.

The mop didn't say anything. It never did. *Stupid mop*.

"Do you think he's found Eric?" said Adeline, but again, the mop was nonresponsive.

Adeline took a deep breath.

"If you don't say anything," said Adeline, "I'm going to throw you into the ocean."

The mop didn't seem to care, so Adeline picked it up and dropped it over the edge of the deck, sending it crashing to the rocks below. She watched a wave carry it out to sea, the rope strands on its head fanning out on the surface of the water.

Now I'm really alone, thought Adeline.

Maybe there was something on TV.

233

Swamster was running, and it felt great. For the first time, he realized just how *practical* his swimsuit was when it came to athletic activity—no wind resistance. The air whipped through the fur on his cheeks, and he felt his gold medals bouncing against his chest—he was moving so fast that he almost believed he had earned them. When the ACORN hideout was safely behind him, he stopped for a moment and used his nose to determine the shortest distance back to Ab-Com City. He got a whiff of wedding cake and streamers drifting down from the north, so north he went. He loved eating both wedding cake and streamers.

234

And then—a stroke of good fortune—he reached a road where a convoy of presidential trucks was ferrying fresh fruits to the wedding. Swamster flagged one down.

"Where you headin'?" said one of the drivers.

"Ab-Com City, same as you," said Swamster.

"Was it rainin' where you came from?" said the driver, nodding to the umbrella.

"No. I just escaped from ACORN," said Swamster. "I know exactly where they are."

"Buncha anarchists, them ACORNS," said the driver. "Come on. We'll get you back to Ab-Com City and you can tell everybody what you know. Hop up front."

Swamster hopped into the front seat with the driver.

"Looks like you worked up a good sweat," said the driver.

"I ran all the way from their tree cave," said Swamster.

"You smell kinda good," said the driver. "Someone should make an air freshener outta you. I'd hang you from the rearview mirror here."

Swamster wasn't quite sure how to respond to the driver's idea. He was slightly uncomfortable for the rest of the ride because the driver kept taking long sniffs, but soon they pulled up to the gates of the Presidential Palace.

Swamster hopped off the truck and raced through the front doors of the palace. The information he possessed was going to change the face of the fight against ACORN, as was the fact that he had managed to acquire this umbrella. President Skeleton's scientists could analyze the solution that the umbrella had been dipped in, and use it against ACORN. Swamster pictured the surprised look on the faces of ACORN fighters as they began to *pop!*

235

President Skeleton was going to be *so* proud of him. *Vice President Swamster. Hmm, why not?*

He raced through the central courtyard, which was now cleared of most of its trees. A team of day workers was in the process of installing a golden carpet, while another group of workers was building a long bar along one of the stone walls.

"What cocktails will they be serving?" said Swamster, racing past the bar.

"Champagne and soda pop," said a talking mime.

Swamster stopped.

"No signature cocktail? Something distinctive?" said Swamster.

"Oh yeah, mint-inis," said the mime. "You know, minty martinis."

Classy enough. Swamster nodded, satisfied.

He climbed the stairs toward President Skeleton's bedroom two at a time, but when he reached the top, a thick arm whipped out in front of him and grabbed him by the shirt. The arm belonged to a baseball player wearing the Presidential Guard insignia on his sleeve and holding a Louisville Slugger.

"NOT so fast," said the baseball player. "This is a private floor."

"I have specific business up here," said Swamster. "I am President Skeleton's beloved assistant."

"And I am President Skeleton's extremely distant cousin," said the baseball player, dragging Swamster by his sweatshirt. "Everybody's got a connection. Talk to somebody who cares."

Swamster was chucked into a small room where Dulfond, a high-ranking advisor to President Skeleton, was sitting at a table, flipping through a copy of *Modern Bride* magazine. Swamster had worked with the goblin for a long time.

"I'd go with the sugared-fruit centerpiece," said Swamster.

"Huh?" said Dulfond.

"I couldn't help but notice that you were looking at centerpieces for the reception," said Swamster. "I think that bowls of sugared fruit can sometimes be a fun alternative to normal flower centerpieces."

"Who are you?" said Dulfond.

"What are you talking about? You know me. I'm Swamster. I've been President Skeleton's assistant forever."

"No, I don't think so," said Dulfond.

Swamster was stunned. He had scheduled hundreds of meetings with Dulfond. He had organized fundraising raffles with him. How could he not—

"Oh," said Swamster, smiling, "I understand what's wrong here. I normally wear a different-colored swimsuit, but you see I just escaped from that horrible ACORN, and my regular suit was stained purple."

"You escaped from ACORN?" said Dulfond.

"I thought you might appreciate that," said Swamster.

"Well, where are they?"

"I'd prefer to deliver my news in person."

"I'm afraid that's not possible."

Swamster shuffled his feet. He had counted on being let in to see President Skeleton immediately.

"If you've got something to say," said Dulfond, "I'll write the message and give it to her. Go on, then."

So Swamster told Dulfond everything he remembered about the layout of the caves and what roads he'd crossed while he was sprinting to freedom and what mountains and forests he'd been able to see on the horizon and how far he'd run. When he was done, there was no doubt exactly where ACORN headquarters was located.

237

"Well done, Swamster," said Dulfond. "Well done indeed."

"Oh, wait, there is one more thing that I found out while I was escaping," said Swamster, running his paw over the handle of the umbrella. "But I insist on telling President Skeleton about it in person."

"Nobody sees President Skeleton without an appointment."

"But she was the one who sent me into the field," said Swamster. "What I have to give her is very important."

Dulfond thought about this and then stood up.

"Come on," he said.

Swamster followed Dulfond to the door outside the library

that served as Persephone's office when she was at the Presidential Palace. A single chair stood against the wall opposite the door.

"Sit," said Dulfond. Swamster did so as Dulfond disappeared into the library. He reemerged a moment later and skittered away busily down the hall.

"Dulfond," called Swamster, "am I—"

"Somebody will be out to deal with you in a minute," said Dulfond, and then he was gone.

Swamster waited outside in the hallway for hours, listening to the scuffling and stomping on the other side of the door. He needed to use the restroom, but he didn't dare get up from his seat for fear of losing his place in line—even though he was the only person in line—so he tapped his foot on the floor and closed his eyes to calm his nerves. At last, the door opened.

238

"M-mister S-swamster?" said a small voice.

Swamster opened his eyes and looked down at a small honey possum barely as tall as his knee.

"P-president Sk-keleton will see you n-now," continued the honey possum.

Swamster didn't move.

"Who are you?" said Swamster.

"I'm B-bugslush," said Bugslush.

"That's your *name*," said Swamster, who was starting to get a sick feeling in his stomach. "I asked who *are* you?"

"I'm P-president S-skeleton's assis-assistant," said Bugslush.

Swamster's world came crashing down.

"You are certainly NOT President Skeleton's assistant," said Swamster. "*I* am President Skeleton's assistant."

"S-sorry, I am," said Bugslush, mad that somebody didn't believe him. He'd worked hard at this job.

"No, *I* am," said Swamster. "And I *have* been for years."

"The P-p-president didn't m-mention a S-swamster," said Bugslush.

Swamster took a deep breath. He and President Skeleton would work out this misunderstanding once he was inside the library.

"Okay," said Swamster. "That's fine. I'll take my meeting now, Bugslush."

Bugslush led Swamster into the library, where President Skeleton was standing on a pedestal, in the middle of being fitted for a wedding dress. The gown was dreadful—one sleeve was sea green and the other was mauve. The middle was made of denim, and the train consisted of long strings of feathers that had been sewn together to resemble glorious plumage.

"Dear me!" said Swamster, momentarily not in control of what he was saying. "This would have never happened on my watch."

239

A multiarmed octopus seamstress stood in front of Persephone, pins in her mouth, fitting the delicate fabric to the president's skeletal torso. She heard Swamster's comment and whipped around, shooting him a scathing look.

Persephone heard the comment too, but all she could do was laugh.

"Oh, my dear Swamster," said Persephone, looking down on him. "You always were terribly conventional."

"I mean, it's, to say, quite unusual," said Swamster.

"It doesn't really matter what you think," said Persephone. "Now, why are you here?"

Swamster was confused.

"Because I'm back," said Swamster. "You sent me into the field, and now I'm back for my job."

Persephone laughed.

"You don't honestly think that I would have sent you into the field if I had *wanted* you to come back, do you?" said Persephone. "I fired you, Swamster."

"But it was temporary."

"The *temporary* part of it was that I figured you wouldn't live very long," said Persephone. "But I am surprised you're back. Well done. Did you hide until you thought enough time had passed?"

"I was captured!"

"Of course you were," said Persephone. "And then your captors threw you back into the world like an undersized fish, without your having learned a thing, no doubt."

"But you said you were going to promote me," said Swamster.

"HA!" said Persephone. "Promote you to what? *Jester?* You weren't promotion material before, Swamster, and you're not now, even after your *field experience*. Give me one reason I should promote you."

Swamster's paw tightened around the handle of the umbrella.

"I suppose there isn't one," he said.

Persephone looked at him like he was something dead on the side of the road.

"That's what I thought," she said. "Bugslush, show Mr. Swamster out."

"V-very good, P-president Skeleton," said Bugslush, leading Swamster to the door. Swamster followed obediently, shell-shocked. He had spent his entire Middlemost existence working for Persephone, only to be laughed out of the room. She was never going to promote him. He'd heard it whispered in coffee shops and seen the headlines in the underground newspapers, but now it had truly hit him—Persephone Skeleton was an awful, awful creature.

And he had betrayed all of ACORN. For her.

241

III

BOOM! BOOM! BOOM!

Ted felt the vibrations of a horrible pounding above and all around him, followed by the shouts of thousands of ACORN fighters running for cover.

VZZZ!

Ted could hear something whirring as chunks of rock were plummeting from the ceiling and fracturing on the floor, firing shrapnel in all directions.

"Stay da calm!" yelled Brother Dezo at the hordes of abstract companions pushing toward the exits.

The falling rocks soon caused entire sections of the ceiling to collapse, cutting off exit routes and sending ACORN fighters leaping for safety.

As he ran for cover, Ted witnessed ab-coms being crushed—right next to him, a porkpie-hatted Egyptian dog and an academic in a turtleneck were squashed. He stopped to try and pull a velvet stork from the ruins, but he couldn't get a firm grip on its wings and had to leave it behind, despite its desperate squawks for help. Next he barely managed to jump out of the way of an entire crumbling wall that had fallen sideways into the corridor. Ted ducked and wove his way past frantic voodoo dolls and rock stars, toward the small hallway alcove that he knew Dwack, Vango, and Dr. Narwhal shared.

Dr. Narwhal was holding up the ceiling while Dwack and Vango stood nearby, watching the narwhal with great concern. His fins were trembling under the weight of the ceiling, which looked like a huge tangled thicket.

"Focus, Dr. Narwhal," said Dwack, as calmly as was possible given the circumstances. "I'm going to help you through this."

"What happened?" said Ted.

"He saved us," said Vango. "The roof fell and he somehow caught it."

"Urrghh," said Dr. Narwhal. Every muscle in his aquatic body was straining under its burden.

"You two should stand back," Dwack told Ted and Vango. "Dr. Narwhal, I want you to try to *move your flippers* along the bottom of the rock and edge your body as *close to me* as possible."

Inch by inch, Dr. Narwhal carefully scooted his flippers underneath the lump of ceiling while Dwack levitated off the ground until he was even with the rock.

"I can't . . . hold itsss weight . . . much longer," grunted Dr. Narwhal.

"You won't have to," said Dwack. "I'm going to count down, and when I say GO, you're going to throw it all forward. In the meantime, *I'll* be pushing it at an angle so that it doesn't come down on top of you."

"Count it, pleassse!" said Dr. Narwhal as he struggled.

"Three. Two. One. THROW!" said Dwack, hurling himself against the branches and tree trunks that were coming down.

Dr. Narwhal didn't do anything, continuing to hold the rocks.

"What are you *doing?*" said Dwack.

243

"You told me you would sssay GO," said Dr. Narwhal. "But you sssaid THROW!"

"Oh for the love of—" Dwack said, and then quickly calmed himself. "No, you're right. I should be more precise. Let's try again."

"Quickly!"

"Three! Two! One! GO!"

"Oof!"

Dr. Narwhal reared back and launched the ceiling chunk as far away from his body as he could while Dwack pushed on it to make sure it didn't split Dr. Narwhal's skull. An avalanche of branches and splinters crashed down in front of them, but Dr. Narwhal jumped out of the way and Dwack soared up and away from the cascade.

"Everybody safe?" said Dwack, out of breath.

"I'm fine," said Dr. Narwhal.

"That was great," said Vango. "I should have painted that."

"Ted?" said Dwack. "How are you doing?"

But Ted didn't even hear the vampire because he was staring at what was coming down *through* the collapsed ceiling— swarms of Presidential Guards.

The guards were cutting their way down into the tree caves. Ted looked behind him to see if there was somewhere to run, but up and down the corridor, President Skeleton's troops were busting through the ceiling and barreling through the ACORN fighters, many of whom were too busy freeing themselves and their friends from collapsed branches to realize they were under siege.

A man wearing Victorian dress and riding an antique

bicycle—huge wheel in front, small wheel in the back—came roaring out of the ceiling toward Ted, intent on running him over.

Ted reached for his badminton racket but he'd left it where he'd been sleeping. The Victorian bicyclist clipped Ted with his front wheel, cutting his leg and causing him to tumble to the ground. The Victorian whirled on his bike, came pedaling furiously back at Ted, and was about to slice him in half when—

"THEO!" said Vango, soaring through the air and colliding with the cyclist. The bicycle skidded away as Vango landed on top of his target.

"Who is—" was all the Victorian managed to get out of his mouth before Vango plunged a paintbrush into his side, and the Victorian exploded into a purple puddle beneath him.

"Thanks, Vango!" said Ted.

245

Dr. Narwhal was grappling with a half dozen Presidential Guards and Dwack was sucking blood from a mandrill. Ted forced himself to his feet and tried hard to imagine the battle away. *What if the floor of the tree cave became a trampoline that launched the guards back to the surface? What if the ceiling grew vines that let ACORN swing to safety?*

"Come on," said Ted to his arm, but nothing happened. Joelle-Michelle had told him that his brain could do amazing things, but she hadn't told him *how*.

All around him, Ted could see that ACORN was being steamrolled by the sheer number of Presidential Guards.

C'mon, brain, do something! Please! he thought.

Down the corridor, Joelle-Michelle was surrounded by fierce Presidential Guards, but as fast as she could kick them with her pointe shoes, new backup guards rushed to join the fight, until there were simply too many coming for her to fight back.

Ted saw a huge locust wrap its wings around her and—WHOOSH!—shoot upward through a hole in the ceiling.

The leader of ACORN had been captured.

"Jo—" yelled Ted, but he couldn't even get her name out of his mouth before a skull-head moth swooped down and wrapped him up in its wings. Ted felt the moth rocket upward through the same hole through which Joelle-Michelle had been whisked away.

As he started to get dizzy from the ascent, he promised himself that if he ever made it back to Cape Cod, he would stick one of those moth-frying zap-lights out on the back porch and watch bugs cook themselves all night long. *Zzzttt.*

IV

Carolina was in a bad mood. Though she had explained to Scurvy Goonda that she was sorry for having tormented Ted and that she was in Middlemost to find him and apologize, when the bird skeleton that seemed to be in charge had returned to the room and ordered that Carolina be taken to the dungeon, Scurvy hadn't objected.

"Please, please tell her that I'm not a threat!" Carolina had said.

"I have observed yer bullyin' ways fer many years, and a bit of jail time might do ya good," Scurvy had replied.

Two guards hauled Carolina out of the room and down three flights of stairs into a dingy basement lit by dripping candles. She had seen places like this in horror movies and books about the Middle Ages, but here there were large cracks in the floor from which geysers of natural gas occasionally exploded: *pfffft!* The guards steered Carolina around the gases, eventually reaching a long row of jail cells.

"In," said the larger guard, opening the cell with a rusty metal key and pushing Carolina inside.

"See you when you're old!" said the other guard. With that, both disappeared back the way they had come.

Carolina looked around her cell. The floor was dirt. A heap

of sticks in the corner served as a bed. A small window was built into the wall, but when she looked through it, all that she could see was a plaque that read: YOU'RE IN JAIL!

As hopeless as her surroundings were, Carolina had the feeling that she wasn't completely alone. Mixed in with the harsh *pfffft* sound of natural gas was the occasional cough or groan—the stone cellar was an echo chamber, and Carolina could hear everything.

"Hello?" said Carolina, and her voice bounced back at her: *HELLO-LO-LO . . .*

The only response was a series of wet, hacking coughs.

"I can hear you," said Carolina.

HEAR YOU—HEAR YOU—HEAR YOU, repeated the echo.

Carolina thought she heard a sputtering sound that could have been somebody or something trying to respond, though it could just as easily have been the normal groaning of a cellar that had thousands of tons of Presidential Palace sitting on top of it. But the sound didn't repeat itself. Carolina sat down in the corner of the cell and wrapped her arms around her legs.

How did I get myself into this? she thought.

For the next few hours, she tried to distract herself from her predicament by drawing pictures in the dirt. The ground felt warm to the touch. She figured that some sort of scalding natural gas was running directly below her, and she could see a deep crack in the floor on the other side of her cell.

Perhaps, she thought, *I'm going to be vaporized?* And with that thought in her head, she began to write her will on the wall, using a rock.

248

To My Family and Friends—

If you somehow get this message— and I don't even know HOW that would happen, but I don't have anything else to do down here—I'd like all of my possessions to go directly to my little brother, except for the more adult stuff like my furniture, which my parents bought anyway, so they should probably keep it.

I'd like whatever money I have in my bank account to be used to set up a scholarship at the high school for kids who have been pushed around. Call it the Ted Merritt Memorial Defense Fund. Just have the other students vote—they know who the unpopular kids are. And more than anything, I'd like for someone to apologize on my behalf for the way I have treated Ted Merritt.

Carolina had ground the rock in her hand down to powder; she began searching the floor for another stone to continue her writing.

She had just dug up a perfect piece of granite when she heard a rumble down the corridor. The noise sounded almost like a party approaching at a very fast pace—howling and stomping and a generous amount of cursing.

Carolina pressed her face against the bars of her cell and saw a herd of abstract companions fast approaching, shackled and irritated, forced forward by a battalion of armed guards. Moments later, the companions were streaming past her cell, and she could hear other cells being opened and clanged shut, filled to the brim with new prisoners. There was a battered-looking narwhal, a painter struggling with a guard for control of his paintbrushes, and a vampire with purple-stained hands and a broken fang.

Carolina had become so hypnotized watching the bizarre parade that she hadn't even *heard* a female voice talking to her from a few feet away.

"Perhaps you vould like to tell Ted yourself?" said the voice.

"Huh?" said Carolina, still watching the procession, realizing that somebody was addressing her. "What?"

"I just read your vill on the vall," said the voice, which seemed familiar.

Carolina turned toward the voice, and when she saw who it was, she nearly broke her head on the bars of her cell trying to rush forward.

"CZARINA!" yelled Carolina. She had her hands tied behind her back, waiting to be pushed forward into a cell.

"My vord," said Czarina Tallow. "Dear girl, vy are you here?"

"It's such a long story," said Carolina.

"NO TALKING," said a guard, snapping his whip and peering back at Czarina over the crowd.

"Don't you DARE yell at her!" said Carolina.

The guard cracked his whip again. "Awfully loud for a prisoner," he said.

The guards began filling another set of cells and Czarina lurched forward with the rest of the group, disappearing into a clanging box somewhere down the line. She tried to wave good-bye; Carolina could see her pale hand sticking out above the throng.

Soon the door to her cell was yanked open, and a guard started yelling "IN YA GO!" at a rabble of ab-coms. The door clanged shut, and Carolina looked around at a dozen new room-mates.

A living statue sat on the floor, fists on his chin, thinking intently. A pink manta ray flew around the cell flapping its fins, trying to fit between the bars. A merman flopped around on the ground until it spiked its trident into the floor and managed to lift itself to a sitting position in the back corner. A large Hawaiian musician leaned against the wall, plucking a ukulele.

In the opposite corner of the cell, a stunning porcelain-skinned ballerina was raising her leg against the bars of the cell, taking her imprisonment as an opportunity to *stretch*.

Carolina was instantly jealous of the ballerina, but she made a point of being civil.

"I'm Carolina," she said.

"*Un moment,*" said the ballerina. "I must do my other leg."

Carolina fidgeted. She wasn't used to being the second-prettiest girl in a room—especially in such a very small room—and the ballerina's fancy accent annoyed her.

"Uh, Carolina? Is that you?"

Carolina turned to find herself face to face with Ted Merritt, who was sitting in the middle of the floor. His hair hung down over his forehead and his entire body was stained purple.

"It is you," said Ted. "Uh, hello?"

"Hi, Ted," said Carolina. "I'm really glad to see you. Even here."

The ballerina stopped stretching and turned to see what was going on. *Ted and this girl know each other?*

"You know my name?" said Ted.

"Of course I know your name," said Carolina.

"Why are you here?" asked Ted. "I mean, this is such a weird place to see you."

"I actually came to apologize."

"For what?" he said.

"For the way I've treated you through high school," said Carolina. "And through junior high."

Ted thought about this.

"And middle school," Ted added.

"What did I do in middle school?"

252

"You destroyed a Christmas ornament I made for my mother," said Ted.

"Wow," said Carolina. "I'm an awful human being."

"Terrible," said Joelle-Michelle, suddenly paying much more attention.

Ted didn't say anything.

"You're not saying anything because you really do think I'm an awful human being," said Carolina.

"I'm not saying anything because I'm not sure what you want me to say," said Ted.

"The whole reason I'm here, the whole reason I tracked you down, is because I wanted to say I'm sorry. For everything," said Carolina.

Ted paused.

"I always wondered how you lived with yourself," he said.

"I can't. I want to change," said Carolina. "Czarina Tallow is my imaginary friend. I didn't want to be treated like you, I—"

"I met her. She's a nice lady," said Ted. "And she's a great fighter with her parasol. You should have seen her during the last battle."

"Do you think there is room for another nut in ACORN?" said Carolina. "I'd like to help."

"*Mon Dieu!*" said Joelle-Michelle. "Now we are taking in bullies?"

"Joelle-Michelle," said Ted. "This is my . . . my friend? Carolina, this is Joelle-Michelle. She is the leader of ACORN."

"Ted is our secret weapon," said Joelle-Michelle. "He is brave. He is imaginative. How could someone like *you* have bullied him?"

Carolina looked at Ted for an explanation.

"I'm much cooler here than I am in high school," he said.

253

V

Trapped with two beautiful girls. Ted wished that Vango were here to paint a picture of this scene.

Carolina tracked me down all the way to Middlemost? he thought. *I never even knew that she was capable of emotion, especially guilt.*

Carolina was clearly happy that he had accepted her apology, but now the mood had turned strange, with the two rivals sizing each other up from opposite sides of the cell.

"So, uh, Carolina," said Ted, "I don't think I've talked to you since that Valentine's Day."

"Valentine's Day?" said Carolina.

"Yeah," said Ted. "Um, Valentine's Day in third grade. You were the only kid in class who put a card in my mailbox. Thanks for that, by the way."

Carolina's face twisted up.

"You're welcome," she said.

"She came all this way for you and you haven't even spoken to her since third grade?" said Joelle-Michelle. "She is very easy, *no?*"

"You're the one who isn't leaving anything to the imagination with that leotard," said Carolina.

"Ah," said Joelle-Michelle. "I forgive your lack of culture. These are traditional dance clothes worn on the stage."

"We're not on a stage," said Carolina.

"I am *always* onstage," said Joelle-Michelle.

Are two beautiful girls actually fighting over me? Ted was totally fascinated and completely unsure what to do. Should he step between the girls and say something cinematic like "Ladies, ladies—"? Should he point out that they needed to figure a way out of this cell before the guards did whatever they planned to do with them?

At a point of mutual exasperation, Joelle-Michelle and Carolina turned to Ted at the same time.

"I can't talk to this girl!" said Carolina.

"This *vache* bores me!" said Joelle-Michelle, calling Carolina a cow.

They both waited for Ted's response.

"I think you should work it out yourselves," said Ted, smiling inside as they started arguing again.

255

But then he heard something.

"Hush!" said Ted, and Joelle-Michelle and Carolina were quiet.

Music. A melody was drifting down from far above; there was no mistaking what it was: *Duh, duh, duh-duh! Duh, duh, duh-duh!* The wedding march.

"Sounds like President Skeleton and Scurvy Goonda have started their wedding ceremony," said the living statue.

"Holy crow!" said Ted. "Poor Scurvy."

The wedding march started again, this time in a different key. *Da, dah, da-da! Da, dah, da-da!*

"No," said Joelle-Michelle. "They are just rehearsing."

Ted knew he needed to help his friend. Fast. If Scurvy was just upstairs . . .

"Use your hand!" said Joelle-Michelle.

"What does that mean?" said Carolina.

"I've discovered that my hand does weird . . . things," said Ted.

Come on, think of a way out of here. He pictured himself turning into a drill and grinding his way upward through the ceiling, or changing the cell bars into chocolate and eating his way through, but nothing happened with his hand, and he felt everybody in the cell looking at him.

"Worthless hand!" yelled Ted, slapping the wall. "Stupid birthmark! Come on, Ted, *think*!"

Ted's outburst silenced Joelle-Michelle and Carolina, who had started bickering again. His voice bounced up and down the corridor, echoing off the stone: *Come on Ted think come on Ted think come on Ted think . . .*

But the only response came in the form of a hacking cough from the end of the cell block.

VI

The courtyard was *nearly* perfect. Dozens of tables with tasteful sugared-fruit centerpieces. Hundreds of chairs for less important guests, and a general-admission standing area for abstract companions who wanted a glimpse of the high life but couldn't swing a formal invitation. There was a stage for the orchestra off to one side, and a mahogany bar off to the other. Dead center at the back of the courtyard loomed a white wedding gazebo decorated with silk bunting and taxidermied doves.

Scurvy and Persephone were sitting on the balcony overlooking the courtyard, at a table piled high with bacon on Scurvy's side and a half dozen glasses of milk on Persephone's. Milk was Persephone's way of getting in shape for the wedding. All that she could improve upon was her skeleton, and she had read in MORE, MORE, MORE magazine that calcium was good for bones. When Scurvy pointed out that the milk wouldn't do anything because she wasn't actually *digesting* it, she shot him such a look that he decided not to mention it again.

"You haven't touched your bacon, Scurvy-Burvy Glopsy-Gurby," said Persephone.

"I know, I know," said Scurvy. "I think I'm gettin' a wee bit *tired* of it. Ya've probably been feeding me tha equivalent of four or five pigs a day."

"Seven," said Persephone. "You've been eating seven pigs a day."

"Seems a mite *excessive*."

"Oh, come now," said Persephone. "I'm just getting my *big man* happy for our *big day*. Doesn't the wedding march sound *wonderful*?"

In the courtyard, a creature in a powdered wig was playing a grand piano specially imported for the ceremony.

"Louder!" yelled Persephone, and the organist responded. *Duh, duh, duh-duh! Duh, duh, duh-duh!*

"Fer me second wedding, we banged out that song on tha side of me ship using cats," said Scurvy.

"Don't let's talk about your other wives!" said Persephone.

"Rightie-o."

"Put your arm around me," ordered Persephone.

"But yer on tha other side of tha table, and I'm all tha way over here."

"Then come over *here*."

Scurvy scooted his chair over to the other side of the table and reluctantly draped his arm over Persephone's bony shoulder.

"Both arms," said Persephone.

Scurvy awkwardly complied.

"Press your face against mine," said Persephone. "It will be so cute."

Her skull bones felt hard against Scurvy's cheek.

"As much as I like planning this wedding," said Persephone, "I can't *wait* until it's over."

"Aye," said Scurvy. "It'll be tha best day of me life when this is over."

"*Oh, Scurvy,*" said Persephone, pressing her face harder against Scurvy's. "You're so sweet."

Scurvy didn't say anything. Persephone waited.

"Sweet . . . on you?"

"*Aww,*" said Persephone. "But do you know the *real* reason I want this wedding to be over?"

"Not sure I do."

Persephone leaned close to Scurvy's ear.

"Our honeymoon," she whispered.

Scurvy's stomach lurched.

"Tha honeymoon," he said. "Where we have tah spend weeks and weeks together?"

"*Please!*" said Persephone. "Ours will be months long. Years. I've planned everything for after the invasion."

"Where are we going?"

"The coast of Brazil. I want to try out a new bikini," said Persephone.

Scurvy shuddered.

"You're shaking," said Persephone.

"Just a wee bit chilly," said Scurvy. "We wouldn't be going on this vacation for *a while*, though, right? Because ya need tah get things in order here in Middlemost?"

Persephone laughed. "Things are well in order here in Middlemost," she said. "No, we're going the *moment* the ceremony is over, and everybody is coming with us."

"I don't think I'm completely understandin'."

"Bugslush!" yelled Persephone. "Telescope!"

Bugslush hustled into the room, carrying an enormous brass telescope on his back. With a great grunt he set it up on the edge of the balcony.

259

"Very good," said Persephone. "That will be all."

"One th-thing I h-have to ask," said Bugslush.

"Well?" said Persephone.

"Th-the raid on the ACORN hideout w-was a s-success," said Bugslush.

"That's not a question," said Persephone.

"W-what do you want to be done w-with the p-prisoners?"

"Oh, just have them taken to a factory and recycled," said Persephone. "There's no need to interrogate them if we're all leaving tomorrow anyway."

"V-very good," said Bugslush. "I'll tell the g-guards."

Bugslush shuffled away from the balcony.

"What do ya mean, we're all leaving tomorrow?" said Scurvy.

"Look through the telescope," said Persephone.

Scurvy placed his eye against the end of the telescope. The horizon came into focus, but all he saw was a field of straw and a quiet lake.

"Pan left," said Persephone. "Next to the bust of our heads I had carved into the mountainside."

Scurvy rotated the telescope until he spotted a mountain that had been chiseled into a sculpture of Scurvy and Persephone locked in a passionate lip-lock.

"Ya had us carved?" said Scurvy.

"Of course," said Persephone. "I had to have my soldiers do *something* while they were waiting around. Now look *next* to our faces."

Scurvy saw it. Persephone's entire military had gathered next to the mountain, armed and ready to move. Scurvy had never seen so many weird creatures together in one place. On the other side of the mountain was an enormous vent. It looked the same as the one he had crawled through underneath the Crusher, but it was twenty times as tall and hundreds of times as wide.

"That's the last open vent," said Persephone. "The one we're all going through. When I had all the other vents sealed, I had that one enlarged."

"Where does it lead?"

"That's the beauty of it," said Persephone. "Our vents always lead to supermarkets and shops and those types of places. So our largest vent leads to the world's largest store."

"Which is?"

"Macy's. It's in New York City," said Persephone. "We also considered a Home Depot in Michigan, but I wanted to pick up some perfume. You'll adore me in Chanel No. 5."

261

VII

It was the middle of the night, and it was the first time that the courtyard had been silent all day, aside from the slight whimpering coming from underneath the mahogany bar. Swamster, who had chewed up a tablecloth to make himself a bed there, was lying down, drinking a mint-ini.

"Oh," he moaned. "You stupid Swamster. You should have known better."

He couldn't believe that all the years he had spent with President Skeleton had meant nothing. A rumor had spread that the ACORN prisoners were going to be transported to processing factories tomorrow morning, and what with ACORN being wiped out and the attack on Earth, Swamster now realized that during the years he'd spent working for a promotion, he had turned a blind eye to Persephone's true nature.

"Here's to me—a total idiot," said Swamster, taking another gulp of his mint-ini.

He closed his eyes and tried again to fall asleep. This time, it wasn't only his thoughts that distracted him. Cutting through the silence of the courtyard, he could hear a pair of female voices echoing up from the palace basement.

"Slug!"

"Porc!"

Swamster climbed unsteadily to his feet and stepped out from behind the bar. He walked to the center of the courtyard, following the voices.

"Ted, tell Joelle-Michelle to place her head in the crack of the floor and wait for a steam blast!"

"Ted, tell this she-swine to find someplace else to flap her snout!"

Swamster realized he wasn't the only one listening to the catfight. He gazed up at the balcony, where Scurvy Goonda stood in his red pajamas.

"You should be resting for your big day, sir," Swamster called out.

"Can't sleep," said Scurvy. "Did ya happen tah hear—were those girls mentioning tha name Ted?"

"Sounded like that to me."

Scurvy considered this.

"How big are ya?" said Scurvy.

"Maybe five feet tall."

"If I was tah jump off this balcony, do ya think ya could catch me? Can't go out through tha room, 'cause there are guards outside tha door."

"I'm not sure I could," said Swamster. "You're quite a bit heftier than you were when we first met."

"Aye, but fer a man my size, I land like a feather," said Scurvy.

Swamster hesitated.

"Please," said Scurvy. "I need tah see if tha Ted they're talking about is me friend."

"All right," said Swamster, walking a little unsteadily beneath the balcony. "Leap!"

Scurvy swung one leg over the balcony and then the other.

263

Swamster looked up at the pajama bootees covering Scurvy's feet.

"I'm gonna let myself fall," said Scurvy.

"I'm not sure—"

WHOMP! Scurvy cannonballed into Swamster from above, sending him sprawling to the ground.

"Not tha best catcher," said Scurvy, holding his hand out to Swamster. "But a better cushion, I've never met."

"Errgh," groaned Swamster. "Thanks." Scurvy pulled Swamster to his feet.

"Which way is tha entrance tah tha basement?"

Swamster pointed with his paw just as Persephone's voice was ringing out into the night above them: "GUARDS! GO GET MY SCURVY!"

VIII

Scurvy knew that once Persephone spotted him sprinting toward the cellar stairs in the courtyard, it wouldn't be long until the guards tackled him and brought him back to her bedroom or perhaps somewhere *worse*.

Scurvy ran, barreling through the basement doors and down the stone stairs, Swamster running beside him. Their footsteps whacked the stairs in unison—*clop! clop! clop!* Scurvy had just enough extra wind to tell Swamster, "This might get hairy!"

BANG! They ran into the first wave of guards rushing up from the cellar. Without breaking his stride, Scurvy snapped a tooth out of a goblin's mouth and plunged it into the shoulder of a tweedy professor. Both fell to the steps in pain. Then he head-butted a harpy and kneed a Neanderthal. A few seconds later, he and Swamster were making their way down to the next staircase, where another swell of guards was dashing toward them.

Scurvy stole a staff from a wizard and cracked it over the head of a fashion model; he took a baker's saltshaker and dumped it over a huge snail; he wrenched a dagger from a sultan and used it to burst a man whose head was a red balloon (which had made him a very impractical choice for a guard).

Swamster had never seen a fighter as brash and fearless as Scurvy, but he could tell that the pirate was running out of gas when he started to gasp and slow down. The guards kept coming, and soon they were leaping all over Scurvy, tearing at his hair and his pajamas and dragging him away up the stairs.

"You were helping him escape!" accused a sheikh, who seemed to be in charge.

"No, I wasn't, I was chasing him!" said Swamster.

Nearby, Scurvy managed to break away from his captors and take off running, yelling over and over, "I AM NOT GET-TING MARRIED TO A PILE OF BONES!"

In the chaos of chasing down Scurvy, the guards let Swamster slip past. While more guards rushed up the stairs, Swamster made his way deeper into the basement, down one flight of stairs and then the next, where the landing leveled out into a long block of jail cells.

"Oh dear," said Swamster.

266

Cell after cell was packed to the brim with wounded ACORN fighters crammed tightly together. Tacked next to each cell was a command:

THIS ONE FIRST!

THIS ONE LAST—NICE GUYS IN HERE.

MAKE SURE TO GET RID OF THESE GUYS RIGHT AWAY!

Swamster realized that the commands corresponded to the order in which ACORN fighters would be taken to the factories.

All of these ab-coms would be exterminated, because of him.

"Hey, over here!" said a voice, and Swamster saw a teenage boy inside the cell marked THIS ONE FIRST!

"You're the hamster-swimmer-thing we captured at the factory," said the boy.

"I am a Swamster. And I'm ashamed to admit that I ratted you out."

"You can make up for it by getting us *out* of here! The guards are coming back. We have to *stop* this wedding and *stop* the attack."

"I know," said Swamster. "Where are the keys?"

"There's an office built into the wall a few cells down," said Ted.

Swamster hustled down the hallway and found a key ring hanging on a hook, abandoned by a guard who must have run to join the Scurvy fight. Swamster ran back to the THIS ONE FIRST cell, flicking through the keys to find the right one.

267

He had his head down when he heard Ted shout, "Look out!"

BANG! Scozzbottle hit him over the head with a rock. Swamster crumpled to the floor, keys clanging next to him.

Scozzbottle bent over and picked them up.

"Traitor!" he said.

IX

Scozzbottle stood outside the cells, staring in. ACORN was totally at his mercy.

"Lookie lookie. Haven't seen you in a while," said Scozzbottle. "Not since you offed my friend Wockgrass, I believe. You know, it's almost daybreak upstairs. Almost time to load you into a truck and send you on your merry factory way."

It was silent on the cell block.

"The sad thing," continued Scozzbottle, "is that this whole ACORN business didn't end up doing much at all, did it? You got together in a tree cave, you were discovered, and here you are in jail, a temporary stopover on your way to being ripped apart. It seems like a lot of wasted effort, doesn't it?"

Scozzbottle grinned wickedly. And then something peculiar happened. The cell block echoed with the same coughing that had been bouncing off the stone walls all night long. But this time, the coughing turned into violent hacks peppered with booming, wet eruptions.

Scozzbottle opened his mouth to continue mocking the prisoners, but each time he did, he was interrupted by more retching.

"So you see—"

HACK!

"The transport trucks are—"

HACK!

"ACORN has been defeated—"

HACK!

Scozzbottle snapped around in the direction of the noise.

"Would you shut up?!" roared Scozzbottle. *"I am trying to destroy morale!"*

That was when Scozzbottle saw it.

When *everybody* saw it.

A pale . . . sickly . . . *birthmarked* . . . arm.

The markings on the forearm were the same as Ted's, and the hand had the same shape. Ted looked down at his own limb to make sure it was still there. It was.

The arm hovered in the air three feet from Scozzbottle and then rapidly fabricated a giant flannel-shirt-wearing fur trapper, probably Canadian. The trapper held a huge cage in one hand and a Taser in the other. He calmly reached forward and zapped Scozzbottle, knocking him unconscious.

269

The trapper stuffed Scozzbottle in the cage, nodded to Ted, and said, "Gonna make me a nice coat out of this one. Eh."

The trapper walked up the stairs hauling his catch, while the arm floated down to the ground and picked up the key that Scozzbottle had dropped. Calmly, the hand unlocked the door, and Ted pushed it open.

"Thank you?" said Ted.

The arm held the key out to Joelle-Michelle, who accepted it.

"It wants you to unlock the other cells," said Carolina.

The arm patted Joelle-Michelle on the shoulder and pointed to Carolina.

"It wants me to help you," said Carolina.

As the arm began to float back the way it had come, Ted *knew* that he was supposed to follow it. He could barely breathe as he walked down the corridor. He made brief eye contact with Dwack.

"Be careful, dear boy," said Dwack.

Each cell Ted passed was smaller than the last, and the corridor was far longer than he had realized. The arm glided steadily along. Finally, Ted and the arm came to a forgotten part of the cell block, where the candles barely burned and the air smelled like mold. Ted was thinking he was going to have to turn around and fetch a torch to help him see, when the arm stopped in front of a dank, lichen-covered cell barely big enough to hold one inmate.

The arm floated through the bars of the cell.

Ted crouched down to see inside.

"Hello?" said Ted, nervously.

270

The arm reattached itself to the elbow of a man leaning against the wall. Dressed in dirty rags, his hair wild, a scraggly beard covering his face, the poor man seemed in danger of crumbling to dust at any moment. A tin cup of water sat in a corner next to a single slice of bread.

The man coughed violently: *HACK! HACK!*

"We'll have you out of here in a second," said Ted. "A girl is coming with the key."

The man nodded feebly.

"Who are you?" said Ted.

The man's rheumy eyes flicked from Ted's face to his arm and back to his face. He wiped spittle from his lip and smiled weakly.

"I'm your dad," he said.

X

By the time Joelle-Michelle and Carolina had finished unlocking all the cells, Ted had barely recovered enough from the shock of learning about his father to tell all ACORN fighters to stay where they were. Guards would be returning to their posts soon. The time wasn't right for an attack—he and Joelle-Michelle had to figure out a plan. Meanwhile, Brother Dezo dragged Swamster out of the corridor while Ted helped his father walk back to his own cell.

Declan Merritt couldn't stop hugging his son. Though Ted's childhood memories of his father were hazy—he had left when Ted was seven, after all—there was no doubt that this was his dad. They had the same eyes and the same color hair. They were about the same height, and their arms were identical.

After seven years, Ted wasn't sure what to feel about his father hugging him. He barely knew him.

"Ted," said Declan. "My Ted. I never thought I'd see you again."

"I thought you never wanted to see me or Mom or Adeline again," said Ted.

Declan released Ted and looked at him.

"I swear to you—I didn't walk out on my family, if that's what you think," said Declan. "Look where you found me."

"But if you could have *imagined* yourself released at any time, why didn't you come home?"

Declan shook his head. "This is the first time in seven years I've had enough strength to do that," said Declan. "I heard what was happening, and I thought it might be you. If I'd managed to find Middlemost, maybe you had too."

"You should have *tried* to get back to Mom, Addie, and me," said Ted.

"You have no idea how many times I tried," said Declan. "It killed me that you might think I left you and your mother. I was chained to a wall for five years. My arm was placed in a steel box. The only thing that kept me alive was thinking I might get to see you and your beautiful mother again. Before I left, I wrote a message on the back of one of your glow-in-the-dark stars."

272

"It said 'here,'" said Ted.

"That's right. It said 'here.' If I didn't come back, I thought you might find it when you were old enough to help, and figure out where I was."

It was a lot to absorb.

"But why did you come here?" said Ted.

"To stop my insane cousin, Lloyd Munch, from running amok," said Declan.

"You failed," Joelle-Michelle pointed out.

"I did," said Declan. "If I had succeeded, we wouldn't be in this mess right now."

"Well," said Ted, "now you'll get another chance to fight."

"I'm too weak."

"Doesn't matter," said Ted. "We can still use you, Dad."

At that word, Declan's eyes dampened. He nodded.

"But first you need to tell me how to use *this*," said Ted, holding up his arm.

"All I know is that it seems to work best when you need it most," said Declan.

"Explain that to my arm," said Ted.

"Can't," laughed Declan. "Mine won't listen either."

Ted smiled. He remembered his father's laugh.

"Brother Dezo," said Ted. "How is the Swamster doing?"

"Swamstah mo bettah, bruddah."

Ted stood over Swamster.

"Swamster," he said. "Can you tell us where the weapons that were seized from ACORN are stored?"

"I'm afraid they've been distributed to President Skeleton's troops," said Swamster.

"All of them?" said Joelle-Michelle.

"A few might have been taken to the lab for examination," said Swamster. "There's a laboratory on the border of the palace grounds."

"Could you take me there?" said Ted.

"I think so," said Swamster.

"Good," said Ted. "All right, Carolina, you're coming with me."

"Why her?" said Joelle-Michelle.

"Since she's human, she won't explode if she gets VIDGA solution on her," said Ted.

"Explode?" said Carolina. "Wait—"

"But I am the *leader* of ACORN!" said Joelle-Michelle.

"That's why you need to be *here*," Ted explained. "What would happen to them, to us, if you didn't come back?"

Joelle-Michelle paused. She suspected that Ted simply

273

wanted to be alone with that Carolina, but she wouldn't throw a tantrum now. She reminded herself that she was a French-woman. She would save it up and find a way to get back at him creatively.

"*Oui*," said Joelle-Michelle. "You go with Swamster, I will stay here."

"It won't take long," said Ted, sliding open the cell door. "Come on, Carolina."

Joelle-Michelle removed one of her ballet slippers and handed it to Ted.

"Use it if you get in trouble, *mon ami*," she said.

At that moment, Ted had never wished for anything as much as he wished to know what *mon ami* meant.

XI

Ted, Carolina, and Swamster barely managed to slide out of the stairwell before the guards returned to their posts in the cell block. Hiding behind a chocolate fountain topped by statues of Persephone and Scurvy dancing in each other's arms, Ted could see a half dozen guards streaming down the stairs, some of whom looked like they had been bruised and broken in the scuffle with Scurvy.

Swamster motioned for Ted and Carolina to follow him. Ducking behind ice sculptures, they made their way off the palace grounds. Down the road, Ted could see lines of transport trucks moving toward the estate—trucks that would be hauling everyone from ACORN off to the processing factories. They needed to find the laboratory quickly.

"See that set of buildings on the edge of the forest?" Swamster whispered. "That's the main lab."

They ducked behind trees and shrubs until they reached the laboratory, where a sleepy-looking guard stood in front of the main door. Pressing their bodies against the outside wall so they wouldn't be seen, they had a clear view of the transport trucks.

"Should we try to distract the guard?" whispered Ted to Swamster.

"I don't think there's time."

Ted removed Joelle-Michelle's ballet slipper from his

pocket, sprinted around the corner of the building, and chucked it hard at the guard. The slipper whacked into the guard's surprised face, and he exploded in a purple gush that splashed against the laboratory door.

"I didn't know I could throw," said Ted, picking up the slipper.

"Can you get us in?" Ted asked Swamster.

"Uh, yes," said Swamster, turning the doorknob. "It's not locked."

Entering the lab, they stayed low to the ground with Swamster in the lead. The rooms were medicinally clean, and random scientists were milling about, all of whom were paying rapt attention to a cauldron in the center of the room. Next to the cauldron was a bundle of ACORN weapons. Ted could see Brother Dezo's ukulele. The head scientist, wearing a WATCHOUT! suit, was scraping solution samples off the weapons and looking at them under a microscope.

"Add another celebrity magazine!" the head scientist commanded.

A pair of scientists dropped a tabloid magazine into the mix. The scientists, who apparently hadn't figured out that the solution was rendered from specific melted video games, were duplicating the formula using other monotonous media.

"Now," said the head scientist. "Let's test it out."

A frightened bison was led out of a crate. Ted recognized the bison as the gravestone-eater from the ACORN hideout.

Oh no, thought Ted, watching as a scientist sucked liquid from the cauldron using a baster, walked over to the bison, and put a few drops on its head.

Drip. Drip.

POP!

The bison exploded in a purple mist. The scientists threw their hands in the air triumphantly.

"Success!" said the head scientist. "Let the army know that we've cracked the formula!"

Ted motioned for Carolina to circle around to the other side of a counter, and for Swamster to stay put. When Carolina looked back at him, he made a *push* motion. She nodded.

As the head scientist reached for the phone, Ted counted down with his fingers: *Three. Two. One.*

"GO!" he shouted.

On cue, Ted and Carolina rushed in from opposite sides of the room. Ted crashed into the head scientist, sending him tumbling into the cauldron. Ted grabbed the baster and sprayed an assistant with the remaining drops, turning him to vapor. Only a WATCHOUT!-suited worker was left, and together Ted and Carolina knocked him to the ground and tore off his hood.

It was Bugslush.

"D-don't h-hurt me!"

Hiding behind the lab counter, Swamster recognized Bugslush's voice and stood up.

"Bugslush!" said Swamster.

"Oh n-no," said Bugslush.

"This possum-thing works for the crazy skeleton-maniac," said Carolina. "I saw him before I was sent to jail."

"He took my *job* working for President Skeleton," said Swamster. "Career thief!"

"Oh d-dear . . . ," said Bugslush.

"What are you doing here?" said Ted.

277

"I have a m-master's degree in c-chemistry . . . ," said Bugslush. "President Skeleton asked me to h-help replicate the f-formula. . . ."

"Throw him in the pot," said Swamster.

"Wait," said Ted. "We're not going to be able to make it back to the cell blocks carrying the weapons and the solution. But if the army brought ACORN to *us*."

Ted looked at the phone on the wall.

"Bugslush, it's time for you to make a call."

XII

If Persephone had had tear ducts, she would have been crying. If she had had a heart, it would have been broken.

This was *not* how she had pictured her wedding day. Yes, she was standing on a platform while her seamstresses whirled around her, draping her wedding dress over her bones. She had already spent an hour in the makeup chair and another hour having an expensive wig fitted to her skull, but none of it was fun or as special as she had hoped it would be, what with Scurvy sitting in a cage in the corner of the room.

"The groom ain't supposed tah see tha bride 'fore tha weddin'," said Scurvy.

"Yes, and the groom is *also* not supposed to fight off dozens of employees of the bride while screaming that he doesn't want to get married!" said Persephone.

"Ya gotta point," said Scurvy.

"I will *not* be embarrassed!" said Persephone, sliding her talons into a pair of high-heeled shoes. "This wedding is *happening*!"

At least, thought Scurvy, *if I'm in me cage, maybe I won't have tah kiss the bride*.

"Here," said Persephone, throwing Scurvy's tuxedo into the cage. "Tux up!"

Dutifully, Scurvy began to strip off his dirty pajamas. There was a knock at the door.

"THIS BETTER BE IMPORTANT!" said Persephone.

A guard peeked his head into the room, holding a telephone on a gold platter.

"Telephone," grunted the guard. "Bugslush."

Persephone grabbed the phone.

"WHAT?" she said.

"Hello, President Skeleton," said Bugslush on the other end of the line. "I have some good news for you."

Persephone paused.

"Why aren't you stuttering?" said Persephone.

In the laboratory, Ted hovered over Bugslush with the badminton racket he had recovered. Bugslush wasn't stuttering because he was so nervous that he had actually *overloaded* the stuttering part of his brain and could therefore speak normally.

"Just feeling relaxed," said Bugslush.

"What do you want?" said Persephone.

"I wanted to let you know that we cracked the formula for the solution."

"Excellent!"

"And we were thinking that instead of taking ACORN to the processing factory," said Bugslush, "you could simply have ACORN fighters brought over to the lab, and we could hose them down. They wouldn't even need to be taken out of the trucks."

Persephone thought about this.

"That *would* be simpler than having them trucked back and forth," Persephone admitted.

"It would also give us the chance to see if the solution works on *everybody*," said Bugslush.

Persephone thought about this.

"Fine. Do it," she said, and hung up. "Have the prisoners brought to the lab," she directed the guard who had brought in the phone.

When the guard had exited, Persephone took a deep breath.

"Could I see that broom for a moment?" said Persephone to a seamstress sweeping up stray pins. When she had the broom in her wing, she flipped it around, walked over to Scurvy's cage, and poked him with the handle.

"Kiss your bacon GOODBYE!" said Persephone. "From now on all you get for your stomach are broom handles! EAT THAT HANDLE!"

"Arrgh," said Scurvy.

XIII

Had Ted failed?

Hordes of guards had returned to the cell block, and he and the others hadn't returned from their mission to the laboratory.

Maybe he and Carolina are under a tree somewhere too busy kissing to save their comrades, thought Joelle-Michelle. *I bet they're picnicking.*

"Ha!" shouted one of the guards. "Look at dis! We accidentally left da cells unlocked and dey didn't go nowhere! ACORN is stupid!"

Joelle-Michelle lowered her head and let herself be forced up the staircase by the guards, feeling the cold stone under her shoeless foot. The rest of ACORN walked next to her, equally downhearted. She looked over at Eric—the bonsai tree growing out of his head was nothing but twigs. She looked at Brother Dezo, whose lei had been ripped to shreds. He was still holding some of the flower scraps in his hand.

When the members of ACORN were forced into the transport trucks, Joelle-Michelle found herself sitting across from Dwack, Vango, and Dr. Narwhal.

"I'm sure Ted did his best," said Joelle-Michelle.

"Certainly," said Dwack.

"President Skeleton has such a huge army," started Joelle-Michelle, "and that Carolina couldn't have been much help to him." The guards shut the back door, plunging the truck into darkness, and she could hear the doors of other trucks slamming shut. The truck started to move.

Joelle-Michelle heard ab-coms weeping. *This* was her ACORN? This was how she led her forces?

"*Non!*" said Joelle-Michelle. In the dark, she could hear the sound of heads turning toward her. "*Messieurs et mesdames!* This may be our last ride, but I want to tell you, I am proud to have known each and every one of you. If we are to face our fate inside a processing factory, it is an honor to think my processed parts might someday be combined with yours. But we will *not* go down with a whimper. And so I say to you: *let us rock this truck!*"

Joelle-Michelle threw her back against the wall.

"One wall, and then the next!" she shouted. "We will topple these trucks, and if they want to take us to our graves, they will have to *drag* us fighting! *Allons-y!* Let's go!"

Joelle-Michelle threw herself against the wall again, and this time, other ACORN fighters joined in, slamming against each other and the walls, rocking the truck back and forth.

"Keep going!" said Joelle-Michelle.

The truck tilted up on one set of wheels and then the other.

Then the truck stopped. There was a banging sound up front, and then muffled shouts from outside of "Hey!" and "What the—" which were followed by more thumps.

"Here they come," said Joelle-Michelle to her troops. "When they open the door, we will rush them. I will lead."

There was the sound of jangling keys outside the door, which then flew open, filling the truck with light.

"*Allez!*" shouted Joelle-Michelle, charging out of the truck with the rest of ACORN at her back. Her body thumped into

283

another body, sending it sprawling, and she heard someone yell "Stop!" at the same moment she found herself flying through the air and skidding across the ground in a purple puddle.

Joelle-Michelle covered her head, but nobody was attacking her. When she looked up, Carolina was standing above her, holding a fire extinguisher, offering her hand.

"Come on," said Carolina. Ted, trying to catch his breath, was lying in the middle of the purple puddle where Joelle-Michelle had barreled into him.

"That's what I get for rescuing you?" said Ted. A fire extinguisher lay on the ground next to him. Farther along, Joelle-Michelle saw Swamster, who was wearing a WATCHOUT! suit and rushing from truck to truck, spraying the drivers with his own fire extinguisher.

"You ambushed the trucks," said Joelle-Michelle, disbelieving. He hadn't let them down—he had saved them?

"We filled the fire extinguishers with VIDGA solution," Ted explained. He took something out of his pocket.

"Your slipper," he said. "Foot up." Joelle-Michelle raised her foot, and Ted slid her shoe on.

"Merci," said Joelle-Michelle, smiling.

Carolina rolled her eyes.

"Get everybody inside," said Ted. "There are no more extinguishers, but I have some other ideas."

XIV

Noon-ish.

The last of the important guests were taking their seats at the tables closest to the wedding gazebo—mostly politicians who had supported Persephone, interspersed with individuals such as the peacock who had done the interior design on her apartment. For additional security, Persephone was using guards as ushers. Once the guards had seated the important guests, they formed a line across the courtyard, behind which common abstract companions could stand and get a peek at the social event of the millennium.

Persephone peered out the window. Her bones were chattering, and she hoped her guests wouldn't be able to tell that she was nervous. After all, this wasn't the *good* kind of giddy, it's-my-wedding-day nervousness. No, Persephone was nervous about what guests would *say*. They were bound to gossip—it was probably never a good sign when the groom was in a cage. But she was hoping that once they attacked New York, all the guests would be too busy exterminating humans and wreaking revenge and those sorts of things to chew over the wedding details.

The bride picked up a pair of binoculars and looked out at the laboratory on the border of the palace grounds. The trucks were still parked out front and there were splashes of purple on the ground—Bugslush and the scientists were apparently doing a nice job getting rid of those tacky ACORN troops.

"Good riddance," said Persephone.

She took a final look at herself in the mirror. Her makeup was perfect. Her plush blond wig sat high on her skull. Her bridal gown hung from her shoulder blades, loose on top and hemmed in around her waist, which gave her the appearance of having *curves*. The effect was dramatic, with that long train that stretched out behind her. Persephone felt pretty.

She checked the clock—ten minutes past noon. In fifteen minutes, Scurvy would be wheeled in his cage to the wedding gazebo, and in twenty minutes, Persephone would walk herself down the aisle.

She lowered her veil, and her world turned white.

XV

In the meantime, ACORN was tearing apart the inside of the laboratory—chairs, counters, plumbing, ceiling fans—salvaging anything that could be swung, shot, or thrown. Ted, Declan, and Carolina were in charge of dipping the makeshift weaponry into the cauldron of knockoff VIDGA solution, after which Swamster distributed the weapons, instructing their new owners on how to hold them without inadvertently popping themselves. Brother Dezo had recovered his ukulele, and he was working with Joelle-Michelle on a battle plan to hit the palace and cut Persephone's army off from the main vent.

Ted caught his father looking at him over the cauldron.

"What is it?" said Ted.

"I'm so sad that I don't know you," said Declan.

"Me too," said Ted. "But after the fight maybe we can fix that."

"Then I'll make sure we win if I have to take down every last one of them myself," said Declan.

"Attention!" Joelle-Michelle commanded.

The ACORN fighters stopped what they were doing and turned her way.

"We have a rough plan," said Joelle-Michelle. "We will be dividing into three groups—Ted, Brother Dezo, and I will each lead one. Ted, unless you can imagine us to victory *now*, you will be leading the assault on the palace."

Ted looked down at his birthmark. Nope. Nothing going on.

"Ah well, perhaps later," said Joelle-Michelle. "For now you'll need just a small group. Your main goal is to draw Persephone's army toward the palace. At which point Brother Dezo and I will flank the army from opposite sides with larger divisions. The only way we'll have a chance against that many troops is by surprising and trapping them from several angles."

"What time does the wedding start?"

Everybody looked at Bugslush, who was tied up in the corner.

"Twelve-thirty," said Bugslush.

Ted's eyes flicked to a clock hanging on the wall. They only had eleven minutes.

"Get your group together," said Joelle-Michelle.

"How many should I take?"

"You probably couldn't even get into the palace with more than ten."

Ted nodded. He looked around.

"Carolina?" said Ted. "You in?"

"Yep," said Carolina. "Can Czarina come?"

"Of course," said Ted. "Dad?"

"Side by side with my boy," said Declan.

"Swamster?"

"At your service."

Ted nodded. "I'll be right back," he said, and pushed his way

288

through the throng of ACORN fighters until he found Dwack, Dr. Narwhal, and Vango.

"Guys?" he said. "Feel like going on a doomed mission?"

"I'm in," said Dr. Narwhal.

"We've done it before, haven't we?" said Dwack.

"Hold on," said Vango, removing a bottle of something from his painter's bag. Vango uncorked the top and drank all that was left. "All right. Now I'm good to go," he said.

Ted spotted Eric.

"Eric?" he yelled. "You in?"

The planda nodded.

"If we're going with such a lean group," said Ted, "we're going to need all three fire extinguishers."

"Take them," said Joelle-Michelle.

"And some decent weaponry," said Ted.

"Whatever you want," said Joelle-Michelle. "And take lab coats with you for extra protection."

Ted had his racket, and he took one of the fire extinguishers. Carolina and Declan took the other two fire extinguishers. Swamster found his umbrella in the pile of confiscated weapons. Dwack took another cane, while Dr. Narwhal grabbed a plumbing pipe. Vango would use his paintbrushes. Eric decided upon a stalk of bamboo he had found in the laboratory.

"If you get tempted, eat the handle, not the part that has touched the solution," Swamster advised Eric.

Ted looked at his odd, brave group, all of whom were pulling on lab coats.

"This should be interesting," he said.

"One more thing, Ted," said Joelle-Michelle.

289

"Yeah?"

Before he could turn around, Joelle-Michelle leaned in and kissed him. On the lips.

"*Bon chance*. Good luck," she said.

"Oh. I mean. Er," said Ted. He turned to his troops. "Let's go."

Carolina shot a sharp look at Joelle-Michelle and got a wink in return.

XVI

Two weight lifters had tossed Scurvy's cage onto a wheelbarrow and hauled it to the wedding gazebo, where the cage sat next to the bespectacled justice of the peace who would be conducting the ceremony. The assembled guests stared at him, whispering to one another.

Once Scurvy's cage was in position, the organist plinked out music as the wedding party entered. Because Persephone didn't have any real friends or family, she had hired the best-looking wedding party she could for the grand entrance and the photographs. The trio of bridesmaids, none of whom Persephone had ever met, looked like they could have stepped off a fashion runway. A pair of enchanting little flower girls, having been paid handsomely for their adorableness, sprinkled lilacs on the red carpet. Three buccaneer groomsmen had been hired as Scurvy's buddies.

"Good luck, pal," said one of the groomsmen to Scurvy.

"Who are you?" replied Scurvy.

Finally, when the wedding party was in place, the organist started the wedding march:

Da! Dah da-da! Da! Dah da-da!

Everybody stood, and there at the end of the center aisle, Persephone appeared.

Da, dah, da-da!

Teetering in her high heels, she walked down the carpet while guests, most of them on the presidential payroll, oohed and aahed and snapped pictures. She reached the gazebo and stood next to the justice of the peace, opposite Scurvy's cage.

Persephone waved coyly at Scurvy, as if it were perfectly natural that he was caged. The justice of the peace cleared his throat.

"We have come together this afternoon to join two individuals who are lucky enough to have found the truest of true love," said the justice. "President Persephone Skeleton."

Persephone curtsied.

". . . and Admiral Scurvy Goonda."

"Admiral!" shouted Scurvy. "I was never *commissioned*!"

"HUSH, darling," warned Persephone.

Scurvy clawed at the bars of his cage.

292

"As Scurvy and Persephone take their vows this afternoon, we are reminded that a necessary component of marriage is a balance of love and commitment," said the justice. "May they remain as devoted as they are now."

Scurvy shook his cage.

"Help!" he said.

"He's just excited," Persephone explained to the justice of the peace. "Go on."

"Persephone Skeleton," said the justice. "Do you take Scurvy Goonda to be your true love, to trust and to honor him?"

"Do me a favor and replace that with 'tell him what to do,' " said Persephone.

"Oh," said the justice. "Well, then. Do you take Scurvy to be your true love, and to tell him what to do?"

"I do."

"And do you, Scurvy—" said the justice.

"Nope," said Scurvy.

"You don't?" said the justice.

"Not a chance," said Scurvy. "No way. Never. No how."

The crowd mumbled.

"Scurvy," hissed Persephone. "Say you do."

"But I don't," said Scurvy. "I won't, and I can't."

Persephone grinned.

"Say '*I do*' or the moment we get to Earth, I send troops to your beloved Cape Cod," said Persephone. "And I'll instruct those troops to wipe out the entire Merritt family—and then they'll sink that sandbox under the Atlantic!"

Scurvy hesitated.

"Ted, Adeline, Debbie, Grandma Rose," said Persephone. "I learned all about where you've been all these years. Say no, and they're the first to go. Say 'I do,' and I'll spare them."

Scurvy considered this. Then he took a deep breath.

"Well," he said, "they're me only real family, so then, I guess, I d—"

"DON'T," yelled a voice that bounced off the walls of the courtyard.

Thousands of heads turned in the direction of the interrupter.

And there stood Ted, with his motley group of ACORN fighters behind him.

"You can do better," said Ted. "She has bad bone structure."

Scurvy grinned.

"AHOY, TED!" he roared. "I *knew* I was right about you!"

"We are trying to get married here!" shouted Persephone. "Guests may not speak!"

293

"We weren't invited," said Ted. "So you see, we're not guests."

"USHERS!" yelled Persephone.

Persephone's thick-necked ushers stomped down the aisle toward Ted and his cohorts.

"Raise extinguishers," Ted told Carolina and Declan, and all three of them lifted their fire extinguishers.

The ushers got closer.

"Hold," said Ted.

Dwack, Dr. Narwhal, and Vango buttoned up their lab coats.

"PULL!" shouted Ted, and with that, he and his father and Carolina dosed the approaching ushers with the fire extinguishers.

A volcano of purple erupted in the center of the courtyard, but it wasn't just the guards who were exploding. Solution also rained on both the spectators and the guests who had been sitting at their tables enjoying their cocktails. All were now spots of liquid on the ground.

"RELEASE!" said Ted. He took his finger off the extinguisher trigger, and Carolina and his father did the same.

The remaining guests were bewildered. Several ushers hid underneath the tables, and the organist peeked out from behind his piano. Where the justice of the peace had been standing, there was only a pair of eyeglasses sitting in a purple puddle.

In the gazebo, Persephone looked completely shell-shocked.

"What the—" she said, ignoring the carnage, looking down at herself. Her bridal gown had a purple stain.

"My dress!" she said. "Oh, this is too MUCH!"

Ted walked toward her holding the fire extinguisher.

"I'd like my pirate back now," he said.

"Oh, I don't think he's yours anymore," said Persephone. "But if you want him, HERE he is!" She zinged the cage and wheelbarrow down the aisle at Ted. The wheelbarrow hit him in the gut and knocked him onto his back, and an usher fell on top of him.

Ted was defenseless. The usher locked in on his neck and reared back with a claw, but before he could attack, he was smashed in the side of the head with a fire extinguisher.

The usher looked up in surprise at Ted's father.

"Don't you touch my boy!" said Declan, giving the usher a shot from the extinguisher. *POP!*

"Thanks, Dad!" said Ted.

Declan helped him up.

"Running bones! Heading upward!" yelled Vango, pointing. Ted saw that Persephone was bolting up the stairs.

"Swamster, go get her!" said Ted. Swamster followed on the president's heels. "The rest of you, take care of any ushers you find, and let the rest of the guests go—we'll be seeing them soon anyway."

Ted looked into Scurvy's cage. He and his friend made eye contact.

It had been so long.

"Hey, Scurvy," said Ted.

"Hey yerself, Ted," said Scurvy. "I kept hearin' things that made me think ya might be here. Seein' ya, it's like seein' the sunrise again."

"I'm so sorry for everything."

"No hard feelin's," said Scurvy. "Yer a stupid teenager. Get me out of this cage and we'll call it even."

"Allow me," said Dr. Narwhal, who reared back with his pipe and—*bang!*—knocked the padlock off its latch.

Scurvy Goonda threw open the door of his cage, brushed himself off, and bear-hugged Ted.

"Too tight, too tight," gasped Ted.

"Ya did good, Teddy me boy," said Scurvy.

"Scurvy, there's somebody I want you to meet," said Ted. "Come here, Dad."

Declan stepped forward.

"Scurvy, this is my father, Declan. Dad, this is my abstr—my *best friend*, Scurvy Goonda."

"I'm honored to meet you," said Declan.

"It's darn good tah meet ya too," said Scurvy.

Most unfortunately, this tender moment was shattered by an earsplitting siren coming from the top of the palace: *Baaa-raahhh! Baaa-raahhh!*

Signal flares rocketed from the top of the palace and exploded in the sky, where they formed letters: C.H.A.R.G.E.!

Ted and the rest of his small group stared at the message.

"Looks like Swamster didn't catch President Skeleton," said Vango. Underneath them, the ground started to rumble.

Persephone's army was coming.

XVII

Persephone took her finger off the alarm button and then calmly looked back at Swamster.

"My goodness," said Persephone. "I thought athletes were faster than that."

"You had a head start," pointed out Swamster, who was standing at the top of the stairs holding his umbrella.

"Yes, but I'm just an old set of bones," said Persephone. "Perhaps betraying our cause has drained you."

"It just took me a long time to see how awful you really were," said Swamster, walking toward Persephone with the umbrella.

"I went easy on you," said Persephone. "A crocodile once worked for me for thirty years, and I had her turned into a pair of pumps."

"You don't care what lives you ruin," said Swamster, getting closer.

"If I'm not mistaken," said Persephone, climbing onto the windowsill, "you wrecked my wedding and turned my guests into purple sludge. But don't worry. My cleaning crew will be here in a moment. And with that, I say goodbye."

Persephone spread her bony wings and fell out the window backward, her wedding dress fluttering above her.

"No!" screamed Swamster, watching out the window as Persephone landed in the middle of three ghosts forming a cradle.

Swirling and translucent, the ghosts carried Persephone over the heads of her charging army. She blew Swamster a kiss goodbye.

"Is she gone?" said Dwack, walking into the room.

"I couldn't catch her," said Swamster.

"Come into the courtyard," said Dwack. "We need to secure the palace."

"I don't think it's going to matter now. Her army is on its way."

"Come on. I want you fighting next to me," said Dwack. "This is the night you're going to earn those medals of yours."

XVIII

Through a pair of field binoculars, Joelle-Michelle watched from the woods as President Skeleton's army charged past her hidden troops toward the palace. There seemed to be no end to the throng of angry, adrenaline-filled ab-coms—even though they had the element of surprise, ACORN was outnumbered ten thousand to one. She could see that many of President Skeleton's troops were holding the solution-coated weapons they had confiscated from ACORN's hideout. No matter what happened, there would be heavy losses.

Joelle-Michelle looked across the stampeding army to a small canyon on the other side of the battlefield, where Brother Dezo would be positioned. Once the army had completely passed by, she and Brother Dezo would attack it from behind with their own forces.

The huge shiny vent loomed at the far end of the battlefield. If President Skeleton's army made it through, Earth didn't have a chance.

Back in the palace, Ted and his small battalion had managed to close the palace gates, but legions of Persephone's troops were hurtling toward them. And all Ted and his troops had to defend themselves were three fire extinguishers and a handful of crude weapons.

Ted, Carolina, and Declan stood behind the gate with their extinguishers pointed determinedly forward.

Dwack, Dr. Narwhal, and Vango stood behind them, along with Swamster, Czarina Tallow, and Eric, who took a small nibble of the handle of his bamboo rod—just a taste in case he never got to eat bamboo again.

"Zis might be an appropriate time for *vun of you* gentlemen to use your imaginations," Czarina Tallow suggested to Ted and Declan. Ted had already been trying to get his brain going: *What if a massive geyser blew Persephone's army into space? What if the outside wall of the palace was carved with a giant Medusa head that turned the army to stone?*

Ted looked over at his father, lost in his thoughts, trying to make something happen. Declan looked back at Ted.

"Sometimes it happens," Declan explained. "Sometimes it doesn't. The only one who figured out how to use it consistently is Cousin Lloyd."

"Who is this Lloyd?"

"A rogue," said Declan. "A bad man who happens to be related to us."

Outside the palace walls, the army was close enough that Ted could hear their howling, and then . . .

BOOM!

A battering ram smacked into the palace gate, followed by the sound of laughter from the army.

Ted glanced at Scurvy.

"Goodbye, Scurvy," said Ted.

"Thank ya fer bein' tha best friend I ever had," said Scurvy.

"Thanks for being my *only* friend," said Ted.

"One good friend is all ya need," said Scurvy.

BOOM!

Ted turned to Carolina.

"If we get back to high school," said Ted, "maybe you'll have lunch with me in the cafeteria?"

Carolina laughed.

"If we make it back to high school, I'll take you to homecoming," said Carolina.

"I hate football," said Ted.

"You have no idea how happy that makes me," said Carolina.

BOOM! The bolts on the gate were almost broken.

"Dad!" said Ted.

"You're all that kept me going when I was in jail," said Declan. "I love you, Son."

"I guess—I mean, I love you too, Dad."

301

BOOOOOM!

The gate fell with a tremendous *THUD!* in front of Ted and his band of soldiers, and the army streamed into the courtyard, claws, teeth, and weapons out.

"PULL!" said Ted, and he, Carolina, and Declan soaked the attackers with the fire extinguishers, holding the triggers until all the solution ran out. The purple dregs of a hundred soldiers pooled at the gate entrance, but there were more soldiers ready to rush in.

Ted wrapped his hand around his badminton racket.

From far away came the sound of drums, followed by a rumbling and a surprised *ROAR*—Joelle-Michelle and Brother Dezo had started their attack from the rear. The soldiers who had been rushing into the palace whipped around to see what was happening, and Ted saw an opportunity.

"Charge!" he yelled, and sprinted forward with his battalion rushing behind him.

POP-POP-POP-POP-POP!

"Keep going!" yelled Ted.

XIX

Joelle-Michelle's forces had slashed their way through Persephone's army, but the enemy had adjusted and was retaliating furiously against ACORN. The weapons the army had taken from ACORN's hideout had been distributed to Persephone's best soldiers, who were cutting energetically through Joelle-Michelle's troops.

Joelle-Michelle saw her best soldiers burst into purple. The tailor who repaired her tutu whenever it ripped fell to a blank-eyed poltergeist. The gardener who took care of her flowers had his hoe torn from his hands and used against him. She saw one of her mummies cut down and one of her magi explode. Rushed from all sides, she was kicking furiously with her pointe shoes. The purple mist hanging in the air around her blocked her view of the other side of the battlefield, where Brother Dezo's brigade was hopefully doing better than her own.

A weight lifter grabbed her by the back of the neck and hurled her into the air. Hanging momentarily above the melee, Joelle-Michelle spotted the massive frame of Brother Dezo, who was swinging his ukulele in the middle of a pack of Presidential Guards. But Brother Dezo was overwhelmed, and as she plunged toward the ground, she saw a chessboard knight come up behind Brother Dezo, raise his sword, and—*POP!*—Brother Dezo burst in a purple cloud.

"Dezo!" yelled Joelle-Michelle. With Brother Dezo gone, the third battalion had lost its leader and was sure to be wiped out. In the distance she could see that the palace was surrounded—there was no way Ted's small group of fighters was still alive.

All was lost.

XX

The palace had been taken.

The platters of food and bottles of liquor meant for the wedding had been toppled and smashed, and the ground was slick and sloppy. Dozens of trays of bacon had been set around the courtyard, and Ted could feel cured meat squishing under his feet. The white bunting and taxidermied doves had toppled from the gazebo, and champagne bottles were being winged through the air, smashing against walls.

Out of the corner of his eye, Ted saw a railroad man enter the courtyard swinging an enormous sledgehammer, barreling straight for the trapped ACORN fighters.

"Watch out for the railroader!" yelled Ted. "His hammer is one of ours!"

But Ted couldn't yell loud enough to make his voice heard above the sound of clanging metal, and he could see that the railroad man was charging toward Swamster, who was trying to bend his wrecked umbrella into a useable form. He reared back to strike.

"Swamster, watch out!" yelled Ted.

Swamster deftly leaped out of the way. The railroad man simply laughed and switched his attention to Dr. Narwhal.

"*No!*" yelled Ted, charging the railroad man, who laughed as he whacked Ted's badminton racket out of his hands. The racket clanged away, and Ted was off balance when the man swung his hammer into his side.

BOOM!

The air rushed out of Ted's lungs, and he crumpled to the ground. He braced himself, expecting to be finished off, but instead, from his horizontal position, he saw the railroad man stomping away.

Toward Scurvy.

Ted tried to lift himself off the ground. Lying in the purple puddle in front of him were a heap of bacon slabs and an empty fire extinguisher.

"Scur-sc—"

Ted saw the railroad man rear back to take a fatal swing at Scurvy, who had his back turned.

Ted grabbed the bacon.

And then he got one. *An idea.* Far faster than it had before, his birthmark became hot, changed colors, and then *SNAP!*

His arm broke off at the elbow and shot forward, grabbing the sledgehammer just as it was about to come down on Scurvy and tearing it from the railroad man's hand. The railroader looked backward to find out what had happened, which gave Eric sufficient time to crack him across the forehead with his bamboo pole.

POP!

"Thanks, Eric," said Scurvy.

Eric took another bite of the handle of the bamboo pole, rewarding himself.

Scurvy looked at the disembodied hand holding the sledgehammer, but its presence didn't seem to surprise him. He just nodded a quick thanks to Ted and went back to the battle.

As a second act, instead of returning directly to Ted with the hammer, the hand hovered over the discarded fire extinguisher that was lying in the puddle next to the bacon. It lowered itself until it was even with the extinguisher and— CLANG! CLANG! CLANG!—brought the hammer down upon the canister until it broke open. Droplets of VIDGA solution spilled out. Ted's hand stuck its pointer finger into one of these globules.

The droplet quickly expanded into a round puddle of solution, enveloping the bacon. The bacon blend started to churn, lengthening into a liquid sheet that stretched straight up out of the palace, touching the sky.

The column then started to harden and solidify, and everybody on both sides of the fight raised their eyes to behold what was now towering above them.

It was simply the biggest slice of bacon ever created. Flavored by VIDGA.

"The mother slab," said Scurvy in awe.

On the battlefield, Joelle-Michelle looked up at the massive slice of bacon teetering back and forth, and at the army soldiers running out of the Presidential Palace. She needed to get her troops out of the way *fast*, and she shouted to the ACORN fighters who were still alive: "RETREAT!"

The few hundred survivors ran.

Persephone's army didn't receive any such instructions from their leader, who was busy using soda water to try and get the stains out of her bridal gown. She had seen that her forces were dominating ACORN, so she'd decided to let her generals finish things up, and trotted off to the vent to get herself in position for the attack on Earth.

307

"GET OUT, STAIN!" she said. "GET OUT!"

The towering slice of bacon wobbled forward and backward, as if it were almost *waiting* for the remaining ACORN fighters to get out of the way. Once they were, Ted's arm floated up to the top of the slab and gave it a little push.

The slice toppled forward like a falling tree, straight down on top of the battlefield.

CRACK!

All at once, the piece of bacon fell on top of President Skeleton's entire army, creating one enormous, synchronized *POP!*

Followed by silence.

Thousands of gallons of purple liquid leaked out from underneath the fallen tower of bacon.

"Lousy wedding," was all Persephone had time to say as the slice of bacon crashed on top of her, permanently—and for all time—staining her dress.

XXI

Ted's forearm reattached itself to his elbow, cooled down, and returned to its natural color.

In the courtyard, Carolina sat in a white wedding chair, catching her breath. Dwack and Dr. Narwhal rested against the stage, where the band had never played, while Czarina Tallow folded some of the napkins that had been mussed by the fight.

Everybody in Ted's battalion had survived.

"Ya got me hungry," said Scurvy, staring at the bacon slab stretching out in front of the palace.

"You *cannot* eat that," said Ted, rubbing his forearm.

"All right. I'll make do with me un-wedding cake," said Scurvy, heading toward the multitiered confection. He took out his dagger, lopped the heads off the bride and groom figures perched atop the cake, and cut everybody a piece. Anything that was left, he took for himself.

"A legendary slice of pork belly, that was," said Scurvy, chewing cake. "Seems we got tha same kinda thoughts running through our heads."

"We do," said Ted, licking some frosting off his fingers.

Scurvy pointed to the slab of bacon with his fork.

"But *that*," said Scurvy. "That's impressive."

"The scale of that piece of bacon is far beyond anything I

was ever able to do," said Declan. "If you could learn to control your abilities, you could run the world."

"I just want to make it through high school," said Ted.

Declan laughed. He looked down at his plate.

"I haven't had cake since your seventh birthday," said Declan.

Ted didn't get the chance to reply. Joelle-Michelle ran around the bacon slab and into the courtyard with her remaining troops, who looked exhausted. She threw her arms around Ted.

"Je t'adore!" said Joelle-Michelle. *"Tu es magnifique!"*

If Ted had spoken French, he would have known this meant "I adore you! You are amazing!" But he got the point anyway.

Carolina put her hand on Joelle-Michelle's face before she was tempted to do any more kissing.

"Dégagez!" said Carolina, which meant "Back off!" "That's my homecoming date."

Joelle-Michelle looked up.

"I'm in AP French," said Carolina.

Then came a sound that made everybody flinch and Dr. Narwhal drop his cake.

POP!

But it was only Vango behind the bar.

"Plenty of champagne back here," said Vango, pouring himself a glass. "Let's get weird!"

"Un verre, s'il vous plaît," said Joelle-Michelle, asking for a glass.

"I'll take a full bottle," said Scurvy.

Champagne flutes were handed around, and at Scurvy's insistence, Ted took one too. Scurvy raised his bottle.

"I propose a toast!" he said. "Tah Ted, our hero, who fer tha first time in his life is tha most popular guy in a room!"

Ted laughed.

"Cheers!" he said, and everybody took a sip.

It had been a long, long day.

XXII

Several miles behind the Presidential Palace ran a sapphire-colored river that was off-limits to the general population. For the thousands of years Middlemost had been around, the river's current had been so violent that if you only stepped *one toe* into it—*WHOOSH!*—you would be whizzed gurgling and sloshing straight to the river's end, whereupon you would be crushed by horrible rapids.

Attempts had been made to build a bridge over the river, but so many workers were swept away that eventually the project managers figured it wasn't worth it. The scouts who catapulted over the river to see what was on the other side never came back, and soon enough, ab-coms simply forced themselves to stop thinking about what was over there. Nobody knew that the scouts never came back because as soon as they crossed the river, a birthmarked arm grabbed them and whisked them into oblivion.

When the arm had completed its task, it floated back to the top of an enormous mountain on which there was a pleasant-looking brick house built in the Northern European Berlage style. The house was large and had the best views in all of Middlemost. And only one occupant.

Lloyd Munch was a small, peculiar-looking man who had been forced—for various reasons—to leave his town in Denmark years before. He had come to Middlemost via a vent he'd found inside an IKEA superstore. Here in Middlemost, he discovered that the birthmarked arm that had gotten him into so much trouble on Earth was quite useful, and he used it to build his house away from everything and everybody.

And he had done so well in this place. He had found a capable leader in Persephone Skeleton and organized her campaign. He had developed the Greenies to draw abstract companions back to Middlemost, and he had mapped out all sorts of plans to crush Earth once they had returned. He had so many imaginative ideas to try out on the people there who had driven him away.

He didn't do the things they said he did. Or at least he didn't do most of them.

But now Persephone's army—*his* army—was no more, and he could see through his telescope that the small ACORN group that had defeated the army was eating cake and drinking champagne. It was all terribly irritating. He had helped pick out the cake—a vanilla chiffon masterpiece—and Persephone had promised to send him a piece following the ceremony. But now it appeared that he wouldn't be getting his slice, which put him in a foul mood.

Lloyd was tempted to destroy the palace immediately, along with everybody inside it, but he had seen the way the boy had destroyed Persephone's army—clearly, the boy had a powerful imagination, perhaps as powerful as Lloyd's. Might they be related?

Let them eat their cake, thought Lloyd. He had been beaten, but only for the moment.

Lloyd walked inside his home. In the spot where there

should have been a fireplace, he had installed a metal vent—
the only privately owned vent in Middlemost. He squeezed his
body into the vent and started to crawl.

It was time to get out of Middlemost for a while and go
somewhere interesting. He'd kill the boy and all the rest of
them.

Soon.

XXIII

Ted, Carolina, Declan, Czarina Tallow, Scurvy, and Eric the Planda stood next to the vent that would take them back home.

Joelle-Michelle, Swamster, Dwack, Dr. Narwhal, and Vango stood on the grass in what a few hours before had been a battlefield.

"Are you sure you don't want to come back with us?" said Ted to Dwack.

"I'm afraid there's too much to be done in Middlemost for us to go back," said Dwack. "Our place is here."

"We need to get the factories going again," said Dr. Narwhal. "It's been a long time since kids have had their ordersss filled, and some kids need replacementsss."

Ted hugged his friends.

XXIV

Screams filled the dressing room at Macy's.

Ted had known that the vent led to the enormous department store, but not that it went directly to the women's changing rooms. A lady trying on a bathing suit didn't appreciate it when Declan crawled out of the vent in her dressing room, followed by a pair of teenagers.

Declan knew that any explanation he offered for why he and Ted and Carolina were squeezing out of dressing room vents was going to sound like a lie, so he just told Ted and Carolina, "Run!"

They went crashing through the department store, upending racks of designer dresses and men's coats as they raced away from security guards. They bombed down the third-floor escalators, down another flight through a floor that seemed to be made entirely of denim, and then across the overpowering cosmetics section. Scurvy, Czarina, and Eric ran to keep up, though they weren't in jeopardy—after all, the security cameras only captured *three* individuals running through the store, not six.

Finally, Declan, Ted, and Carolina barreled out onto Thirty-fourth Street and hopped in the back of a cab while Scurvy, Czarina, and Eric crammed into the front seat.

"Ya smell good," said Scurvy to Czarina.

"Vatch it," replied Czarina.

"Where to?" said the cabbie.

Ted leaned over to his father.

"Do you have any money?" he whispered.

"I was in jail," said Declan. "Any money I had, I ate it a long time ago."

"Do you take credit cards?" said Carolina.

"Yup," said the cabbie.

Carolina pulled her wallet out of her pocket and removed a platinum American Express card. Ted raised his eyebrow.

"My mother gave it to me," said Carolina. "My parents divorced and she feels guilty."

"She really doesn't care?" said Ted.

"She just pays the bill," said Carolina.

Ted leaned forward and gave the taxi driver an address that made the driver's eyes widen.

317

"The ultimate ride," said the driver.

In the cab, Declan asked his son about the family, and about school, and about all the things from the past seven years that were important to him. Carolina listened to Ted and Declan talking and realized just how wrong she had been to ridicule Ted.

In the front seat, Scurvy, Czarina, and Eric tried to get comfortable, to no avail.

"Forget it!" yelled Scurvy. "I'll make me own space!"

Scurvy climbed out the window and onto the roof of the taxi, where he had all the room he wanted. He loved the feeling of the wind whipping through his hair. It was even better than riding on Ted's bike.

Five hours later, the cab pulled up in front of Ted's house—the first stop. The rate meter was flashing the fare: $3,740. Ted got out of the cab, followed by Declan and Scurvy, who filled his lungs with the good sea air, and then Eric, who stretched his legs and ate some leaves.

Ted looked at the meter, and then at Carolina.

"Trust me. I've got it covered," she said.

"So, see you at school on Monday?" said Ted.

It sounded so bizarrely normal.

"Yeah," said Carolina. "I'll see you at school. And at homecoming."

"Right," said Ted. "Homecoming."

"Hold on," said Carolina. "I think you left this."

When Ted poked his head through the window to see what he had left, Carolina kissed him.

318

"Atta boy, matey," said Scurvy. "Atta boy indeed."

"Monday?" said Carolina.

"Muh-muh, Mund—" said Ted, totally dazed.

The taxi pulled away down the street.

Ted looked at his father, who was staring at his decaying home.

"You're still here," said Declan.

"Mom never wanted to go anywhere else," said Ted. "She's been waiting."

Declan took a deep breath.

"Okay," he said. "Let's go inside."

Ted walked up to the front door, his father behind him. He pushed the door open and looked into the house.

"Mom?" he said. "Anybody?"

Grandma Rose was sitting at the kitchen table, playing solitaire. A look of shock crossed her face when she saw Ted, and then she stood up when she realized who Declan was.

Ted had never seen her stand.

"YOU'RE BACK!" said Grandma Rose. "EVERYBODY COME QUICK! I'M STANDING! AND THEY'RE BOTH HOME!"

Ted stepped forward and hugged his grandmother.

"Hi, Grandma Rose," he said.

Declan did the same.

"Long time, Rose," he said.

"I MISSED YOU!" she yelled.

Adeline walked into the kitchen from her bedroom, holding a picture that she had been drawing. The picture was of her family all together, with Eric and Scurvy, but Ted didn't notice this as he ran forward and lifted her up.

"Adeline!" said Ted.

"TED!" she yelled. "TED! YOU'RE BACK!"

Behind Ted, Eric the Planda waved to Adeline.

"*ERIC!*" yelled Adeline, squirming out of Ted's arms and running to Eric. The planda wrapped his arms around her, and the bonsai tree on his head turned bright green.

"Who's that?" said Adeline, pointing at Declan.

Declan's eyes were wet as he walked up to Adeline.

"Hello, Adeline," he said.

"You know my name?" said Adeline.

"I'm your dad, Adeline," said Declan.

Adeline didn't know how to react, so Declan just wrapped his arms around her. The last time he'd seen her, she wasn't even three months old. She was still the most beautiful thing he had ever seen.

"Declan," said Debbie, standing at the bottom of the staircase, stunned. "Ted."

319

Declan lifted his head and looked at his wife. He put down Adeline, walked toward Debbie, and lifted her up, kissing her.

"You have no idea how long I've waited to do that," he said. "You are more perfect than I even remembered."

"Oh, my Declan. My Declan my Declan my Declan."

"I'm back," said Declan. "For good. I'm back."

"I can't believe it," said Debbie. Her eyes were wet.

Ted walked up and hugged his mother, and Adeline followed. Slowly, Grandma Rose shuffled over and joined the embrace.

It was the first full-family hug the Merritts had ever had.

XXV

Monday.

Ted nervously walked into school. His and Carolina's return had been all over the local news, and since they'd come back together, it was just assumed they had run off with each other. Neither of them said anything to curb the rumors, because it was by far a more believable explanation than the truth.

Between classes, everybody looked at him like he had just returned from the moon. No one approached him, and in general, he was treated with awe. Many of the students in the school had younger siblings, and over the weekend, they had been listening to their siblings' shrieks of happiness as their abstract companions returned.

In Mongolia, Oochkoo Bat awakened in her drafty room to discover that her miniature fire-eating yak, Mandoni, was once again sleeping in his normal spot on the floor of the closet.

In Iceland, Halldor Gundmondsson pulled open his window blinds and saw his rhinoceros friend, Bjarni, stomping around in his yellow raincoat and a new pair of galoshes.

In the African country of Eritrea, Natsinet Tenolde found her leaf-nosed bat, Gongab, sitting on top of her house.

Though none of Ted's fellow students said anything, many of them simply had a feeling that Ted's return and the arrival of thousands of imaginary friends were somehow related.

Halfway through the day, Ted took a deep breath.

"You ready, Scurvy?" said Ted.

"Aye," said Scurvy. "Let's go."

Together, they walked into the cafeteria.

Ted stood in line to get his food—meat loaf with a side of macaroni and cheese, and an apple juice—and then took his tray and walked into the seating area, where *everybody* was staring at him. He looked around for a table and spotted one in the far corner where his exchange student friend Kettil was eating alone. As Ted walked over to Kettil, the cafeteria was so quiet that Ted could hear his own footsteps.

"Hi, Kettil," said Ted.

"Hej," said Kettil. That meant "hello" in Swedish.

Ted sat down and started to eat, trying to ignore everybody's eyes. And then . . .

"Hey, want some more company?"

It was Carolina, holding her own tray.

"Sure," said Ted.

Carolina sat down next to him and the cafeteria gasped.

"May I sit?" said Czarina Tallow to Scurvy.

"Please do, m'lady," said Scurvy.

"A YO YO AND A HO HO!" yelled a familiar voice. It was Duke, marching over from the popular table. "LOOK WHO HAS RETURNED FROM THE SEVEN SEAS."

"Quit it, Duke!" said Carolina.

"You've had your fun, Carolina, but you're at the wrong table," said Duke. "Come on."

"I'm sitting with my boyfriend," said Carolina.

"YOUR BOYFRIEND?" said Duke.

"Really?" said Ted.

Carolina nodded.

"Don't be stupid," said Duke, grabbing Carolina's arm. "Come on."

"Don't you touch her," said Ted.

"Oh?" said Duke. "You're telling me what to do?"

Ted thought about this.

"Yes I am," he said.

Because Ted's hands were under the table, Duke couldn't see that his birthmark was rapidly changing color. Ted could feel the limb getting warmer, and then—*snap!*

Ted willed his arm to stay underneath the table and not fly around freaking everybody out. Down by his knees, Ted could hear it rapidly building something, plucking atoms out of the air.

Then Duke realized that something was grabbing his shirt.

In its talons.

An enormous bald-headed condor stepped out from underneath the lunch table and spread its wings.

"Rrrack!" said the condor, tightening its claws around Duke. "Rrrack!"

Ted's forearm quietly reattached itself to his elbow, its job done.

"What the—" said Duke.

Scurvy leaned close to Ted.

"I think tha condor wants tah go out," said Scurvy.

Calmly, Ted walked over to the cafeteria's outside exit and opened the door. With Duke firmly in its claws, the condor took a few hops out the door, stretched its wings, and soared off into the afternoon sky.

Ted closed the door and walked back to his table, where he took a bite of his meat loaf.

323

"Where's it going?" whispered Carolina.

"I believe condors are native to California," said Ted.

Everybody in the cafeteria was staring at Ted. The lunch ladies stood motionless, holding their spatulas. The popular kids were trembling. Ted needed to say something.

He stood up.

"Hi," he said. "For those of you who don't know me, I'm Ted Merritt."

Silence.

"It's been a weird couple of months."

End of Book One

Chris McCoy

grew up on Cape Cod and graduated from New York University's Tisch School of the Arts. He has contributed to *McSweeney's*, and currently lives in Santa Monica, California. This is his first novel.